JUST WAR

DOCTOR WHO – THE NEW ADVENTURES

Also available:

THE NEW
DOCTOR WHO ADVENTURES

JUST WAR

Lance Parkin

First published in Great Britain in 1996 by
Doctor Who Books
an imprint of Virgin Publishing Ltd
332 Ladbroke Grove
London W10 5AH

Cover illustration by Nik Spender
Original concept by Mark Jones

ISBN 0 426 20463 8

Phototypeset by Intype, London

Printed and bound in Great Britain by Mackays Paperbacks,
Chatham, Kent

This book, like its author, is dedicated to
Cassandra May.

Acknowledgements

Special thanks to Cassie and Mark Jones for, well, everything really: advice, constructive criticism, proofreading, support, punctuation, encouragement. The nun and the giant rubber hamster were Mark's idea, by the way. Thanks to Michael Evans for inspiration, John Langdon and Mark Clapham for historical snippets and David Pitcher who would never forgive me if I didn't mention him. As subscribers to rec.arts.drwho will know, Benny's birthday was astrologically determined by Jim Sangster. Thanks to Paul Cornell for settling the matter, and to everyone else who took part in the discussion.

Once upon a time, when the world was black and white . . .

Prologue

'Doctor. It's been a long time.'

'Yes, Ma. Even longer for me. Too long. But this still feels like home.' The Doctor stared into the hearth, the light from the flames flickering in his eyes. He sipped at his cocoa, and watched as the firewood blackened and curled. No doubt, thought Ma Doras, he was divining patterns in the smoke and messages in the crackling of the flames. At times like this, Ma really could believe that he was as old as he claimed. At times like this, the Doctor scared her. Ma turned to the young woman crouched at the fireside. Her daughter, Celia, whom the Doctor had brought back from the dead.

'Are you warmer now, Celia?'

'Yes, Ma. I'm sorry, we've just been somewhere a lot warmer than this.' The young woman looped a strand of blonde hair back over her ear.

'My dear, this is a tourist resort. People come here for their holidays. You're right, though, this is what we'd call the "off-season". It has been since June.'

The Doctor finished winding his pocket-watch and lent forward. 'Tell us.'

'You must know. You must have read about it. An historic moment: the first successful invasion of the United Kingdom since 1066. The Day the Nazis Came.'

Celia sat alongside her, looking puzzled.

'It's not the same as hearing it from someone who was there,' the Doctor said.

1

'No? Well, there isn't much to tell. The British government gave up. The Germans swept across France in a matter of weeks. You must remember Dunkirk?'

'I was there,' said the Doctor quietly. 'Refugees from Paris were blocking the roads. The British army was stuck in traffic and running out of petrol. Messerschmitts wheeled overhead mowing down the civilians. All the time, German tanks were getting nearer. Every fishing boat, every little barge on the south coast of England had been commandeered. The army was being evacuated by civilians: fishermen, old men in yachting club jerseys. All the time, their little boats were being fired at by the German guns. Even British propaganda afterwards admitted that it was a massive defeat.'

Ma continued. 'After that, it was clear that there was nothing we could do to stop the attack. The Cabinet decided to pull all the soldiers back. Demilitarize, and we might be able to stay out of the war. Ships were sent to evacuate everyone that wanted to go. A second Dunkirk. Within a couple of days around a third of the population had gone; the rest of us decided that we couldn't afford to leave our homes or farms, a few stayed out of patriotism. Many of the young men who left vowed to join the armed services: they'd come back and liberate us. Some stayed. A few have even come back since.'

Ma looked down at Celia, who smiled nervously. She was so tall, so pretty. Celia shivered again and Ma handed her a poker. Celia looked uncertainly at it for a moment, until the Doctor took it from her hands and jabbed at the hearth with it. The fire began to flare up again. The Doctor handed the poker back to Celia, who smiled and began prodding the fire experimentally for herself.

'At a quarter to seven on June twenty-eighth, the Germans attacked. I was there, most of us were. It was Friday, the warmest evening of the year. We were just coming back from church and Mayor Sherwill was making a speech on Smith Street, trying to reassure everyone. There was a droning noise, a squeal, and then a thud. We'd never heard a sound like it before, so we didn't realize at first

2

that the Germans were bombing the harbour. A lot of vans were down there, and the planes targeted them. The drivers didn't know what to do. A lot of them sheltered underneath their vehicles. They died. We all saw it; there was nowhere to go. We just didn't know what we would do. Do you know, there wasn't a single bomb shelter in the whole town? It just shows how naïve we were. It's odd: my main impression was of the colour pink. The explosions were a sort of salmon pink. I don't suppose that fact will ever make it into the history books. Noise and panic. Confusion. Screaming and black smoke.

'Look, it's not really much use remembering. We had to piece together what had happened afterwards, anyway. For nearly half an hour, half a dozen bombers soared and dived overhead, strafing the area with bullets and dropping bombs. Then, it was over. Twenty-seven men and four women had died and forty others were wounded. Two hours later, at nine, we all listened to the BBC news, and learnt that the government had demilitarized us and hoped to keep us out of the war.

'Later, the Germans said that they regretted the deaths – the purpose of the raid had been simply to prevent the shipping of a consignment of tomatoes, the deaths had been incidental.

'The real invasion wasn't long in coming. We were all terrified on Saturday. We thought that there would be another raid. Or a gas attack. We were very worried about being gassed. On Sunday afternoon, three German planes landed at the airstrip, but they were scared off by an RAF patrol. I learnt about that later. The Germans returned in force at six in the evening, most of us heard the plane circling. They must have been looking for ground defences. There weren't any. Half an hour later, Major Lanz had assumed command, and had set himself up in the Royal Hotel. Most of us didn't learn this until the day after, when we read the declaration. Some people, the ones in the outlying farms, well, some of them didn't find out for over a week. All private transport had been

3

outlawed. The curfew was in place. The Swastika was raised from every flagpole.

'It was so strange that it didn't sink in for a couple of days, until the planes came. Wave after wave of troop transports, Junkers, barely clearing the rooftops. One hundred and seventy-eight huge aircraft bringing thousands upon thousands of Nazi soldiers. We just stood around, watching them arrive, watching all these young men pouring off the planes, then marching in regimented lines.' Ma couldn't think of anything else to add. Celia had turned to the Doctor.

'Doctor, what's happening?'

'You know, it's so long since one of my travelling companions asked me that. It really takes me back to the good old days . . .' There was a toothy grin all over his face. Ma sighed, hadn't he been listening?

'Well, it's a long time since you gave a straight answer to a straight question. Perhaps that's why we stopped asking. This never happened, did it? Britain won the war. History has changed.' Ma listened to Celia's cultured accent, the sort of voice you heard on the Home Service.

The Doctor's voice was a whisper, there was no trace of his grin now. 'Well, strictly speaking, according to "real" history, you died on Hallowe'en 1913. You were three years old. A lovely young girl. I couldn't prevent it.' Was that a tear in his eye?

'Stop it, you're giving me the creeps.'

'This isn't a parallel universe, this isn't an alternate timeline. History is running exactly as you know it. This is Guernsey, late December 1941. Merry Christmas, Celia.'

1

Resistance is Useless

The woman who called herself Celia Doras woke early, half-past six on the morning of 1 March 1941. She could hear planes flying overhead. Four of them, bombers, nothing out of the ordinary. They had spent the night on a bombing raid, and now as the dawn approached they were returning to the aerodrome at St Villiaze, three or four miles away. Just as the droning had died down, a second wave arrived, five or six of them this time. She pulled the sheet back and lay flat on her back, staring blindly at the ceiling, listening to them. Everyone on Guernsey had grown used to the planes; most islanders could identify the different types by their propeller sounds. Usually, about sixty-five planes would leave during the course of the evening. Rather less returned the next morning. The islanders no longer resented them; truth be told, they hardly even noticed them.

The planes were German. It had been nearly a year since the Nazis had invaded. Celia hadn't been there, hadn't seen the invasion. She reached under her pillow and fished out a small hardback pocketbook. She'd been reading it the night before, and had forgotten to put it away. The title was embossed in gold letters on the damaged spine: *Advice For Young Ladies*. The book did contain a great deal of useful information – maps, codes and so on. One chapter, Chapter 8, recounted the events of the invasion in some detail and she'd pieced together the rest by talking to islanders.

Celia stared at herself in the mirror. She looked pale, her face sallow due to worry and rationing. No, it was more permanent than that. She was beginning to get old. She had her first wrinkles now: traces of worry lines across her forehead, crow's-feet around her eyes. She wasn't particularly old, but three months here had taken their toll. All the children had gone last year, all the young islanders. Something vital had been sapped. All that remained now were the middle-aged and the elderly, people waiting to die. The British government had told the Channel Islanders that because the islands weren't of military importance there was no point committing acts of sabotage. They needn't risk their lives, or those of their families, by organizing resistance. Could they resist anyway? There were Germans everywhere, in every house, in every shop, lining the coast, filling up the towns. In France, if you sabotaged a railway line you could be two hundred miles away before the Germans noticed. On an island only twenty-four square miles in area, there was no escape. So the islanders sat out the war – not co-operating with the Nazis any more than they were forced to. It sounded so easy. Some tried more than passive resistance. Marcel Brossier had cut a telephone line. Celia thought that she had met him a couple of times: he was a quiet man, an ordinary man. The Nazis discovered him and shot him without even the pretence of a trial. Everyone had a story like that, everyone had lost a friend. What could be done, though? The Nazis were everywhere. Young, fierce and ambitious, it was as though they'd come from another world. Celia had never been so aware of her own mortality.

Just before Christmas last year, much to the astonishment of the German authorities, Celia had come back to the islands to help her mother at the family boarding-house, or so she claimed. Until she arrived, the full extent of the horror of what was happening here hadn't struck her. She hadn't realized that the Germans might deport her to a labour camp just because she was born in England. If she had been Jewish, she'd have gone, if she made even the slightest anti-German remark. She hadn't been prepared for the oppression that began the moment you woke, that surrounded you as you fell asleep. For months now her dreams had been filled with droning black aircraft, the sound of marching, the feeling that she was being watched. The irony was that this was, in the words of Mayor Sherwill 'a model occupation' – even though the situation had turned for the worse recently as the winter ate up the food and fuel supplies, not too many had been shot, the troops had been ordered to keep their hands off the local women, medicines had been imported from the Continent. Life continued as normal. What could it be like in Poland, or France?

Celia stood stiffly and scooped up her book. There was a large pine dresser alongside the bed. One of the drawers had a false back, and she kept *Advice for Young Ladies* behind there along with her diary and some other things. Both books contained information that would compromise her. A euphemistic way of describing what would happen if the Germans discovered them, but the only one she could bear thinking about this early in the morning. She eased into her underwear and tried to suppress her fears. Under German Law, 'Local commanders of occupied territory may pass summary sentence on persons who are not subject to Military Law if the facts of the case are self-evident and if this procedure is adequate in view of the guilt of the offender' – in other words she could be shot here and now if a German officer felt that she ought to be.

Celia took her work clothes out of the wardrobe, her heart beating faster now. She pulled the plain blue dress over her head and struggled into it. That done, she stood still, breathing deeply. Finally, Celia felt ready to step out onto the landing, she locked her door, and went downstairs. On the way down, she pulled back the blackout screens and drew back the curtains.

As she entered the kitchen, two of the young Nazi boarders abruptly stopped their conversation. They were sitting at the kitchen table in their dressing-gowns sharing a cigarette, which they offered to her. She declined. There were tens of thousands of German troops like these infesting the island. By her reckoning there were as many Nazis on Guernsey as there were native islanders. They all had to stay somewhere. The Doras could almost be described as 'lucky'. They had not been turfed from their house without notice, they hadn't had any furniture stolen. The small boarding-house had currently got a dozen soldiers billeted there. Twelve young privates, none older than nineteen, two to a room. They had, for what it was worth, behaved in the proper fashion. Ma Doras and her daughters Anne and Celia had not been badly treated. They were paid, albeit in useless German Occupation marks, the boarding-house was still in one piece, and they hadn't been abused. Celia knew that others had not been so lucky. She had heard about one girl killing herself after getting pregnant. That girl had hated the Germans. As Celia walked past them to the kettle, one of the Nazis made a comment about her body, but the other quickly shushed him.

'I'm the one that speaks perfect German, remember?' she said sternly. She was careful to sound a little stilted. Both leered at her. It was an impossible situation. Normally she'd tell a young lad like that exactly what she felt about him, but if she did that here they could imprison her or beat her up and no one would bat an eyelid. She had adopted a stern approach to them, making it clear she was unapproachable, never letting them see her in her night-clothes or into her bedroom, never talking to them or accepting the small gifts they continued to offer her. She was well aware that this air of untouchability made her all the more attractive to the young soldiers. It did seem to keep them on their best behaviour, though, and they treated Ma and Anne the same way. She'd heard that another hotel owner insisted that the Germans entered his premises through the back door, and made them wipe their feet when they did so. Apparently he made a point of always coming through the front door himself. That's right, show them who's boss.

Celia kept her eye on the kettle as it boiled on the stove, although she could hear them whispering about her. She carefully measured out a third of a teaspoon of coffee, just enough to flavour the water. Another advantage of living with Germans: they hadn't confiscated the large catering jars of coffee, or the big boxes of tea leaves. Supplies were beginning to run low now, though. With a scowl, Celia realized that the Germans had each taken heaped spoonfuls for themselves. She glanced over at them, but they weren't looking at her any longer. Someone else had come into the room.

'Hello, Celia.'

It was Anne, her sister. She was shorter than Celia, and was a redhead. At sixteen, she was half Celia's age. They didn't look like sisters at all, really. Over the months, though, they'd learnt to look out for each other. Anne's fiancé had left the islands and had joined the British Army. She hadn't heard from him in over a year; he could be alive or dead, he could have a desk job in London or be serving in the jungles of Burma. Anne had a worn grey dressing-gown pulled tightly around her. The German boys gawped at her, and she recoiled. They were just acting like young men throughout the world would, but their uniforms gave them power, literal and psychological. Anne came over to Celia, shielding herself from the Germans. As she passed their eyes met and Anne gave a faint smile, a moment of recognition and understanding.

Anne helped her mother at the boarding-house. Cleaning up and cooking for the Germans billeted there was a full-time job. Celia did the same sort of work, but at the 'town hall', what had been the Royal Hotel. After a couple of slices of toast (no butter) and a quick wash, she headed there. It was a ten-minute walk along the seafront. St Peter Port, the largest town on the island by quite some way, looked like most British seaside villages, with tiers of gaily painted hotels and shops piling up from the harbour. As might be expected, there was an odd mix of architectural styles: provincial French alongside Georgian, with a large contingent of Victorian hotels and public buildings marking the age when the islands became a tourist destination. Not forgetting the more recent concrete pill boxes and gun emplacements.

There was a strong sea breeze, although the weather looked set to improve. Celia strolled along, looking out past Castle Cornet to the open sea. There was a hazy black shape on the horizon, a German ship, probably a frigate. The sense of violence was all-pervasive: war machines filled the skies, patrolled the seas, both on and under the surface, artillery swarmed over and under the land. All along the beach German soldiers with rifles oversaw construction work. The sea wall was being fortified by Todt workers. Slaves, as they used to be known, before slavery had been abolished over a century before. These were men from Georgia, who had been captured on the Eastern Front. They were over a thousand miles from home and all wore drab work clothes that were now little more than rags. They were undernourished, permanently on the verge of death, yet they had to work throughout the day under threat of summary execution. The Nazis considered them subhumans. All that mattered was the victory of the Reich – since all enemies of the Reich would die, it was best that they died working for the Reich. The Georgians grunted rather than spoke, never smiled and grimly accepted their fate. As Celia walked past them to work they hardly seemed human: the Germans had worked a chilling self-fulfilling prophecy. No one really knew how many slaves there were on the island – they were used, as here, to fortify the island, to work the fields and to maintain the roads. No one was entirely sure where they slept. No one ever talked about them, not even in the relative privacy of their own homes. Celia looked away, and turned into Smith Street. She walked up, past the shops.

A swastika flag flapped in the sea breeze over the Royal Hotel. Celia climbed the steps, where two guards with submachine guns always stood on duty. They recognized her, but checked her identity papers anyway before opening the doors for her. She entered the hotel lobby where a dozen local women stood around waiting for their shift to start. There were more guards in here and uniformed German officials and secretaries were already buzzing around.

When their supervisor, a stocky German woman, arrived, they were set to work. For the first couple of hours they worked together, silently, sweeping up the restaurants, scrubbing the kitchen floor. At eleven, Celia began cleaning the rooms on the first floor. These were nearly all bedrooms being used by senior German officials and military personnel. She opened up each of the rooms in turn, scrubbed the surfaces, beat the carpet, opened up the windows to let some fresh air in. Hard repetitive work, but it helped take her mind off things.

She knocked on another door and opened it up with her pass-key. As she stepped into the room she realized that an officer was still asleep in there.

'I'm sorry,' she said in German, 'I'll come back.'

The officer stirred, quickly realizing she was no threat.

'Come in. You can work round me, yes?'

He spoke in English though with a thick accent. Celia recognized him as Herr Wolff, but couldn't remember his exact job. He must have been working late last night to still be in bed at this hour. He was slightly younger than her, nearer thirty than thirty-five, with cropped blond hair and blue eyes. Typical Aryan stock. He smiled as she came into the room. Thankfully he was alone – it was always a bit awkward when they weren't.

'May I open the window?'

'All the better to see you with,' he said, shifting himself upright. Celia pulled back the curtains, letting the light stream in. She turned to face Wolff who was shielding his eyes. He wore striped pyjamas but was powerfully muscled underneath. She set to work, starting at the window-sill. He kept a keen eye on her as she moved around. Instinctively, Celia put her head down.

'I'll leave the window shut for the moment, it's a bit cold outside.'

She bent over the bedside cabinet, wiping it down. He

looked up at her, making her feel self-conscious. At least he was keeping his hands to himself.

'What is your name?'

'Er . . . Celia, Celia Doras.'

'There is no need to worry, you've done nothing wrong.'

'Glad to hear it.'

Celia moved over to the dressing-table, started to polish it, whistling a tune she'd picked up. She could see Wolff still watching her in the mirror.

'Do you like watching people work?' she asked, trying to keep her tone neutral.

He grinned. 'That song you are whistling: "Hang Out Your Washing"? I bet a couple of years ago you'd never have guessed that the Siegfried Line would be coming to you?'

It was an old joke, but she managed a thin smile. Wolff was sitting up, his hands behind his head. Celia watched him warily in the mirror. There was a mark on his forearm, a tattoo. In the mirror it looked like 'ZZ'.

The lighting-bolt insignia: SS. Only members of the Waffen-SS, the most feared soldiers in the whole of the Reich, would have that tattoo. This man was an SS officer. Celia felt sick, she didn't want to stay in this room any longer. If he was SS, then he had killed civilians, he had tortured people.

She tried to sound relaxed. 'I'm finished. Be seeing you.'

Celia glanced back as she closed the door, and saw Wolff pulling himself out of bed. She moved on to the next room. And the next. She finished her round about ten minutes early, at ten to twelve, and went down to the canteen for lunch. She was handed a dollop of potato and a small cube of meat. Food was getting scarce now, unless you knew a farmer who'd managed to stash something away. She sat next to a woman about her age, Marie Simmonds, who lived a couple of doors down from the boarding-house. She leaned over to Celia.

'The Germans shot someone near the airport last night.

12

Said he was a spy from England.' She sounded almost enthusiastic.

Celia shrugged. 'The Germans shoot a lot of people.'

'Celia, Anne's told me how you stand up to them.' Marie gulped down her food. Her short brown hair emphasized her fat little cheeks. She'd got black-market supplies from somewhere – and not necessarily from one of the islanders.

'Leave it to the experts.'

'Are you saying that you are an expert?'

Celia tried to look non-committal.

'Because, "Miss Doras", I don't remember you from before the war. You're the same age as me, right? You said you've been away for fifteen years, but that doesn't explain why we weren't at school together.'

'You must have forgotten about me. I sat in the middle and kept quiet. A bit like most of the islanders nowadays.' The judgement was a little harsher than she'd intended.

'I think I'm on your side. I think I can help. Not all of us are as passive as you think.'

Celia pulled herself back abruptly. 'I think that you'll get us all shot.'

She left the canteen, trying to contain herself. Marie pulled Celia's plate across and scooped over the potato she had left.

At four o'clock, Celia walked home, stopping off at the greengrocer's in Smith Street, next to the post office. The small shop was only open for three hours a day now, and the shelves were pitifully bare. As Celia made her selection, an armoured car rattled past. The young girl behind the counter was a brunette called Collette or Charlotte, something like that. They shared a conspiratorial glance, and the young shop assistant scooped another couple of small spoonfuls of flour into Celia's bag. It was a deal they had, unspoken but powerful none the less. Celia left the shop, feeling ever so slightly guilty about taking more than her ration. The post office still proclaimed that it delivered the 'Royal Mail', but it wasn't the King's head on the stamps it sold.

There was a disturbance up ahead. She saw an elderly couple sitting at the bus shelter. No buses ran, of course, but it was a cold day. A man was confronting them, voices were being raised. As she passed she heard snatches of conversation.

'That brooch is the emblem of a hostile power,' said a young German voice.

'It's an RAF badge, son. Royal Air Force.' A woman's voice.

'You will remove it.'

'I will do no such thing, my son's RAF.'

Things were getting heated now. Celia shoved her hands in her pockets and carried on walking. As she went past she glanced at the scene: the younger man, presumably a German plain-clothes policeman, had drawn his revolver.

'Remove that brooch or I shall tear it off you!'

The elderly man was standing now. 'Don't speak to my wife like that!'

A German military policeman ran past Celia to help his colleague. Celia heard the old man being dragged off, but didn't turn back to look. She could see the boarding-house now, and kept her eyes fixed on it.

Ma was cooking dinner for the Germans, and she didn't like anyone around her when she was cooking, so Celia just dropped off the provisions in the kitchen and went into the front room where Anne was sitting.

Upstairs, Celia could hear some of the Germans shouting, singing and getting drunk. Two of the new German privates sat down here in the front room, playing cards, talking and laughing, occasionally glancing up at the ceiling. Neither of these two could speak any English, which was important to bear in mind. Anne was sewing up some shirts. There was always plenty of darning and laundry to be done, and the Germans paid the women of the island with loaves of bread. It didn't feel like part of the German war effort, but technically it was aiding the enemy.

14

Opinions were divided on whether it was collaboration, but most islanders thought it was acceptable.

'Do you need any help?'

'You can't sew,' Anne reminded her. 'The Germans would shoot you for insubordinate sewing.'

'Fair enough.' She glanced over at the two 'lodgers'. 'Why aren't you in your room, Anne?'

'With that lot upstairs?'

'You're not worried about –'

Anne blushed. 'No, it's just that I wouldn't be able to hear myself think.'

'Do you mind if I read?'

'Of course not.'

Celia stood and squeezed past the Germans to the bookshelf. She bent down to examine its contents. As ever, there were only three books there: an anthology of poetry by Edgar Allen Poe, *Three Plays by Christopher Marlowe* and *The Invisible Man*. The Doras didn't read much. Celia had read all of these books cover to cover several times.

Anne cleared her throat.

Celia glanced back at the Germans, who quickly looked down. It was a prearranged signal: the Germans had been gawping at her again. What was it they found so interesting about her bottom? Celia gave them a disapproving look, and they looked suitably repentant. Then she noticed that the pack of cards they were using had crudely drawn pornographic images on the back.

Celia plucked the Marlowe from the shelf and slipped back over to Anne. She smiled reassuringly at her sister, and opened up the book at a random page.

Why this is hell, nor am I out of it.

Celia slammed the book shut and went back to the bookshelf for the Poe. On the way over, she decided to take *The Invisible Man* as well, to save her a trip. After a couple of minutes she realized that she couldn't work up the enthusiasm to read either of them. She rested the books in her lap.

'Are you friends with Marie Simmonds?' she asked Anne.

'No, I am not,' Anne said harshly. Then, 'We met in the village last week.'

'Not a friend of yours, then?' Celia surmised.

'She's a jerry-bag.' It meant that she slept with the Germans. The islanders didn't distinguish between those doing it for money or those who did it out of love. Either way, it was the ultimate form of collaboration, and the worst thing you could call a woman here. As such, of course, the phrase was used to describe any female whom people didn't like. No one on Guernsey, or anywhere else for that matter, led a blameless life. It seemed a strange double-standard: married women whose husbands had evacuated to the mainland could have affairs with fellow Guerseymen without anyone batting an eyelid, but if they had an affair with a German then they'd be stigmatized.

'How do you know?' Celia didn't like Marie Simmonds, but didn't want to think the worst of her without a bit more evidence.

'I heard, that's all,' Anne said crossly.

'Fair enough.' How many women's lives had been ruined by unsupported allegations? On a small island like this, it was the sort of reputation that stuck for decades. Simmonds would be branded as a collaborating whore until the day she died.

'Marie Simmonds should be shot,' Anne concluded.

Celia looked over at her sister. Pretty little Anne. She was still only a little girl, with a child's body and a playground mentality.

Celia picked her Marlowe up again and began reading.

By half-past ten, the Germans finished their singing. Celia silently made her way upstairs, unlocked her bedroom door and slipped inside. As she got undressed, she tried to work out how many had died on Guernsey since she had been here. Not that many, but the deaths were taken for granted. Murder was so routine, so arbitrary, that it had become the subject of idle canteen gossip. She

16

wrapped a towel around herself, locked her door and headed across the landing to the bathroom.

'Nice legs.'

A young German's attempt at English. His name was Gerhard; he was staying in the room next to hers, sharing with another young private called Kurt. Gerhard was one of the nicer ones: always courteous, always willing to lend a hand. He had developed something of a crush on Celia. He was probably missing his mother. Gerhard sat on the landing, smoking a cigarette by himself, still in uniform. She could feel her towel slipping. Celia cursed herself.

'We go date?'

Celia shook her head, smiling condescendingly. The German leapt up, startling her, but he quickly backed off.

'Need help with bath?'

He couldn't be more than seventeen. Had he ever kissed a girl? He'd certainly not had much practice with chat-up lines. She walked past him without answering, bolting the door behind her.

Ten minutes later the bathroom door opened. Celia emerged onto the landing from a cloud of steam, her skin glistening, damp hair draped over her bare shoulder. Gerhard gaped at her.

'Second thoughts, Private, we go date. Give me ten minutes to dry my hair and you can take me for a walk. Wear your uniform, but bring a coat, there's a storm coming.'

2

The Start of Something Big

The police box's survival was little short of miraculous. The night before, a two-thousand-pound German bomb had crashed through the roof of Portland Street library and exploded. No one had been killed, but one wing of the large Victorian building was now a burnt-out shell. As a small group of local people worked at clearing away the rubble and broken glass early the next morning, they noticed that although the windows of the shops opposite had been shattered by the blast, the little frosted glass panels of the police box had remained intact. Cushioned by the sandbags piled up its sides, the blue box had withstood the full force of the blast – indeed it had deflected some of the debris. What was it made of? Wood? Concrete? Whatever it was, it could withstand anything the Hun could throw at it.

Captain Roslyn Forrester made her way through the fallen masonry, a task not made any easier by her high heels. *Usiyazi*, the Doctor, was there already, just as he said he would be. It had been a week since she had last seen him. He was dusting down the police box with his handkerchief.

She dispensed with the pleasantries. 'The War Office took us in without even checking up, just like you said they would. You'd think that in time of war people would be more security-conscious.'

The little man smiled. 'They checked your file and found that everything was in order, exemplary, in fact. "FORRE-

STER, Roslyn Sarah: Born 1900 in Port Elizabeth (South Africa) to wealthy parents, educated at Fort Hare College, showed remarkable aptitude in applied mathematics and philosophy, joined the army at sixteen, has risen through ranks, despite background, an officer of the highest calibre. Has LONGBOW clearance." '

Roz was unimpressed. 'You've gone back a couple of months and filed away fake documents?'

'I hardly need to. The SID isn't that old yet: they're still on the lookout for bright people from anywhere they can find them. They think that Chris is a Canadian secret agent, of all things. "CWEJ, Christopher –" '

'Yeah, okay, I get the point. Look, I don't want to stand around here all day, it's so damn cold. Watch this.' She exhaled, her breath condensing in front of her. 'Correct me if I'm wrong, Doctor, but you aren't meant to be able to see what you breathe.'

The Doctor laughed. 'Are there any other problems?'

'The uniform itches. I dread to think what sort of chemicals they dye and wash their clothes with here. Cwej, of course, thinks that the "costumes" are wonderful. Apart from that, no problem at all.' Her face had remained straight, but the Doctor gave one of his secret smiles. He knew. Roz continued. 'I'm working with Chris, Lieutenant Reed and a civilian scientist called Lynch, analysing German air-raids, of all things. I take it that events are running to schedule?'

'I've just received word from Bernice: everything is falling into place.'

'But you can't tell me what's happening yet?' Roz had lit herself a cigarette, much to the Doctor's obvious annoyance.

'I don't know precisely what myself. Something big. I'll need you and Chris here, watching my back.' He had been watching her cigarette all the time he had been speaking.

'What do you want us to do?' Roz asked, business-like.

'Find out if anything unusual is going on,' the Doctor said vaguely.

She looked around. 'Well, my initial findings suggest

that Earth War Two is in progress, the planet is at war and that thousands are dying every day. Does that count?'

'No.'

'You won't tell me where you're going. That's fine by me, but are you taking the TARDIS?' Roz didn't mind the Doctor wandering off, but she wanted to be told the ground rules.

The Doctor patted the side of the police box affectionately. 'She's staying right here.'

'It . . . she wasn't damaged last night?' Forrester wasn't particularly surprised, but needed to know.

'It takes more than an Esau dropped from a Dornier to do that. I'm leaving the TARDIS here for you' – he handed her two keys from his waistcoat pocket – 'and these are the only things that can open the doors. One for you, one for Chris. I've preset most of the controls, but if you're not sure then just pull a few levers and press a few buttons at random.' The Doctor leant over and said confidingly, 'That's what I do, and it seems to work most of the time. I'll be back at eight o'clock tomorrow morning, and I'll know what's happening by then, and what our next move will be. Try not to get up to any mischief while I'm gone.'

Forrester glanced up at the reassuring shape of the TARDIS as she pocketed the keys. The Doctor was looking the other way.

'Here comes Chris,' he said.

Forrester glanced over her shoulder. Lieutenant Reed and Lieutenant Cwej were clambering across the rubble towards them. George Reed was younger than Forrester but older than Chris: he must have been about thirty. He looked every inch the heroic type: lantern-jawed, with neatly combed brown hair. He came from a rich Kent family, worked at the War Office on counter-intelligence, and was currently showing them the ropes of the job. Despite herself, Forrester quite liked him; he had a narrow view of the world, but was basically honest. Chris liked him, too. As George arrived, he saluted her – despite her rank there was precious few at the War Office that would do that. Chris stood behind him on a pile of rubble, hands on his hips, surveying the bombsite like a tourist at a theme park.

'Inspecting the damage, Captain Forrester?' asked Reed.

Roz turned to introduce the Doctor, but he had vanished. George apparently hadn't seen him. Her cigarette had disappeared, too. 'That's right. Looks like it was done by an ... Esau dropped from a Dornier. No one was injured – the firemen had to let the fire burn, though: St Kit's hospital and Paddington station were both hit, too. By the way, permission to call me Roz when there's no one else around.'

George grinned. 'You're billeted around here, aren't you?'

Roz glanced up at the TARDIS. 'I am, yes. Hardly recognize the place at the moment.'

Reed lowered his voice. 'It was heavy last night, Roz. A lot of the planes came from the Channel Islands according to radar. Jerry was damned lucky, too; virtually everything they dropped hit something important. There wasn't even a bomber's moon. We can't hit them back without hitting civilians too. Kendrick wants to brief us at 08.45, so you're coming back with us.' He moved away, wanting to inspect the damage for himself.

Chris stepped over. A week ago, when they had first arrived in London, he had been very taken with the fashions of the time. Overnight, he had grown himself a thick handlebar moustache, which he assured Roz was 'just like they have in the air force'. Thanks to his body-bepple, Chris's teeth and nails were always distinctly sharper than human normal. The combined effect of his pointy teeth and new facial hair was to make him look like a gerbil. Roz hadn't the heart to break the news to him.

'It was quite a night, wasn't it?'

Forrester looked up at him. 'Yes, twenty-three dead, two hundred injured.'

'That's not what I meant,' Chris whispered.

'I know. I just met the Doctor.'

21

He perked up. 'Where?'

'Just here. Don't get too excited, he's off somewhere again. He'll be back tomorrow at the same time. He gave me this for you.' She handed over one of the TARDIS keys.

Chris held it up to the light and frowned. 'What's he playing at?'

Roz wished she knew.

The Scientific Intelligence Division Headquarters were part of the War Office, on the banks of the Thames. From the outside the building was imposing – a seven-storey building in white stone. Inside, the rooms were smaller, perhaps less impressive, but nevertheless Chris thought that the third-floor office he shared with Roz and Reed was wonderful. Oak panels, an antique (even relatively speaking) globe, a full drinks cabinet. There was a lovely musty smell that centuries of air-conditioning had erased by the thirtieth century, his and Roz's native time. A large oil-painting hung on one wall – Daedalus and Icarus soaring. Chris couldn't identify the artist, but could appreciate the skill that had gone into its crafting. Although the windows had been taped over to stop the glass shattering during an air-raid, the room afforded a view of the rest of Whitehall. The office was cluttered with files and maps, the largest of which permanently filled a vast round table in the centre of the room.

Admiral Kendrick entered the room. They all stood, saluting. Kendrick acknowledged this, but marched straight over to a composite map of Northern France pinned to one wall. Kendrick was a large man, in his late fifties now. He had an almost regal bearing, and a heavily lined face. Chris had quickly learnt about his commander's military record. Kendrick had proved himself escorting convoys across the Atlantic during the Great War, over a quarter of a century ago, where he had learnt to second-guess the U-boat commanders. He was respected throughout the armed forces. Kendrick glanced up.

'The Channel Islands.' He said nothing more. Chris

grinned, and looked over to Roz, but his partner appeared not to recognize the name. She returned his glance with a mocking look that made him turn away.

Reed piped up, 'I thought we'd agreed that the Germans were holding them for propaganda value only, sir?'

Kendrick grunted. Chris watched Roz glancing between them, bemused.

'Yes, we did, but it doesn't mean we were right. Latest reports show heavy air and naval activity. I think there is something big going on. Cwej?'

Chris mulled it over, pretended to predict what might happen. When he finally spoke he was quoting from one of the books he'd found in the vast TARDIS library. 'The Germans would be foolish not to use the islands for training. They could practise amphibious landings. How far is it from France?'

'About fourteen, fifteen miles to Jersey,' George answered automatically, his eyes still fixed on the map.

'About half the distance to the south coast of England. They could iron out the bugs in the landing procedures, find out who gets seasick, which new landing craft don't work, what supplies they will need, that sort of thing.'

Kendrick looked enthusiastic, but Reed merely looked curious. ' "Iron out the bugs"?'

Chris bit his tongue. It was so difficult to know which phrases were being used and which weren't in any given year. In the end, he'd approached Benny – who after all was a seasoned time traveller as well as an archaeologist. She'd turned out to be quite an aficionado of the cinema of this time, and had recommended half a dozen war movies. They had given him as much insight as any academic textbook. It had been there that he had learnt that all officers had moustaches, something he hadn't found out about in any of the books. Kendrick had one, although it wasn't quite as magnificent as his own. 'A Canadian expression, George,' he said quickly, 'it means "to solve the little problems".' Reed seemed to accept that.

Kendrick was nodding thoughtfully. 'You could be right, Cwej. There's something else: they seem to be testing

23

some totally new weapon there. One of our operatives on Guernsey thinks that Hartung was there last week.'

Kendrick handed Reed a buff folder, which he began examining. This time, Chris was puzzled. When the Doctor had told him that they were going to 1941, he'd spent quite some time researching the period – nothing he'd read had mentioned this Hartung person.

'I've not heard of him,' he heard Roz admitting.

Kendrick didn't look surprised; indeed he hardly seemed to notice she had spoken. Chris was baffled: he had noticed that for some reason, Kendrick often ignored what Roz had to say. As a result, his partner had become noticeably quieter in the last couple of days. He made a note to ask her about it when they had a spare moment. Kendrick certainly reacted when Chris also admitted he knew nothing about Hartung.

'The German avionics expert,' Kendrick offered.

They both shook their heads.

'Used to be a racing driver, built his own cars?'

Chris apologized, but still didn't recognize the name.

'I'm surprised. Perhaps he's a bit before your time. We're expecting a lot from Hartung in the future, though. He's an expert in all sorts of fields: aerodynamics, physics, rocketry, mathematics, metallurgy, even radio waves. A genius. They usually keep him very safe. Rechlin, is it, George?'

Reed looked up from the folder he had been flicking through. 'That's right, sir, on the Mueritzsee, north of Berlin. He has his own team of boffins there. He's been there since November 1936 and the Luftwaffe give him anything he wants – men, materials, money. We're not even sure what he's working on these days. This is the first time he's left Rechlin since Christmas '39.'

'He could be taking part in the landing trials,' Forrester suggested. Kendrick didn't acknowledge her.

'It's not what I'd expected at all. Even with the number of paratroopers they have, the Germans couldn't possibly launch an aerial assault on the British mainland, it would have to be naval. Besides, there hasn't been anything like the build-up of planes they would need. George, show Lieutenant Cwej and Captain Forrester to the File Room. See what you can come up with. Hartung may be a red herring, but it can't hurt to check. You know what it might mean if it isn't.'

Chris watched George's reaction. The two men were keeping something from them. Hardly surprising; he and Roz had only been in the job for a week so he didn't really expect to be privy to the deepest secrets of British Intelligence straight away. Still, it was something to keep in mind. A glance at Roz confirmed that she was thinking the same thing.

The File Room was in the sub-basement, far below the reach of any bomb. Reed knew that it was the first time that either Cwej or Forrester had been down there. He hoped they wouldn't be disappointed. Bare bulbs cast pools of harsh light across the large room. Row upon row of metal shelving strained under the weight of piles and piles of identical buff folders. Every so often the pattern was broken by a small box of index cards. A handful of men and women, some in uniform, some in neat dark blue suits, stood at strategic points, rummaging through boxes, sorting through reams of paper. The air smelled musty, and a thin layer of dust coated every surface. George effortlessly navigated his way through this colourless world. To the untrained eye, this might not have seemed like much, but this was one of the most important rooms in the world: a repository of knowledge about the enemy. Information from this room had saved thousands of lives, and it might yet turn the course of the war.

'How are things filed?' asked Cwej. Reed grinned; the Canadian lad seemed genuinely keen to learn.

'At the end of the day, someone brings the box down with all the papers in. Hopefully, it's in some kind of order. Analysis, reports written by someone here, aerial photographs, that kind of thing, is in the grey files, information from the field is in the buff ones. It's not quite as crazy as it sounds. Normally Kendrick would fill in a docket for you, and one of the office girls would get the file you wanted, but they don't start until nine-thirty.'

'What a wild and wacky world you lead,' he heard Forrester mutter. Reed glanced over to her. The African woman was staring into space, arms crossed. Forrester was an odd one, he thought. She was unlike any woman he had ever known, and was certainly very different from the few other negro women he had encountered. She was jolly civilized, and knew so much, but she seemed so distant. Roz was an African who knew as much physics as their own boffins. But it wasn't just that: Reed recognized something in her unique to those who had seen active service. Cwej was strong and well trained, but Reed instinctively knew that he'd hardly ever fired a shot in anger. Roz? Roz Forrester had seen friends die, she'd faced the enemy a dozen times, she'd led her troops over the top. Reed recognized a kindred spirit in this exotic creature. She was a riddle that he wanted to solve, and a woman he found profoundly attractive.

'Don't they have filing where you come from, Captain?'

'No. We've not used paper files for centuries,' she said casually. She gave one of her rare grins, her teeth so white against her ebony skin. George realized that he was staring at her, and looked away. They had reached the box he was looking for. It was on a high shelf, and together he and Cwej began to ease it down to the ground. They both turned down Forrester's offer to help. Sure enough, they soon managed to get the box down onto the floor. Now Cwej knelt down and helped Reed look through it. After a couple of fruitless minutes, George looked up.

'Found it.'

As Roz trudged back to the office behind George and Chris, it occurred to her that this job would be a lot easier with even a rudimentary computer terminal. In her time, police computers could collate all the surveillance and forensic information in a case and seven times out of ten they'd manage to name the culprit from just that. In 1941, and she supposed for a couple of decades still to come, the job still involved some physical effort. Soon this file room would be gone, replaced with one of those big antique processors. George's successors would simply tap their request into a terminal somewhere and reams of computer paper would spew out. A couple of decades after that, the computers would do most of the analysis, indeed most of the spying, for them. Paper would become a thing of the past and a whole new order of crimes would evolve: computer fraud, hacking, aggravated flaming, narcoware, blackemail, intermeshing.

They had arrived back at their office. Immediately, George moved over to the drinks cabinet and smiled. 'Too early in the morning for you, Cwej?'

Chris seemed momentarily confused by the question, so Forrester stepped into the breach. 'He doesn't drink, Lieutenant. I do, though.'

George handed her the folder, reaching into the drinks cabinet for a narrow-necked bottle.

'Is it OK if I look at this?' Forrester asked, resting the folder on her lap.

'I wouldn't have handed it to you if it wasn't.' George had located a couple of glasses.

Forrester nodded and opened the file. For Chris's benefit, George recited the details without needing to refer to it: 'Born June twenty-sixth 1898, his parents were a dentist and the daughter of a prominent industrialist. Served in the Luftwaffe in France during the Great War, then went on the Heidelberg. Worked on the design teams of all the major German automobile companies, was a racing driver from the late twenties until about five years ago. His first love was really aerodynamics – there are over two hundred individual patents in his name covering all aspects of planes: engines, guidance, construction. But the man has a secret.' He leant over. 'His grandmother was Jewish. Couple of people from the racing world remember talking to him in the 'thirties, and they say he's not that fond of the Nazis. Kendrick reckons, and he's not usually wrong, that Hartung is ready to defect.'

George handed Roz a generous measure of brandy and

took a sip from his own glass. She flipped through the file. There were a couple of old press clippings, and a more recent photo that had been crudely torn from a news- paper. The caption said it had been taken at a race meet- ing in January 1936. Hartung was a handsome devil, thick black hair slicked back, with dark eyes. In this picture he wore a very sharp suit and leather gloves. What remained of the caption read '(Photo M. Jarvis: Emil Hartung in Cairo with his latest travelling companion, Miss Bu–'. Miss Bu was missing from the picture, although Roz could make out that there were Arabs in the background.

'I can see why Scientific Intelligence would be interested,' she offered.

The Scientific Intelligence Division had been formed late the previous summer, on Kendrick's recommenda- tion. Its job was to co-ordinate the various pieces of specialized technical information that came the way of British Intelligence. At this early stage, the Division con- sisted of around a dozen officers and half a dozen scien- tists. It was the first organization that linked the two groups (officially, at any rate). Military technology was becoming more and more advanced by the day: only a specialist could hope to really understand cryptography, radio technology and electromagnetism. Field operatives continued to radio in even the slightest thing they felt was important. The SID read everything that was picked up by radio operators in Bletchley, both intercepted German messages and information sent by field agents. Aerial reconnaissance was producing hundreds of photographs every day. Millions of pieces of information were being collected, and it was becoming increasingly difficult to understand what the Germans were developing, predict when it would be ready and work out a defence. The SID was designed to deal with the unknown weapon, the unexplained German radio signal and to report directly to the War Cabinet. The military officers came from all three services, the scientists only from the finest universit- ies and private research labs, from all the Allied countries. Forrester and Cwej had been brought in from abroad, from South Africa and Canada respectively, or so the SID thought.

'Hartung's defection might in itself be enough to turn the tide of the war.'

Roz bit her lip. This was something big. Was this what the Doctor was looking for? She pondered this for a moment, then, 'Couldn't it be a bluff? He could be a double agent or might not want to defect at all.'

George shrugged. 'That, Roslyn, is the question.'

The phone rang, surprising Chris.

'It's only the telephone, Cwej. Hello?' George listened intently for a second, then put the handset back. 'Kendrick wants a word, won't be long.'

George got up and left the room hurriedly.

'He seemed worried,' suggested Chris. Roz was having none of it.

'Will you please explain what is going on? What are these islands, who is this Hartung and what on Earth has his Jewish grandmother got to do with anything?'

Chris looked pleased with himself. 'You shouldn't skimp on your research, Roz, we learnt that last time. The Channel Islands are a small group of islands off the French mainland – they belonged to the Normans about two thousand years ago, the Great British held them for virtually the whole of the Second Millennium, although they were briefly held by the Germans, and that's the period we're in now. Later, they were captured by the Spanish in the Gibraltan War. They're part of the Undertown now, of course. Spaceport Seven, I think.'

'Thank you, Lieutenant Database. They're not exactly the centre of the universe, though, are they?'

'No.'

'Have you heard of Hartung?'

'Not at all. I mean, to be fair, I'd not heard of Franco, Mussolini or Stalin until we came here.'

Forrester only recognized two of the names. How could the Doctor leave them in such a temporal backwater? This was a full millennium before they were born, an age when radar and rockets were state of the art. There were still cavalry regiments, for Goddess's sake. How could anything important happen here?

George came back through the door, and he looked flustered. Kendrick came in right behind him. Behind him was a pipe-smoking civilian, in a tweed jacket: Eric Lynch, the research scientist from Cambridge. Roz and Chris saluted.

'I have just received word from one of our top agents on Guernsey. Hartung is conducting tests there of a new aerial weapon. Our agent doesn't know what this weapon is, but has established that the tests involve the frigate Vidar. Hartung has been seen a number of times on Guernsey, but we believe that he is based at the airfield just outside of Granville.'

George nodded thoughtfully. Kendrick continued. 'The team working on the problem, that's Davis and young Lynch here, suspect that the Germans have a new type of airborne weapon, a superbomber that could devastate our cities with minimal losses to their forces. We had a report of such a programme as long ago as 1939, but we never located the research site or had any confirmation of the weapon's existence.'

'A superbomber?' Chris said curiously. 'What exactly do you mean?'

'I mean a bomber much larger and faster than anything else in the sky. It will be the Dreadnought all over again, only this time the Germans will have it first.' Kendrick could see that Roz was confused, so he explained, 'In 1906, the Navy put the HMS Dreadnought to sea: it was the fastest, most heavily armed ship that the world had ever seen. It was so powerful, in fact, that it could outclass any other ship on the oceans. Now, you'd think that this would have strengthened the British Navy, but instead –'

' – when the Germans built one, it made every other warship in the Navy obsolete,' finished Roz. 'Whoever built the most dreadnoughts would win the arms race, regardless of how many centuries of naval tradition they had.'

Kendrick nodded. 'Well done. Thankfully, we could

build more than the Germans, so we could keep control of the seas and win the last war. It's an open secret that the RAF are trying to develop a heavy bomber that will really be able to take the fight to the German cities, but we are still over a year away from seeing one of those in action. Until a couple of weeks ago, though, we thought that the Germans had other priorities. Now it looks as if Hartung is building a superbomber after all.' Kendrick paused, looking at Cwej in a way that made Roz feel distinctly uncomfortable. It was the sort of look that her superiors always used to give her before sending her off-world to adjudicate on a planet where the two sides were already holed up on different continents firing photon bombs at each other. Sure enough:

'This is our last chance to bring Hartung over before his project is complete. We need to snatch him from them. A commando raid is out of the question; we need something smaller to get through coastal defences. Likewise, Downing Street can't spare us any paratroopers, not without better evidence. Lieutenant Cwej, I want you to go over to France on your own and bring Hartung back to London. I've checked your file and you are the most qualified person in the SID for such an operation. I have arranged to get you down to Plymouth for this afternoon, there you will join the submarine Prometheus. Commander Hobson will take you to the French coast, and you'll receive a further briefing from MI5 on the way. Any questions?'

Roz stood. 'With respect, Admiral, I'm far more experienced than Cwej. I should go.'

'It's far too dangerous for a woman, and your skin makes you just a little bit conspicuous, don't you think?' The response was disdainful, and Roz wouldn't have talked to a child like that. She tried to appear calm. A hand touched her shoulder and she almost ripped it off. It was Chris.

'Don't worry, Roz, I'll be fine.' He beamed his gerbil smile.

Forrester looked at him, eager to go off to war. Oh Goddess, she thought, please let him come back.

3

Bang on Time

Celia had changed into a thick floral dress. Gerhard thought that it suited her, and it must help to keep her warm. He had told her as much, but she hadn't seemed to hear him. The cold wind that had been blowing all day had finally developed into a thunderstorm. Celia also wore a heavy navy-blue coat, unlike Gerhard who had been trying not to shiver ever since they'd left the boarding-house. It was dark now, and as usual there was a blackout in force. All over the island, the street lights had not been lit and curtains were in place. If it had been a clear night, it might have been possible to see the odd light on the French or even the English mainland, but tonight the horizon was black as pitch.

Gerhard had the distinct impression that Celia was steering him away from the town and out into the country. He could understand this – with the age difference between them the islanders were sure to gossip, and the local people would have thought of her as a collaborator. It was good that she was brave enough to risk that. They'd been walking along a narrow lane now for three-quarters of an hour. They talked as they went, and as a special dispensation, Celia had let them speak in German.

'It is cold, isn't it?'

This was not the first time that he had pointed this out on their walk.

'Don't worry, it'll be nice and warm where we're going.'

'And where is that exactly?'

They stopped and she looked him straight in the eye. Gerhard was five foot eight, which was above average height for his age, but Celia was a little taller. For the first time, he found this disconcerting.

'Trust me.'

He moved a little closer. Celia took a step back. 'You can't kiss me yet.'

Gerhard's eyes lit up. 'Then later?'

Celia gave a sly smile. 'Let's keep walking, find somewhere quiet.'

'Who goes there? Declare yourself!' was shouted from twenty yards away, then torchbeams. Gerhard held his hand above his face.

'It is me, Gerhard. Is that you, Franz?'

It was indeed Franz, another one of the young soldiers boarding at the Doras'. Gerhard offered him a cigarette and explained about his date in German. Obviously, Franz recognized Celia. Technically, the curfew wasn't due to start for another couple of minutes, but Franz reminded them both that they shouldn't be out here this late. Couldn't they have picked better weather for a walk? Solemnly, Celia and Gerhard agreed. Then Franz and his (unseen) companion disappeared into the night. Gerhard reached out for Celia.

'May I hold your hand?'

'I'm sure I can allow that. Follow me.'

Gerhard watched as Celia clambered over a stile. He followed, but found the thin footboard a little more slippery. He negotiated his way across it and jumped down into the small field. It had been raining for a while, but the ground underneath his boots was still firm. Before he had been posted here, Gerhard had taken part in the devastating assault against France – the Blitzkrieg. He'd marched hundreds of miles with his regiment. Gerhard knew that the thousand-year Reich would be based on such victories. The history books might not mention him by name, but Gerhard knew that he had played a part. He had been one of the first soldiers into Paris. He remembered the victory marches, past the Eiffel Tower, past the

Louvre, past Notre-Dame. His children would know: fifty years from now his children and his grandchildren would be proud of what he had done for Germany. The Brandenburg Gate would be a symbol, it would be the centre of the largest empire the world had ever seen. Celia was still young enough to bear those children.

She was running ahead of him now. As Gerhard watched, she unfastened her coat and let it fall to the ground. She was so sure of herself. The girls in his home town of Waiblingen were not like her at all. The populations of small islands such as this tended towards the simple-minded, but this woman was as sharp as they came. She was beautiful too, with a wide, kind mouth and flowing blonde hair.

To his surprise they had reached a gorse-covered clifftop: the dark sea glistened twenty feet below them. This was one of the small coves that lined the coast of these islands, but not one that he recognized. He was surprized that no barbed wire had been laid here. For a moment, Celia stood poised on the edge of the cliff, and Gerhard could have sworn that she was about to throw herself off. She was staring into the distance, oblivious to everything around her: the rain, the sea, Gerhard himself. Then she turned to him, grabbing his hand again.

'Are you scared?'

Gerhard realized that he hadn't been breathing for the last few seconds. 'Yes. No. Where are we going?'

'Follow me.'

They scrambled down a steep rocky path onto the beach. The sand was damp.

Celia noticed his hesitation. 'What's the matter?'

'Celia, this beach will have been mined, so will the sea.'

'Don't worry. It's too small and out of the way to bother with. I've been here a couple of times before. What time is it?'

'Aren't you wearing a watch?'

She leant over and whispered in his ear, 'I'm not wearing anything at all apart from this dress.'

Gerhard fumbled for his wristwatch. 'It's about midnight.'

'Just before or just after?'

'Just before.'

Celia nodded thoughtfully. 'Shall we go for a swim? We could go behind those rocks and get ready. We won't need costumes, it's so dark and there's no one else around.'

Gerhard nodded dumbly, and followed her. They worked their way across the sand, reaching a pile of rocks that had fallen from the cliff last winter. Behind the largest of these they were sheltered from the worst of the storm. Celia leant against the cliff face. Gerhard stood close, mesmerized.

'What's the time now?'

'Why worry about –' He edged closer. Celia pushed him away.

'Just tell me the time.'

'Just gone midnight. For God's sake, why?' Gerhard was baffled. Did Englishwomen have to wait until a certain time at night? It wouldn't surprise him. Before he could formulate any suspicions, Celia was speaking again.

'Can you hear something odd?' she asked softly, her head cocked to one side.

Gerhard listened, but all he could hear were the waves and the wind. No. There was something else. A noise from the sky. It was too quiet to be a plane ... it was unlike anything he had heard before. He glanced at Celia who was staring over his shoulder, a look of astonishment on her face. Gerhard turned.

There was a huge explosion.

Gerhard's training kicked in automatically and he fell to the floor, his hands over his head. It had been a comet, or some shooting star. A blossoming orange light, burning his eyes. It was too high up to be a shell or a bomb. Celia was already crouching alongside him, covering her ears, staring past him. Gerhard kept his head down. A deep resonant boom echoed from the granite cliffs, repeating

35

and repeating. The ground rocked in sympathy. Celia stood shakily, dusting the sand from her skirt.

Something hit the sea.

There was a terrifying crashing noise, Gerhard could hear the waters surge and boil. A small tidal wave washed across the beach, swirling over Celia's bare ankles, drenching him as he cowered at her feet. A second later a rumbling underwater explosion sent plumes of water dozens of feet into the air. Tiny fragments of what looked like wood and leather clattered against the cliff face. Red-hot pieces of metal rained from the sky. There was the unmistakable smell of death.

Celia stood pressed against the cliff face watching this scene. Finally she said something and Gerhard didn't understand it.

'Cruk!'

Bernice Summerfield watched the fire falling and felt the adrenalin that she had spent so long trying to suppress flow through her, warming her. For three months she had not dared to think like this: she had hidden herself in someone else's clothes and someone else's name. The beach was lit now by hundreds of tiny burning pieces of debris that threw evil shadows across the cove. She could feel the heat from here; she could feel the rain and the wind and the rock against her skin. The earth still trembled from the explosions. God, she felt younger already! Gerty had scrambled to his feet, but now stood watching the spectacle, his mouth open.

'I suggest you get out there and see what's going on,' Benny said, trying to look suitably apprehensive.

Gerhard looked at her for a second, then nodded, scurrying across the beach to the shore. The Doctor's note had warned Benny about the explosion, but that hadn't stopped her jumping out of her skin when it actually happened. And she had absolutely no idea what was going on, as per usual. For starters, it would be nice to know exactly what had exploded. Well, there were enough clues lying about.

While Gerhard busied himself, Benny looked around. It didn't take her long to find a flat piece of metal debris. It was still red-hot despite the driving rain, so she piled wet sand over it with her hands to cool it down. After a minute she retrieved it, slipping it into her dress pocket. She could feel it warm against her leg. Gerhard was peering out to sea, but it wouldn't be much longer before his Nazi pals arrived. She recovered her shoes and hurried away.

Benny went straight home. She had to dodge only one Nazi patrol on the way back to St Peter Port, an armoured personnel carrier that had been heading for the crash site. Air-raid sirens were blaring, and carefully orchestrated drills were being performed. Every dog on the island seemed to be barking. Everyone on the island would have been awoken by the explosion, fearing that it was an air-raid. The only planes flying overhead were German, though, heading for England. Benny clambered over the high garden wall of the guest-house, and let herself in through the unlocked back door. Home security was lax in the 1940s and burglary was hardly a major problem on a Nazi-occupied island. She'd found that she could come and go almost as she pleased. She quickly secured the blackout curtain behind her and went straight to her room.

Once she had bolted her door, Benny moved over to the dresser. She fished what looked like a radio out from the hidden compartment. A couple of months ago, the Germans had confiscated all the radios they had found. She might have guessed that listening to German military transmissions was not allowed, but it was a criminal offence just to listen to the BBC, although most people still did it. If the Germans had discovered Benny's radio, though, they would be preoccupied with how technically advanced it was. The Germans led the world in magnetic tape-recording, yet they were years from producing anything so compact. A German scientist would find it almost impossible to explain even in the broadest terms how the radio receiver or the tuning mechanism worked and would have a few questions to ask her. How could such a high-quality speaker be manufactured? Where was the battery? Benny often took the Spatio-Temporal Alarm Beacon on her field-trips: it was her link with the Doctor and it allowed her to monitor local transmissions. She looped the headphone over her ear and flicked it on. The BBC World Service came up with the usual blend of made-up and heavily censored stories, concentrating on the one battle the British had won, making no mention of the twenty they had lost. The war sounded so much more heroic on the radio than in real life. She flipped open a small panel on the side and punched in a code number. A second later the 'message sent' LED lit. Benny glanced at the LCD clock on the side: 00:52.

It was late, and she was exhausted. It had been a long day – technically it was already tomorrow. Rationing was so tight now that most islanders couldn't summon up the energy to walk very far, and Benny had just made a five-mile round trip. She unbuttoned the dress and shrugged it off before towelling herself down. She slipped into bed and was asleep within minutes.

Outside a man was walking up the sandy beach, straight from the sea. No one saw him arrive, and so no one saw that as he strolled up the beach he left no footprints in the sand.

For the first time in months, Benny slept through the return of the German bombers. She woke as the door handle jerked downwards. She was instantly alert, reaching under her pillow. With her other hand she grasped the mattress, without really knowing why. They always came when your guard was down.

The door opened. She had bolted it.

She tensed. To have come so far . . . It was a friend,

38

it was her only real friend. He raised his hat, closing and bolting the door behind him with his free hand.

'Good morning, Miss Doras. That is your name, isn't it? How are you?'

Benny relaxed again, sinking back into the sheets. She smiled too, her first real smile for far too long. It was good to see him again, to hear his voice.

'Mustn't grumble.'

She saw the Doctor's eyes flicker with pride.

'Sorry I took so long, but I had to stop off on the way for your milk, and I took a bit of a wrong turning. Anyway, I thought you could do with a good night's sleep after all you've been through.' He handed her a plastic bottle of semi-skimmed milk, a litre not a pint. The use-by date was '27 April', but it didn't say which year. She hadn't asked him for any milk. The container was icy cold. Benny sat up to take it from him.

'The door was bolted,' she noted.

The Doctor was examining the leaves of a house plant which sat on the window sill. 'Um?'

Three months ago, she'd found this aspect of his behaviour infuriating, now it seemed almost endearing. He was also the only person she'd ever known who didn't notice when she was naked.

'I could have killed you. I had a gun under my pillow. I might have flunked the odd class during my military training, but even I could blow your head off at point-blank range.'

'If you did that, I'd just grow a new one,' the Doctor joked. At least Benny assumed it was a joke.

'Pick a less bendy one next time. One whose eyebrows occasionally stay in the same place for more than two seconds.'

The Doctor deliberately contorted his face. Benny laughed. She leant over and hugged him. It was so good to see him.

The Doctor seemed embarrassed. 'Please, Professor Summerfield, put some clothes on, I have a reputation to maintain. You'll get me struck off.'

The Doctor extricated himself and sat on a small wooden chair, hands clasped over his umbrella. Benny looked at him. He hadn't changed in the last three months of course. Unlike her, he hadn't aged a bit. A decade from now, they'd look the same age. A decade after that and everyone would assume that the Doctor was her son. She had always known that he was an alien, an immortal being who resembled a scruffy little middle-aged man, but most of the time the knowledge sat at the back of her mind and she didn't let it bother her. Once, just once, in the last three months, she had questioned his motives, wondering why he should leave her totally alone for so long. For a little while she had even wondered whether he had abandoned her to die in this time, for some inscrutable alien reason of his own. Perhaps she was turning into a racist. Or alienist. Whatever Roz was. As Benny watched him, the Doctor glanced down at the floor, then poked at something with the point of his umbrella.

He broke into a grin. 'Nice dress.'

Benny pulled herself up and swung her legs over the side of the bed. 'Check the pocket.'

'You know, I'd forgotten how ratty you were first thing in the morning. Ah, this is interesting.'

The Doctor turned the knobbly piece of metal he'd found in the dress pocket over and over in his hand. Benny stood stretching, and stepped over to the dresser. She caught a reflection of her gaunt face, her dead eyes and her skinny arms. The Doctor hadn't looked up.

'Just a guess, Doctor, but I bet that Chris and Roz have had a better three months than me.'

'They're in London, with the TARDIS. And they've only been there a week. We had to attend to the political situation on Troxos 4. I'll tell you about it one day, or better still I'll show you. Er, won't you get cold like that?'

Benny shrugged indifferently. After a second, she looked up from her clothes drawer.

'The TARDIS is in London? How did you get over here then?'

The Doctor smiled enigmatically, and she decided not to press the point.

'I'll meet you downstairs when you're dressed.'

The Doctor lifted himself up and left the room. Benny reached over to bolt the door, but it was already bolted. Rather than think about it, she reached for the holowig, and brushed the filament into her hair. She stood back, watching herself in the mirror as her hair lightened. Naturally brunette, she still wasn't used to seeing herself as a peroxided blonde. She'd tried to bleach her hair when she was twelve, an act of defiance that had gone very very wrong, so badly wrong that she'd worn a plastifez until it grew out. She'd been blonde a couple of times since, over the years, but it had never really suited her. The holowig was less fuss, a gadget from a short-lived late-twenty-first-century craze that used fibre optics and a simple holographic projector. Her hair was naturally longer now than she would normally wear it, shoulder-length. Benny remembered writing a paper on fashions in the twentieth century. As she applied her make-up, Benny recalled a relevant passage; 'Whereas most clothing now' – the mid-twenty-sixth century – 'tends to be fairly androgynous, in the first half of the twentieth century in the Anglo-Saxon territories clothing was used to emphasize sexual difference: women wore skirts, and low-cut blouses, that emphasized their breasts and hips. Men wore jackets with square shoulders and often wore hats, to emphasize their size and physical presence. This can best be seen in the military uniforms of the period (see illustration). Gender roles at all levels of society were more strictly defined anyway, with a –'. Typical Summerfield prose, Benny mused: wandering punctuation, too talky, and it wasn't really about anything. Ace had once managed to get hold of that paper. She had been particularly taken with 'Mods were so named due to their love of modernist poetry'. A mistake that anyone could have made. It was hardly fair, anyway. Archaeologists should be able to get away with generalizations and guesswork without representatives of long-dead civilizations coming along and laughing at them.

The Pharaohs hadn't phoned Howard Carter up and corrected him on points of detail, had they? No, they jolly well hadn't. This period was as distant to Benny as the Hundred Years War was to Ace – the occasional error was bound to slip in every so often. Benny finished getting dressed and packed her belongings – including the milk – into a small travel bag.

When Benny had finished, she made her way downstairs to the kitchen and the Doctor. Ma Doras was sitting at the kitchen table, mugs of tea ready for them. She was a stout woman nearly sixty years old, with great wide hips and thick ankles. As ever, a cigarette hung from her lip.

The Doctor was in the middle of an anecdote. '. . . and when he turned round they were all wearing –'

'Morning, Celia. The Germans have all gone, trouble down at St Jaonnet. Something to do with the explosion last night,' Ma said quickly. The old woman turned her full attention to the new arrival, apparently relieved that she didn't have to hear any more.

'I saw the explosion happen,' Benny said. Ma didn't look surprised.

The Doctor sipped at his tea, chuckling to himself. Suddenly, his expression clouded over. 'Celia is going now, Ma.'

The old woman's expression flickered. 'I'll miss you, Bernice.'

It was the first time that she'd ever used that name. Benny gave a thin smile. She would not be sorry to leave Guernsey, but would certainly miss Ma and Anne. Before she went, though, she had to ask a question. 'Why did you help us? The Germans could have you killed.'

Ma Doras and the Doctor shared a conspiratorial look.

Ma spoke softly. 'I can remember the last time the Doctor was here, a long time now. Back before the first war. He saved the islands then, and those of us who were there know what he had to go through to do it. There's worse out there than Nazis, believe it or not, and there's worse than dying. That's when Celia, my baby Celia, died. Will you tell me something now, Doctor?'

He nodded, and she continued. 'It's going to get better, isn't it? We'll win the war?'

Benny watched the Doctor, expecting his usual knowing silence. Instead he spoke in a low voice. 'It'll get better, Ma, but it will get worse before it does. More islanders will be deported, tens of millions of people will die across the world, soldiers and civilians, men and women, Jews and Gentiles. Great scars will be left on history, wounds that will take generations to heal. Terrible weapons will be built. But there will also be courage, technical innovation, hope for the future. This will be the last war of its kind for a very long time. Anne's children will live all their lives in peace and safety and so will their children.'

They had left shortly afterwards. Benny took one last look at the boarding-house, then they set off for the crash site. After a few minutes it became obvious that the Doctor knew the way.

'What is the size of the German occupying force?' The Doctor sounded almost conversational as he interrogated her.

'It varies; somewhere between twenty and twenty-five thousand.'

The Doctor seemed to work something out with his fingers. He chuckled. 'More per square mile than in Germany! What are they doing here?'

'Most are just barracked here. The islands are being heavily fortified. The sea defences at St Peter Port have been improved, there's some sort of underground hospital complex being built and there's unusual activity, and very high security, up at the airstrip.'

She peeked at him to check his reaction.

'Good.' He nodded absent-mindedly, as if he already knew the answers. 'Did you know that Victor Hugo wrote *Les Misérables* in St Peter Port? I told him to change the title, but he wouldn't listen.'

'There's a statue of him in the Candie Gardens. Doctor,

I may be talking out of turn, but what are we doing here?' She had waited long enough, and now the Doctor was here she wanted some answers.

'It's all to do with that explosion.'

Benny rolled her eyes. 'You don't say. I won't ask how you knew where and when it would happen. I take it it's alien?'

'Um?' The Doctor was checking his pocket watch.

He was annoying her again now.

'The piece of metal. It's from a spacecraft. The same spacecraft that I saw this time last week.'

With a magician's flourish, the chunk of metal appeared in the Doctor's hand. He tossed it to her. 'You're the archaeologist. See for yourself.'

Benny turned it over, peering at it. It was black, twisted. She couldn't make anything of it, she couldn't tell what type of metal it was, what that weird stuff it was coated with was or how it had been manufactured. She told the Doctor as much. He took the fragment back and it vanished with a flick of his wrist.

'Is it alien? Well, that's a very subjective question, isn't it? I think it's chronistic, though. I know for a fact that it was manufactured near here.'

She was puzzled. 'Then our work here is done, surely?'

'Um?'

'Concentrate, Doctor. We've finished here. If this is man-made and from this time period – I don't think "chronistic" is a word, by the way, and the archaeologist in me would prefer "concurrent" – then no one's changing history. Therefore, the Doctor and Benny leave in the TARDIS, pausing only to pick up any policemen from a thousand years in the future that they may have left lying around.'

The Doctor stopped in his tracks and laid his hand on her shoulder. 'Take a deep breath, Benny.'

'I'm perfectly calm, I just . . .'

'Close your eyes and take a deep breath. Do you feel the air surging into your body? Your lungs inflating? New oxygen pumping around your body and into your brain?'

44

Benny nodded, her eyes still closed. The Doctor's voice was almost hypnotic. 'By breathing in those air molecules you've changed history. You've left footprints that wouldn't have been left, eaten food that someone else could have eaten.'

She shifted uncomfortably. For the last couple of months she'd lived under rationing. Last night, she'd only allowed herself two inches of water for her bath, and felt guilty about that.

'Yes, well, I couldn't help it.' She paused, then stamped her foot. 'Hang on a minute, your hypocritical old fraud! You told Ma the outcome of the war, so don't blame me for breathing.'

'I wasn't. There are billions of humans on this planet, all of them eat, all of them breathe. All of them, some more than others, are changing history every second of their existence. So many choices, so many possibilities. Something is wrong here. That piece of metal is a clue.'

'What are you saying?'

'Not only evil aliens change history, Benny. It's more subtle than that sometimes. That piece of metal should not be here. That is why we're here. Pinpoint the problem, and remove it before it has a chance to alter history.'

'The Doctor on a surgical strike,' whispered Bernice.

'What was that?'

Benny looked down at the little man. How long had she been travelling with him now? She had been thirty when she had met him, and she'd thought that she'd seen it all. She didn't know for certain how old she was now. Time is relative, as the Doctor kept saying. When she was in a philosophical mood – three or more glasses into the evening, usually – she liked to say that you were as old as you felt. Flying around saving the universe she felt a decade younger than she did scrubbing floors in a hotel.

They had reached the stile. Benny could see over it into the field. A ring of German troops surrounded the cove, an armoured car sat in the middle of the field. More unarmed troops were bent down collecting debris, placing it in large paper sacks. From this angle, it was impossible to see down into the cove itself. They were safe where they were, though, for the moment. She ducked out of sight, but the Doctor popped up his head.

'There are a lot of them,' he remarked. 'Too many. Three dozen? That's just what I can see.'

'Is there another way down?'

'The ones on the cliff will see us if we get down that far, and they'd have the high ground. We'd be sitting ducks.'

The Doctor was crouched, leaning on his umbrella, his eyes closed. Benny looked around. No one had seen them, but it was hardly the time or place to go into a trance.

The Doctor's eyes snapped open. 'Could you arrange a diversion?'

'Bernice Summerfield versus the massed Nazi hordes. Oh yes, an even match there.' The Doctor looked disappointed, so she continued. 'I'll do my best to outwit them. After all, I'm old enough to be their mother.'

'Sign you're getting old that, when the Nazis start to look young.'

Benny winced.

'I'll need to get down onto the beach. Even I can't slip past so many people, not when they're alert.' The Doctor was already sizing up the situation.

Benny nodded thoughtfully as she pushed her travel bag into the hedge. She pulled the holowig from her head and stuffed the filament into her pocket. Her hair dark again, she vaulted over the stile.

'Hello, everyone. Have you see my coat? I left it here yesterday.'

Some of the troops stepped forward. A couple of them had raised their machine pistols, but not many of them considered her a threat. All of them were looking at Benny, though, and she was right – they were all younger than her. There didn't seem to be a commanding officer. She didn't recognize any of them. One of the troops had come up to her.

'This is restricted place,' he announced in a very thick accent.

'Oh, sorry, I was looking for my coat. Big blue thing.'

Before he could reply, Benny had yanked the rifle from his hand and pulled him in front of her, shielding herself from the rest of the troops. It all happened too fast for the other Germans. Just as they were realizing what was going on, Benny had fired above their heads. But not that far above. They fell to the ground for protective cover, pulling their guns up. Benny leapt for the armoured car.

The Doctor was stepping carefully across the beach when he heard the crackling of gunfire. It mustn't distract him. There was heavy lifting machinery down here, and something huge had been dragged from the sea. Whatever it was had been covered by a large black tarpaulin. The handful of troops on the beach were scrambling up the narrow path to assist their comrades.

The Doctor rapidly moved towards the tarpaulin. It covered an object the size of a tank, or small shuttlecraft. The Doctor poked at it experimentally with his umbrella. There was a satisfying clank. Whatever it was, it was made of thick metal. The Doctor moved forwards cautiously and lifted the sheeting. A grenade detonated above him with a soft crump.

Thankfully, as Benny had hoped, there was no one inside the German vehicle. She slammed shut the hatch, bolting it, and slid over to the driver's seat. It was dark and reeked of sweat. The only light came from a couple of slits at the front. Through those, Benny could see troops running towards her.

As they reached her, she discovered how to start the engine. The armoured car roared into life, lurching forward, and the troops scattered. Just as Benny was working out how to change the gears, a rifle bullet richocheted off the roof.

She had better start thinking about tactics. There were three groups of Nazis, one to the left, two to the right. The unarmed men had fallen back, but weren't heading for the beach. The Germans were as disorganized as she was. It didn't really matter, though: she realized that she'd effectively boxed herself in. She just needed to buy a little time for the Doctor. Who knows, she might even have supplied his getaway car. A grenade bounced off the roof, clattering past her sight. She pulled hard left on the steering wheel, and the car swerved out of the way. There was an explosion to her side and a shower of soft mud, but the axle held.

Damn. One of the groups was falling back, heading for its original position. They'd soon be back at the clifftop, and they were bound to see the Doctor if they got that far. Benny steered the vehicle towards them, its primitive suspension almost throwing her from her seat. Military vehicles throughout history had never been built for comfort. The other two groups were now behind her, out of view, and she was getting too close to the cliff edge for comfort. She mustn't let her mind wander. Damn!

The Doctor peered into the murk under the tarpaulin. He wrinkled his nose as the smell of salt, rotting leather and charcoal wafted out. He ran his finger along a metal panel which had blackened and warped in intense heat. His brow furrowed.

'Do you know what it is?'

The Doctor shrugged. 'It's the most advanced piece of hardware this planet has seen. It's years ahead of its time. Whoever has this will almost certainly win the war.'

Puzzled, the Doctor looked over his shoulder to see who had asked the question. A powerfully built German officer held a pistol to his head. There was no one else on the beach. The man was wearing the neat black uniform of the Schutzstaffel. The pistol was a standard SS-issue Mauser. The Doctor recognized the German officer as Standartenführer Joachim Wolff, the Butcher of Mallesan. The Doctor hadn't heard him arrive.

'Keep silent.'

The Doctor closed his mouth.

'Drop the umbrella.'

It fell to the wet sand.

'Keep your hands on your head.'
The Doctor raised his hat mournfully.

4

Death and its Ramifications

It was a situation that required quick thinking. The Doctor lowered his hat and smiled disarmingly at the German officer. 'You look like the sort of man who would like a Kola Nut. Would you? I have a bag of them in my pocket.'

'I've already eaten.'

At least he was listening. The Doctor decided to change tack and indicated the wreckage. 'I know all about that.'

'So you say,' the German replied calmly.

'And you are Joachim Wolff.'

'You have me at a disadvantage.' Wolff chuckled, but he didn't lower the gun. The Doctor stared down the barrel, nervously licking his lips.

'I'm the Doctor. Now you'll want to question me, won't you? Interrogate me? Grill me? Give me the works?' suggested the Doctor hopefully.

'No.'

'I could be useful.'

Wolff began to squeeze the trigger.

'Er . . . before you shoot,' the Doctor gabbled, 'I think you ought to know that you'll actually miss me pointing the gun there. You'd never live that down, would you, not hitting me at such close range?' His voice was suddenly calm. 'Aim eight inches more to the left.'

'Thank you.' Throughout the exchange, Wolff had kept his gun level. Now he adjusted his aim and fired at point-blank range.

* * *

Benny had forgotten what it was like being with the Doctor. Without him you kept regular office hours, you had a lunch break, pension rights and holiday pay. With him you tended to find yourself driving at high speeds along muddy clifftop fields in unfamiliar military equipment being chased by heavily armed Nazis. Benny had forgotten how much she enjoyed it. After months of bottling up her feelings, it was so good to feel the adrenalin rush, to know that at any moment she might die in a blaze of glory, defending the universe from some unknown terror.

The terrain was rough, and she found herself being lurched from side to side. A burst of machine-gun fire peppered the rear of the armoured car. Her plan was working, though, all three groups were moving further and further away from the cove and the Doctor. At this rate, they were bound to run out of bullets soon. Benny was feeling cheered by this thought when the rear driver's side tyre burst and the vehicle gave way. Instinctively, she let go of the steering wheel, throwing her head between her legs and her hands over her head. The armoured car toppled over on its side, quickly crashing to a halt in the mud.

She only had seconds to act. She wasn't hurt, but she could hear boots splashing towards her. They'd be here soon. It was then that she heard the single pistol shot from the beach.

Benny wondered what she should do next.

The bullet blasted two inches past the Doctor's right ear, temporarily deafening him. Before Wolff could react, the Doctor had hurled himself behind the wreckage.

It took Wolff a second to respond. The Doctor had used some form of suggestion on him. A dangerous opponent. A threat. Wolff dived to his left after the little man. The Doctor stood there, facing the other way, poised in wait. When he glanced back and saw Wolff he simply looked annoyed.

'Oh, for heaven's sake, a right-handed combat-trained

human should instinctively dive to the *right* in a situation like this. What are they teaching you these days?'

Wolff punched him hard, straight in the kidneys.

'There ... was ... no need ...' coughed the Doctor crossly. Wolff tried to silence him with a swift kick to the stomach.

'I would appreciate it if you'd stop hitting me,' said the Doctor, who seemed to have recovered his breath.

Wolff held the Doctor down, his knee pressing against the little man's ribcage. An explosion rumbled above them. The two men looked at each other, although it was clear that neither knew precisely what had happened. Wolff didn't loosen his grip.

'I was going to kill you, but now you're going to live. For a little longer. But you'll suffer first,' he whispered.

'Well, there's an original sentiment. Frankly, I'm not impressed.'

Wolff eased the pressure on the Doctor's back, then pulled himself upright. 'Get up.'

The Doctor struggled to his feet. He stood for a moment, dusting himself off.

Then Wolff punched him squarely in the jaw, and the little man fell back, clutching his mouth.

'Frankly, Doktor, I don't care whether you're impressed or not.'

Benny kicked open the hatch of the armoured car and threw herself clear. Splashing down into a muddy puddle, she allowed herself to roll to a halt. There was a moment of calm, then a noise, like a stick clattering across a tin roof, a sound that she couldn't quite place. A repeat of that sound. And again, followed by a more solid clunk. Metal on metal. They'd thrown something metal.

Simultaneously, all three grenades detonated. Before her eyes, the armoured car threw itself apart, its sides were thrown clear of the chassis, the remaining tyres burst explosively. As the fuel tank gave way, the armoured car was lifted five feet into the air, before crashing back to the ground. And then, as quickly as it had happened, there was calm again, just the crackle of fires dying down and choking black fumes in the air.

Benny saw a figure materializing through the smoke as it cleared: it was Gerhard, his pistol raised. Without needing to think, she grabbed his trouser leg and yanked him down. He flailed in the mud, and Benny scrabbled for his gun. She found it and levelled it at him, her heart beating furiously. The lad looked terrified. Her face was covered in mud, her hair was a different colour, there was no way he'd be able to recognize her. He spoke.

'Celia?'

With a dreadful clarity, Bernice realized that Gerhard would have no choice but to betray her. Gerhard knew where she lived: he lived there himself. He had to die, to save the lives of Ma Doras and her daughter. Before she had even completed that thought, Benny felt the trigger give way and her pistol pull upwards. The bullet ripped through the boy's stomach, and he fell to his knees, gasping, coughing up blood. Gerhard slumped, his eyes open. Dead.

Suddenly shocked by what she had done, Benny dropped the pistol and scrambled away. Gerhard was dead. The armoured car shielded her from the main group of Nazis; she just needed to reach some better cover. She had killed Gerhard. She pounded towards the dry stone wall marking the edge of the field. Behind her there were cries for a doctor. It was too late, though. She concentrated on what was ahead.

Benny threw herself over the dry stone wall, grazing her legs and crashing to the tarmac road on the other side. Ignoring the pain, she forced herself up, and hobbled back behind a patch of vegetation, sliding herself down into a muddy ditch. She peered out from her hiding place through the short branches. She was shaking. Benny wanted to cough, or to scream, but couldn't do either of those things. The main group of Nazis had been a full twenty seconds behind her, and hadn't seen her. As she had hoped, only a handful of troops came over the stile, thirty yards away. The others had to stay back to guard

53

that thing on the beach. Whatever it was down there, these leaderless troops knew that it was even more important to guard it than to capture the murderer of a German soldier. Those few that had followed hadn't seen her, and couldn't work out where she had gone. They broadcast their ignorance in loud shouts in German, instinctively assuming that she wouldn't speak their language. Three minutes later and they had pulled back to the field.

Benny hauled herself upright, and allowed herself to cough. She'd bought herself some time: there had been a radio in the armoured car, and that had almost certainly been the group's only link with any reinforcements or search parties. She couldn't take that for granted, though, and it wouldn't be long before a runner was sent. Her little diversion had made a great deal of noise, and so it was entirely possible that every German patrol on the island had already been drawn this way. There seemed little chance of doubling back and meeting up with the Doctor here; she'd have to head back to the boarding-house.

She remembered the shot she had heard. A single shot. Someone must have come across him. She wasn't worried, because the Doctor was quite capable of looking after himself. Had the Doctor had time to find out what he needed to know, though? There was no way of telling, and she certainly wasn't in any fit state to go down there and help him. She'd done all she could. She flexed her muscles, tried to figure out how badly hurt she was. Nothing broken, but virtually everything cut and bruised. Mud caked her dress, her legs and half her face. She was colder than she had realized, her feet already numb, her legs in the first stages of cramp. She stamped her feet, trying to improve her circulation. Her hands were still shaking. She wasn't badly hurt, but she was far too distinctive. She would be picked up by any German patrol she came across. Even at a brisk pace, it would take her three-quarters of an hour to get back to the boarding-house, but she really couldn't think of anywhere else to go, and she couldn't wait here. She set off, circling back while also giving the cove and surroundings a wide berth.

Had they invented the helicopter by now? Benny tried to remember as she fled across country. A century from now the jet helicopter would be the principal form of transport, and she had seen for herself that they were certainly around in the 1960s and '70s, but she couldn't remember seeing or hearing any on this visit. The Germans hardly needed them: when the alarm was raised, they would bring in tracker dogs, foot patrols, roadblocks. Guernsey was so small that search parties could be set up in no time at all. Benny decided that, on balance, it might well be better to stick to the roads: there would be no risk of getting lost, and she wouldn't leave a trail of footprints. Thanks to the restrictions imposed by rationing, only the Germans could run motor vehicles now, so if she heard the noise of an engine, it would have to be them. There were plenty of hedges and ditches to hide in. If she was careful, she ought to be able to get back safely. If there were roadblocks, she could dodge round them.

On the way back, Benny didn't encounter any patrols. At first this didn't make her feel any safer, just paranoid that the Germans were saving themselves the effort and that they would be waiting for her at the boarding-house. Finally, she decided that she ought to consider herself lucky, not worry too much about it. There was no sign of the Doctor anywhere. The Doras' boarding-house was right in the centre of St Peter Port. Security in the town was a lot tighter than in the country, but it tended to be in fixed positions: guardposts at road junctions, outside the town hall and by the post office. With no organized resistance, and no real threat of invasion, there wasn't any point wasting resources on stricter security. She'd had three months of practice at sneaking to and from the Doras', and there were good hiding places lining most of the approaches. She picked her way across the town without much effort, by sticking to the backstreets and alleyways. Now, Benny stood with her back to the wall, two doors down from Ma Doras' front garden.

It was time to become Celia again. She rummaged through her pocket, quickly finding the holowig filament. She brushed it hurriedly into place. There wasn't any way of seeing herself, so she didn't know whether it was working or not. She assumed that it was, but waited a moment, for luck, before stepping out. Benny approached the imposing front door of the boarding-house with mixed feelings. She liked Ma Doras and Anne, but had said her goodbyes. She did not want to go back there, not now. Not back to a life dominated by rationing and randy young troops in the bathroom. Perhaps the Doctor could take her to Guernsey after the war was over. It would be good to visit Ma and Anne in better times, to see Anne's fiancé, and the children she hadn't had yet, to see holiday-makers back in the guest rooms.

Ma Doras opened the door, a cigarette in her mouth.

'What's the matter, Bernice? Where's the Doctor?'

'You had better call me Celia.'

'Celia, you need to get changed.'

Brushing past Ma Doras, Benny pulled herself upstairs, locked herself in the bathroom and peeled off her dress. The mud would wash out. In normal circumstances, her shoes would have been ruined, but this was wartime, and shoes were in short supply, so they'd be mended. She kicked them off. Then she caught a glance of herself in the mirror, covered in mud and scratches, with stupid 1941 blonde hair a mess, stupid 1941 make-up running down her cheeks, stupid 1941 underwear pushing and squeezing her in awkward places. The reflection didn't look like her at all, it looked like some bimbo on the cover of a lurid true-crime novella. THIS ISSUE: CELIA (NOT HER REAL NAME) – HELPLESS VICTIM OF NAZI TERROR. She had thought she was going to get away. She really thought that the Doctor would come along and whisk her away from all this oppression. It was never as straightforward as that, was it?

Anne was sitting on the big sofa in the front room, cradling a mug of tea, her head leaning against the antimacassar. She managed a smile as Benny sat alongside her. Benny had washed and changed, and she was feeling a little better.

'Back so soon?'

'The Doctor and I got split up. It's not exactly the first time. He'll come back and get me when he's finished what he's doing.'

'Were you over at St Jaonnet? That's where our Germans have gone.'

Benny had forgotten about Gerhard. He'd died – no, don't deny it, she'd killed him – less than an hour ago, and already he'd slipped her mind. Perhaps now in Waiblingen, Gerhard's lover or mother or sister was sitting in her front room waiting for news. Did any such woman exist? Bernice had lived with Gerhard for three months, but didn't know anything about him. He must have a family, though. Across the world, women sat alone in houses and factories, anxious for letters, waiting for their men to come home, dreading the thought they might not. Of course, Anne was in the same situation, not knowing where her lover was. Benny couldn't describe how she felt about Anne. Sympathy? Sorrow? Respect? Such little words. This young woman had drawn on some internal source of strength and carried herself with nobility. Although she would never win a medal, she was at least as heroic as the millions of conscripted men her age. But Anne's experience was a common one. Like her, most of the women in the world were at home now, desperately hoping that the doorbell wouldn't ring. When the doorbell rang it was someone from the police or the army to give you a telegram. There was no need to read it, someone else on the street had had one the previous week, and their curtains had been drawn ever since. It is with great regret that I have to inform you . . .

The doorbell rang. Without giving Anne a reply, Benny jumped to her feet, her heart surging with relief.

'I'll go. It'll be the Doctor.'

Benny went to the door and opened it. A German officer stood on the doorstep with Franz. Benny tried not to show her disappointment. It was the younger man who spoke first. He had been crying.

'Celia, Gerhard is dead. He was killed.' He always spoke in primary-school German, straightforward sentences, not a hint that his was the language of Goethe and Schiller.

'You speak German?' The officer, a Hauptsturmführer she had never seen before, spoke now. He was a slight man in his forties, with greying hair. His chest was lined with various campaign medals that Benny wasn't in the mood to catalogue.

'Yes.'

'Good.' And that was the end of the conversation. The two men came into the house and wiped their feet on the mat. Ma Doras had come into the hall. She regarded the officer warily.

'Is everything all right, Celia?'

'Bad news, Ma. Gerhard was killed.'

There was genuine sorrow in Ma's reaction. 'At the beach?'

'Yes,' Franz and Benny replied together. An awkward pause before Franz continued. 'We are here for his possessions. They will be returned to his family. Would you help us pack them, Celia?'

Benny nodded dumbly and led them upstairs to the first floor. She opened the door to Gerhard and Kurt's bedroom. The room was small, just a couple of beds, a wardrobe and a chest of drawers. The bed had not been made, a fact clearly noted by the German officer. Benny opened up each of the drawers in turn. Gerhard had left nothing remarkable: underwear, a fountain pen and writing paper, a tatty postcard of the Eiffel Tower, an unopened packet of cigarettes, a book of regulations, a magazine featuring photographs of healthy Aryan women in various states of undress. Benny laid each of these out on the bed and the officer meticulously listed them in a notebook.

'Not much, is it?' he commented.

'He was young. Seventeen or eighteen.'

'Sixteen. Seventeen in July. Not much for a life.' He

had removed a paper bag from his overcoat pocket and now dropped everything but the magazine and cigarettes into it. He handed the last two items to Franz and carefully closed up the bag with some sort of official seal.

'Thank you, Miss Doras. Private, I shall be waiting in the car.' He marched from the room.

'Yes, sir.' Franz handed the magazine and cigarettes to Benny. 'Could you take these to my room?'

'Of course. Then I'd better get to work.'

Franz hesitated for a second, then whispered, 'I would not.'

'Why not?'

'Well, you and he were . . . friendly.' There was no doubt what he meant by the word. At least he had the decency to blush.

'We were not.'

'You went out last night. He told me.'

She fixed him with a stare. 'We went for a walk, nothing more. And I am going to work.'

Chris Cwej was in love.

The radiator was a vast silver slab, the bonnet an equally solid expanse of green-grey. Huge wings arched over the narrow tyres, then stretched back to the very rear of the car. The car's roof was bulky yet elegantly rounded. The windscreen and other glass was thick, lined with brass. The headlamps and other fittings were carefully polished. Chris came from an age when automated factories churned out thousands of functional transport units. Each model was designed according to strict rules, principally the laws of aerodynamics and the demand for energy efficiency. Computers made sure that each flitter conformed to the rigorous safety and emissions standards required by law. The car in front of him wouldn't. It was the fossil fuel this car used that contributed to the fog that shrouded London every morning. The tyre treads were worn, the vehicle had no back-up computer. In a crash, all that metal would crumple, all the glass would shatter. It must weigh several tonnes; most of that huge engine would surely be needed just to move it. Chris changed his mind: this car would move. This car would be one of the fastest things on the planet at this time. He loved this car.

He looked back at Roz. 'Magnificent, isn't it?'

'Yeah, great. But trust me, it'll never get off the ground.' Roz didn't share his love of machines, and in the past had proved unwilling to acquire it. Chris turned back to the car, and saw the driver holding the rear door open for him.

'It belongs to a lord of the realm, sir,' the driver said. 'He volunteered it for military service. We were hardly going to turn him down.'

'It's a beautiful vehicle,' Chris breathed. 'Do you think I could sit in the front?' There was a snort of derision from somewhere behind him.

'Yes, sir.' The driver sounded delighted at the admiration his car was receiving, and was closing the rear door as Chris clambered into the driver's seat. The driver looked around helplessly.

George Reed shrugged. 'Let him drive if he wants to, Harry. Just don't let him get lost.'

'No, sir.'

Chris was running his hand over the black leather seats and the walnut trim. 'This is just superb. Hey, Sergeant, how do you start the engine?'

The driver showed him. The engine surged into life.

'And then?'

'Drop the handbrake, put it in gear and push down the pedal, sir.'

'Are you sure you don't want to come for a spin with us, Roz?'

'Chris, there's a war on.' Her tone was sharp, but there was an underlying tenderness there that Chris couldn't fail to spot. She was worried about him.

'Don't worry, Roz, I'll be OK.' He grinned reassuringly. Then he slammed the driver's door shut, pushed the pedal right down to the floor, and the Bentley roared away. Harry, the driver, was thrown back into his seat, grabbing for his cap. When he had recovered, he grinned at Chris, who grinned back. The car threw itself past St James's Park.

'How long will it take to get to Plymouth?' Chris asked, shouting over the roar of the engine.

'About half as long as it should take!' laughed Harry.

An islander had killed a German officer: there was only one possible course of action. At a quarter-past nine, on the cold morning of 2 March 1941, German troops silently moved into position, blocking off Smith Street in front of the post office. Islanders were allowed to enter the area, but none were allowed to leave. They had become used to such inconveniences and thought little of it. When the Germans insisted on checking the identity papers of everyone present, most people in the crowd concluded that this was simply a routine security matter. Accepting this, the crowd did as they were asked, and stood in line. Then, a senior SS officer, Sturmbannführer Schern, came forward. Reading from a typed sheet of foolscap paper, he informed the crowd that a German officer had been shot and killed in the course of his duties that morning near the airstrip at St Jaonnet. The crowd became noticeably more anxious at this news. A reward was now offered for information leading to the arrest of this *traitor*: 25,000 Occupation marks. The crowd murmured at this figure. Some had already calculated that this would be enough to buy a car, no, enough to buy a house. The German continued to speak: as a reprisal for this action, firstly, rations were to be cut further. The officer read out the precise details of which foods and materials would be affected. Secondly, half a dozen villagers were to be shot. Six shots were fired. Six islanders were killed instantly. Any future resistance would be met with a similar response. The German troops stood down, and the crowd of islanders quickly dispersed. Boots the Chemist, next to the post office, opened as normal at half-past nine.

* * *

The Doctor was looking out from the third-floor window, rage and sorrow surging across his face. Wolff watched him staring down into the square. By now, the bodies would have been cleared away, life would have returned to normal. There was nothing to see but workers scrubbing away the blood. When this 'Doctor' spoke, his voice was low.

'There was no need. Why?'

Wolff was dismissive, and he replied in German, 'Because I can.' He smiled as he saw the Doctor's reaction. Outrage, indignation, horror. In many ways the Doctor was extraordinary: he was an exceptionally intelligent man, the bruise around his mouth was already healing, and most remarkable of all he didn't seem remotely worried about his arrest. Yet his reaction to witnessing the massacre was tiresome and predictable. The usual, impotent, rage. Mindless sympathy for the weak, knee-jerk concern for the unimportant. No sense of history.

'Your accomplice killed a German soldier, Herr Doktor. You crossed the line first.'

'You just don't see it, do you? You killed six innocent people. Men and women who had done nothing.' The Doctor strode towards him, menace in his eyes. Wolff remained where he was. They were alone in the room together. Wolff turned to face him. Even when Wolff was sitting down, the Doctor was barely taller than him.

'They, or people like them, harboured you.'

'I arrived this morning and went straight for the beach.'

'If you did that, then you were acting on information passed on by an islander. The sentence stands.' Wolff broke eye contact. The Doctor hovered at his shoulder, unsure how to respond. Before he could continue, Wolff spoke, 'Herr Doktor, I would have shot you on the beach without a second thought, like a stray dog' – he paused as an amusing thought crossed his mind – 'and if I had, then there would have been no need for those people down there to have died.' The Doctor showed no signs that he appreciated the irony, so Wolff continued. 'You know of Oskar Steinmann?'

'Yes. The torturer.'

'The art collector. The professor of philosophy. The chess grand master. The family man. Steinmann is many things.'

'I don't doubt it. Just as you don't deny it.'

Wolff smiled. 'Steinmann wants to talk to you about what was down on the beach. Your plane leaves at six-thirty. It's only a short trip to Granville. You'll find out there exactly what Steinmann is.'

George Reed glanced out of the window. It was getting dark again: it was nearly time to pull down the blackout curtains, ready the searchlights, brace oneself for the air-raid sirens. Soon, on both sides of the Channel, the bombers would leave their concealed hangars, setting out on carefully prearranged flight patterns with their fighter escorts. They wouldn't pass each other mid-Channel. The British squadrons would head out over the North Sea to the industrial centres of the Ruhr and the Rhine; the German bombers would head across the Channel, targeting the ports and the factories of the Midlands. On the great round table in the centre of this room, lines of toy planes marked the routes of the German bombers as they flew straight through the grey hatched areas of radar coverage, past the anti-aircraft batteries marked by red pins and the airfields marked in yellow. Their targets were easily visible on this map, green pins indicating where clusters of barrage balloons were concentrated. The same went for the British, little model Wellington bombers lining the route to Europe, but on this side the pins only marked where defences had been discovered by spies, reconnaissance flights or bitter experience. Next to the huge map, tally charts mapped the estimated damage to industrial sites and compared the number of lost planes on each side. The rows and rows of statistics on those sheets reminded George a little of Wisden's Almanac. The great round table was almost a huge watch face – its hands wave after wave of bombers, sweeping across the map with the precision of clockwork – or maybe one of those carefully choreographed production numbers in an MGM musical.

Admiral Kendrick was over by the far wall, plotting something on a vast wallchart. Forrester was staring into the middle of the tabletop map, as though she were trying to find her own place on it.

'What's the matter, Roz?' he whispered.

'I'm worried about Chris,' she said, distracted.

'It looked like Cwej could handle the Bentley.'

'I'm not worried about that, he's got a car in every port. I'm worried about him in France,' she snapped.

'Well, yes, I know. Sorry, that line about the Bentley, it was meant to be a joke.'

'I don't like jokes.'

Reed tried to suppress a smile, but couldn't quite manage it. He turned away, only to face Kendrick, who had stepped over to the map. His face fell quickly, and he winced as he saw Kendrick's disapproving look.

'Smile when you've worked out the solution, George, and not a moment before. Do try to remember that there are lives at stake here.'

'Yes, sir.'

'Forrester, could you make a jug of coffee?'

Reed heard her acknowledge the order and turned to watch her head for the small kitchen just outside their office. Kendrick was bent over the map.

'How can we defend against this? We've got radar, a string of observers. There must be a way of predicting what the Luftwaffe will do, and reacting in time to stop the bombs falling. When I was on the Atlantic convoys, we could second-guess the U-boat captains, and we should be able to do the same with Hartung and Steinmann now.'

Kendrick was right, George thought. It ought to be possible to trace the flights of individual bombers by the trail of destruction that they left. Untangle the web, and you could tailor your defences accordingly, find out which planes were targeting which sites. At this rate it would take them months to work it out, by which time there wouldn't be any factories left to defend. George looked at the map again. Sometimes he thought their task was hopeless.

As it was all my fault, I thought I might sacrifice myself. For the rest of my life, I will regret that I never got the chance. It was all over so quickly. I tried to dive into the path of one of the bullets, but they only fired six, all at once. It was eerie: people just got up afterwards and carried on to work. They were glad that it hadn't been them, I suppose, and didn't want to hang around. I was a little shocked. I didn't stay either, I didn't want to arouse too much suspicion, and I know what a dead body looks like. I went straight to the town hall, finished my rounds, ate my lunch. All around me were islanders who had been lined up with me, but no one discussed what they had been through. Everyone chatted at lunch, as usual, but no one spoke about what the Germans had done. Everyone just kept their head down and avoided eye contact with each other. I did the same, I'm not claiming I didn't.

Slowly, as the day went on, I managed to shut up the rage inside me. So, when I opened up Room 214 and found Marie Simmonds on the bed underneath some sweaty little Hauptsturmführer, I didn't kill them there and then. I could tell that Marie had recognized me, I saw her expression, and I could hear it in her breathing: *Oh, I'm all right, Celia, I was already up here at nine o'clock, safe and sound. Oh yes, I've been here all day. Very safe, and, oh, so very sound. I did hear some shooting, though, somewhere in the distance.* I felt a primal urge to kill them both that transcended law and consequence. I wanted Marie to watch me kill her lover, then hear her scream as I tore her apart. I could have done it, I know I could have done, but instead I mumbled my apologies and left. I closed the door and walked away. Cleaned some rooms, scrubbed some wash-basins. As I left the town hall, my rage had dissipated into a vague sense of annoyance. And I managed to walk a full hundred yards past the flowers resting on those peculiar new circles of sawdust in Smith Street before I remembered why they were there.

I'm a strong person. I've faced death before. I've laughed in the face of fear, as they say. I've been surrounded by evil – not just crime and injustice, but pure, stark evil. I've gone through a lot in the last couple of years: I've been stabbed, tortured, starved, blasted, mauled, betrayed, absorbed, poisoned, possessed, lacerated, bruised, conscripted, electrocuted, impregnated, drugged, abandoned, abused, battered, probed, burnt. Blown up, shot down, kicked in, thrown out. I've done it all. I even died once. But I always bounced back within a couple of weeks, ready for my next exciting new adventure. Sticks and stones may break my bones, but bones mend if you're young enough and you've got a good doctor. This time it's different.

'It's over.'

Celia had been crying for the last hour. Sobbing, trying to speak but unable to form the words. Ma Doras had cradled her in her arms, and Celia had sobbed like a baby. Now, Ma watched as the younger woman wiped her eyes and sat up.

'I have to go, I'm putting you at risk.'

'Nonsense, dear.' Ma Doras poured herself another cup of tea. 'Besides, where would you go?'

Celia unfurled a small piece of paper. 'I got a note this morning. It was pressed into my hand in Smith Street after the shooting. I didn't see who gave it to me. It's from the Resistance.'

'There isn't a Resistance. Not one of us likes the Germans, you know that, but there isn't a Resistance. In France there might well be groups hiding out in barns, blowing up châteaux and sabotaging factories, but there's nothing so romantic here. Celia, there isn't even a railway line to sabotage yet. The best we can manage is to water down the Germans' beer a bit more than our own, or to huddle together and listen to the BBC News when we think the Germans won't be looking.'

Celia seemed shaken, and said uncertainly, 'They've promised me passage back to Britain.'

'And then?' Ma knew she didn't need to remind her of the threat of betrayal, of mines and naval patrols, the plain fact that she almost certainly wouldn't get as far as the mainland.

'I've got some friends in London. I should be able to trace them.'

'London's a big place. Have you got valid papers?'

'I can get hold of papers, and Roz and Chris are pretty distinctive. If I can't find them, there's a house outside Canterbury. I'd go there and wait for the Doctor.' Celia paused, then, 'Ma, I killed Gerhard. I did it to protect you.'

The old woman considered this revelation for a moment. 'Yes. Yes, I thought you must have. This morning, you already knew about it when Franz came to tell us. Luckily, Hauptsturmführer Rosner didn't notice. You took Gerhard to the beach last night, too, didn't you?'

'It's probably just as well that he died. He'd have been able to identify us all.' Benny didn't sound convinced.

'Why did you take him in the first place, for heaven's sake? I know you're spying on the airstrip for the Doctor, so why on Earth did you take a German with you?'

'A couple of nights ago I was nearly caught by a patrol there. You know the curfew rules: I'd have been shot if they had seen me, especially there. The night before last someone else was shot up there, or so I heard. I led Gerhard on. That way, if we'd been caught up there he would have covered for me – he genuinely thought we were on a date. That was the plan, anyway. To be honest with you, I was scared I was going to be caught, it was a snap decision, if I'd had a couple of days to think about it I'd have chosen differently, and I made a mistake.'

'Yes.' The word hung in the air for a moment. Ma looked at Celia – Bernice, she corrected herself. This woman didn't look like a killer. Then again, neither did the young soldiers, nor the Doctor. Bernice had stood, ready to leave.

'I'm going first thing in the morning. Don't worry, I won't wear my wig, so they won't recognize me. Say good-bye to Anne for me.'

Ma stared after the young woman as she closed the door behind her, listened to her footsteps climb the stairs, then turned to the window. The evening was drawing in, a chill was heading up from the sea as it did every night. A transport plane flew overhead, probably bound for France, or perhaps Alderney. Ma watched its running lights recede into the evening sky. Someone was leaving the island, at any rate. She wondered who it might be. Across town, the church bell rang six-thirty. A tear ran down Ma's cheek, as she thought of Celia, and what she had done.

5

Things to Come

The patrol had spotted the dark-haired woman as she entered the harbour at ten past six, and had notified Standartenführer Wolff by telephone. Within five minutes, Wolff had intercepted her as she made her way to the quayside and the fishing boats moored there. She was unarmed and didn't struggle as she was handcuffed and gagged with thick adhesive tape.

Wolff examined this enemy spy. She wore patched trousers and a thick fisherman's sweater, but underneath those clothes she was a very shapely young woman. Her hair was raven-black. She had beautiful fiery eyes, with long, curly lashes. He caught a whiff of her perfume.

'Are you going to make this easy on yourself?'

The girl shrugged. Wolff released his grip, and she struggled to undo the top button of her trousers. Wolff ran his finger methodically around her waistband. Finally he found a couple of sheets of cigarette paper concealed there. He motioned to the girl, who refastened her trousers. Wolff studied the sheets. Two sketch maps, a couple of sheets of gibberish: clearly some code or other. The girl stood by, waiting for him to react.

'The hospital complex?' he asked.

The girl nodded.

'And this is the airstrip?'

Again, she nodded.

'You drew the maps on cigarette paper so that you could swallow or smoke them if caught. You were passing this on to Arthur Kendrick's Scientific Intelligence Division in London?'

The girl's sullen expression faltered for just a second.

'We know all about your operation. You are part of the so-called "Tomato" network that covers these islands and the coast of France that faces them. It is especially concerned with German defensive capability. The network comprises some thirty people. You only know the name of two other people in this chain.' He reached into his pocket, and held a typed sheet of paper up to her face. 'Those are the rest. Your name is fourth on the list. You'll see that the previous three have been crossed off. That is your name: Colette Mallard? Occupation: Shop assistant at the greengrocer's on Smith Street?'

She nodded, the trace of a tear in her eye.

'You see, I know even more about you than you do yourself. So, I'm afraid, there would be no point interrogating you.' He paused, gesturing round theatrically. 'This street is the Rue des Vaches. Do you know why it's called that? In years gone by, cows from Jersey couldn't be unloaded on the quay, so farmers would push them into the harbour. They would be forced to swim ashore, then they would be herded up this way to the abattoir. Those poor, pretty, long-lashed cows.'

He broke her neck.

The Doctor awoke in an eighteenth-century four-poster bed. There was no one else in the room. He was wearing a knee-length night-shirt. Outside, overhead, were a number of bombers on descent trajectories: German planes coming back in to land after a hard night's bombing. Judging by the amount of light coming through the curtains, it was nearly dawn.

He had only been unconscious for about twelve hours, then. They'd drugged him just before putting him on the plane. So, this must be Granville. He pushed aside the laundered bedsheets, and stood. The effect of the sedative – unless he was very much mistaken, simply chloroform – had completely worn off. He peered around the room.

The decoration was French, but anachronistic: most of it was about one hundred and fifty years too early, the sort of thing he would have expected to see in Napoleon's time. The Doctor ran his fingers over a delicate glass nymph, *circa* 1830. Presumably, this townhouse had been some sort of museum before the Nazis had requisitioned it.

He pulled one of the curtains back slightly. This house was in the centre of Granville, and the town looked much as it had the last time the Doctor had been here, a decade or so in the future. This guest bedroom was on the second floor. An armoured car drove past in the street below. The antique glass rattled. The Doctor tried to open the door out to the balcony, but as he suspected, it had been locked and bolted. He drew open the curtains.

His clothes had been washed and ironed, and now lay neatly folded on a dresser. The Doctor crumpled up the jacket and trousers, then put them on. The pockets had been completely emptied, except for the folded hat and his abacus. He would have to find some more dog biscuits, he reminded himself. He began searching the hatband for his TARDIS key before remembering that he had given it and the spare to Roz the morning before. The slip of paper was still secreted there. When he had finished dressing, he looked at himself in the full-length mirror by the dresser, placing his hat on his head and adjusting his scarf. The sun had almost fully risen over the horizon. The lights were going out all over Europe. Church bells nearby struck seven o'clock. The Doctor checked his watch.

There was a knock at the door. Without waiting for a response, a young female Gefreiter stepped in, closing the door behind her.

'Herr Doktor, your breakfast is ready, in the main dining-room. Oberst Steinmann will join you shortly,' she announced in slightly awkward English.

'I speak German,' the Doctor replied. 'What is your name?'

'Gefreiter Fegelein.'

'Your real name,' he said gently.

'Ulrilda,' she smiled a pretty smile.

'From Falkenstein?'

'Yes, however did you know?'

'A lucky guess. Time for breakfast.' He took a last look at his reflection. 'Don't go avay!' he ordered it in a mock-German accent.

He stepped from the room. If Ulrilda had glanced back at the mirror at that moment, she would have seen the Doctor's image raise his hat, a broad grin on his face, before he slowly faded from view.

The Doctor hadn't been there.

He had arranged to meet her by the TARDIS at eight, but he hadn't arrived. This worried Roz more than she cared to acknowledge. It was an hour later now, and she was safely behind her desk at the Headquarters of the Scientific Intelligence Division, with work to do. Principally she was keeping her mind off what had probably happened to the Doctor and Chris. Annotated aerial photographs of London were scattered over her desk. Each crater was marked in tiny white writing, a record of each explosion which gave the location, the time it happened and the yield of the bomb used. Even with a computer, working out the course of events last night would be virtually impossible. Of course, this office hadn't got a computer. When she'd asked about requisitioning one, they didn't even seem to have understood the question. Why, then, did she have the nagging sensation that she was on the verge of making a major breakthrough? Wishful thinking, probably. The British were dreading spring, thinking that as the weather got better, the Germans would dust off their plans for invasion, shelved last winter. The British had a codeword, 'Cromwell', meaning that an invasion had started, and they expected to hear it very soon. As far as Roz could tell, this war was deadlocked: the Germans had a powerful air force and army, but lacked the navy to carry through an invasion, and their bombers just weren't powerful enough to do more than superficial damage. Britain had the navy, it was building up the air power, but Germany controlled so much territory on the Continent that invasion was out of the question for a long while yet. Had Hartung found a way to break the stalemate? If he had, what was it? His field of expertise would suggest some new aerial weapon, but it might not be the superbomber that Lynch thought it was. She made a mental note to research the state-of-the-art at this time. With her knowledge of the future, it might be possible to predict which technological developments were due in the next decade or so. Had they got atomics yet? Orbital platforms? Ballistic missiles? Any of those would tip the balance. For the moment, all she could do was to stare at these photographs a little longer.

Her eye caught something she hadn't seen before. Lynch was busy with something called a 'crossword', and so she asked George to come across and pointed out one of the bombsites.

'That's St Kit's.'

Reed peered into the picture. 'Yes . . .' he said uncertainly. Roz heard Kendrick coming into the room behind them. He began talking to Lynch in a low whisper.

'It is, look, that's Paddington station, that's Portland Street, there's the library. I live around there, remember?'

'Yes, I think you're right.'

'Well,' Roz continued wearily, 'this gives the time of the bomb dropping as last night at 21:00. But that's wrong. It happened the night before last, the first of March; remember I told you about it when we looked at the library?'

'Are you sure you're not getting confused? I picked you up there this morning as well.'

'Cwej was there when I told you.'

Reed considered this. 'By Jove, yes, he was. Well, that first night, the Germans were particularly lucky. Lots of fluke hits. The spotters must have got mixed up. We've had cases before where they've got the day mixed up. You know: it fell after midnight, so it's a different date.'

'And if that observation is wrong, then they all could be.' Roz sat back, frustrated. Reed scratched his head.

'It is rather complicated, isn't it, Captain Forrester?' Kendrick said, coming over and laying his hand on her shoulder. 'Could you make us a pot of tea, and we'll try to help you work our way through it?'

'Admiral, I don't think that will be possible. It's a classic chaotic system. These planes might all be following strict orders but they are all subject to random factors. Bombers get lost in the dark and drop their loads at random. High winds, heavy ground defences, mechanical problems all alter what a plane is doing. Add to that the unreliability of our eye-witnesses and the length of time it takes to get reports here it –'

'Thank you, Forrester,' rumbled Kendrick.

'Sir, it's a fact.'

'There is absolutely nothing wrong with our communications,' he said calmly. 'Those chaps risk their lives. Do you know how many wardens were killed last week? What would you prefer? Smoke signals?'

'I don't know, they might help. What are they?' If they had some sort of encoded-vapour transmitter, why weren't they using it?

'If you don't have anything useful to contribute, Forrester, then kindly let George and me get on with our work.' His tone had changed.

'Begging your pardon, sir,' – her emphasis on that last word was so scornful it was mutinous – 'but all you have me doing at the moment is making the drinks, a spot of typing and watering the office plant. I was brought into the Scientific Intelligence Division on the understanding that I would be able to put my scientific and analytical talents to use. I remind you, sir, that I outrank both Lieutenants Reed and Cwej. I've been here a week. In that time, you have welcomed their contributions, but you're treating me like some third-grade Servobot fit only for housework and preparing snacks. Well, sir, I've had enough.'

A vein on Kendrick's neck pulsed, but when he spoke, his tone was conciliatory. 'Captain Forrester, your talents may seem very impressive back in Africa and I'm sure that your teachers were delighted that someone with your background could do so well. But I did not give you permission to speak freely. Please be civilized.' To emphasize his intentions he smiled.

Roz, however, exploded. 'Civilized? Your state-of-the-art around here, as far as I can make out, seems to consist of cavalry regiments and bayonets. You attempt to work out the tactical analysis of a Continental war by pushing toys around a tabletop. You rely on a network of doddery old men on bicycles to bring in reports of bomb damage. Your air defences seem to be based on the principle that if we all draw our curtains at night then the Germans won't be able to see us. And don't you dare question my background, I can trace my ancestry back to Nelson Mandela himself which is –'

Kendrick just smiled, and said, 'Captain, is it or isn't it true that you once ate someone's identity papers?'

'Well, yes.' The remark wrong-footed her, as Kendrick had intended it to.

'Is that the mark of a civilized lady?' he asked. It was, by anyone's standard, a reasonable enough question.

'It was the –' Why the hell had Chris told them?

'Yes or no?' he pressed.

'It was . . . Listen, Admiral, I'm trying to help.' Roz had realized that not only had she overstepped the mark, but that she was in an untenable position. Kendrick swept from the room. Reed kept his eyes fixed on the desk. Roz covered her head with her hands. Bad day just got worse.

The Doctor was munching a triangle of toast when Steinmann entered.

The dining-room was on the floor below his guest quarters. The view of the sea was better down here and the decoration was just as opulent. There was a dark patch on the ceiling where a crystal chandelier must have swung before the war, discoloured patches on the wall where paintings had once hung. A row of bullet holes in one of the walls, presumably acquired when the Germans

75

captured the building, had been crudely plastered up and repainted.

The Doctor continued to eat, but sized up the new arrival. Oberst Oskar Steinmann was in his fifties, his white hair was thin and combed back over his scalp. He had a Roman profile: aquiline nose, high forehead. He was not a tall man – then again, mused the Doctor, who am I to speak? – but he was thin and well-proportioned. He carried himself like a man born to command. Naturally, not a single part of his ironed and pressed uniform was out of place.

'I take it your English breakfast was satisfactory?'

The Doctor dabbed his top lip with a napkin and replaced it on his silver tray. 'Perfectly.'

'Like they serve in England?'

'Oh yes.' Steinmann beamed, but the Doctor went on, 'I'm not English myself, but this is definitely a breakfast like they serve in England. Herr Steinmann, please don't try to ask me trick questions, because I'm cleverer than you and I'll see through them.'

Steinmann's face fell. The Doctor stood, paced the room for a moment, then whirled to face the German officer. 'I don't mind direct questions. Here's one: why didn't Wolff shoot me on the beach? It's obvious I know exactly what you've got down there. It would be safer to have me shot.' The Doctor realized what he had said, and gave a nervous smile that he hoped would be disarming.

'Doktor, you mustn't judge the Reich by the standards set by the English. If you were a German agent captured in England, you would indeed have been shot. We, however, choose to keep all spies sent to the Channel Islands alive. Unlike your own government, even the British agents we pick up in plain clothes are treated as military prisoners of war, with all the rights and privileges that status entails. The same goes in France and the Netherlands.'

'Of course, you want to find out exactly what they know. What I know.' The Doctor had moved back to the window,

76

and stood staring out to sea. He heard Steinmann come up behind him.

'Naturally. But we are a more civilized people than the English,' he said quietly.

'Forgive me if I don't believe you.'

'You mustn't believe the propaganda of our enemies: we observe a Christmas cease-fire, the British do not; unlike Britain, women don't serve in our armies, they stay at home where they belong; we only target industrial and military sites, the RAF deliberately bomb German civilians; the British use phosphorous bombs and dumdum bullets, we have banned the use of both. And, of course, it was the British and French who started this war by refusing to negotiate back in October '39'. Steinmann counted these examples off on his fingers.

'You invaded Poland.'

'A state created a mere twenty years ago by the Allies in a draconian treaty, in order to punish us, a state that contains millions of German people. Already in this war, the British have conquered Iceland, Iran and Madagascar: once neutral countries, now part of the British Empire.'

'What about the three concentration camps on Alderney, in which Russians are used as slave labour, and are expected to survive on scraps of food and clothing?'

Steinmann nodded his head, gracefully conceding defeat on that issue. 'You're an exceptionally well-informed man, Doktor. So why can't you see that the world has changed? We are witnessing the twilight of the ancient regime. This is obvious to every German person, because of what has happened to us during this century. Our colonial possessions were taken off us after the last war; we saw our economy collapse. But we rebuilt and now we have grown stronger than ever before. Capitalism is dead; imperialism is dead; democracy is dead. What remains? Communism? Do you have any inkling what hardships the Russians are suffering under Stalin? How that once great country has collapsed? The British intelligentsia idolizes a man who has killed millions of his own people, both deliberately and through his own incompetence. Food sits rotting in fields. Cement is shipped from one city to another, but it sets before it arrives. I predict that when we attack, the Russians will turn on their own leaders and that they'll refuse to fight us. In the slums of England and France, illiterate children die of preventable diseases. What "freedom" do they have under bourgeois democracy? That era is over!'

Steinmann was only inches from the Doctor, and he kept his voice level. His eyes were a piercing blue, his profile and bearing made him imposing, but the most frightening thing about him was that he looked so ordinary. This man wasn't mad, or a fanatic; he was in complete control of himself.

Steinmann continued. 'When this war has finished, the British and French empires will be gone, and a new Europe will have sprung up, a vast area controlled by Germany, the greatest empire the world has ever known. We shall enter a new golden age of technological achievement. Fascism is the future. Not just a fusion of all the old styles of government, but also something new and glorious. Have you seen Albert Speer's plans for Berlin? By the end of the next decade it will be the greatest city the world has ever seen. Every sign of decadence and corruption will be burnt away from Europe. The slums and ghettos will be cleared, criminals and degenerates will be eradicated, moribund economies will be resurrected. In Fascist cities, grand palaces, great amphitheatres, vast offices and factories, superb autobahns, huge public spaces will be constructed. Every city in the world will be a monument to Fascist victory, to the invincibility of the Reich. That, Doctor, is why our armies were welcomed by cheering crowds in Austria, Czechoslovakia, Poland, even in Paris itself. That is a fact.

'The British pretend that the German people are, what was the phrase? – "writhing under the Nazi yoke". Nonsense, we have never been more prosperous, have never had such firm leadership, such belief in our destiny. I heard word this morning that we have entered Bulgaria. We march onwards. I am the son of a Dresden shoemaker:

78

could any Englishman of my upbringing have risen as far through the ranks? You see: we are not ogres. I am not an ... alien. I am a reasonable man.'

'A man of wealth and taste,' murmured the Doctor.

'Is that a quotation?' Steinmann asked, trying to place it.

'Not yet, no. But it will be in the future.'

'You see, Doktor? You are already thinking like a Fascist, thinking of what is to come. A reasonable man such as yourself has nothing to fear. I understand your moral objection: you see the war, you see the people dying – on both sides – and you wonder whether there is another way. There isn't. The world must be purified by the flames of this final battle. The war will be swift, though. See how the Netherlands fell in four days and how we swept across France in less than a month? When the time comes, our paratroopers will take London in a day and our eastern army will be at the gates of the Kremlin in three weeks. It is inevitable, before a new age can rise from the ashes.'

'How very Wagnerian,' remarked the Doctor dryly.

'I loathe Wagner. This is not some adolescent fantasy, Doctor. This is not a scientific romance like Mr Wells' film. Nazism is fact, Nazism is the future. The Shape of Things to Come. You have a simple choice, Doktor: join us or be destroyed.'

'You want me to join you?' the Doctor spluttered. This was not what he had expected.

Benny passed the Gaumont cinema. She had never been inside. From an historical point of view it would have been fascinating to see all those Nazi propaganda films. Last week they'd put on a Rienfenstahl documentary, no copies of which existed in her century. Most scholars agreed that the last existing print had been destroyed in 1945. Withdrawn, de-accessioned and junked. The islanders, though, found it difficult to be objective, and anyone who went to the cinema these days was labelled a collaborator. Takes one to know one. She'd been here three months, but had not visited one of the dolmen or tumuli that dotted the island. The prehistoric ruins didn't seem terribly relevant in 1941, a year that was quite capable of creating ruins of its own.

There was a wind blowing, and it whipped the breath away from her face. Even the air here was rationed. Clouds dashed across the sky like Zeppelins.

God, when you're drunk you don't half get maudlin, Bernice Summerfield. She'd been saving her bottle of Scotch for a special occasion. One hadn't come, so she'd drunk it early that morning before leaving the guesthouse. It was her first alcohol for three months, and she'd forgotten how much she enjoyed it.

Come on, Doctor, if you're coming.

She was walking through the harbour now. That would explain the smell of fish. She giggled, and turned a corner.

Herr Wolff was standing over the body of a young woman. The Nazi turned to face her.

Benny made a run for it, but he had caught up with her within twenty yards. Expertly, Wolff kicked Benny's legs from under her and she fell to the pavement.

'I have done nothing. I'm just drunk. I'm lost,' she stammered. Wolff bent down, trying to place her face. He mustn't find out about Ma and Anne. She'd told him her name, her false name, at the hotel a couple of days ago, hadn't she? The game was up. Give him the answer.

'I am Bernice Summerfield. I am an agent of a hostile power. I am unarmed. I surrender.'

Christopher Cwej ordered himself another coffee and a croissant. There were half a dozen other patrons outside the café, most of them octogenarians. Chris had been here for just over an hour. Twenty minutes ago, a Nazi had asked for his identity papers. The soldier had peered at the document for a minute or so, checking it very carefully, but had been satisfied.

You would hardly need to be a secret agent to realize that the Nazis had something planned here. There was a steady stream of armoured cars, motorbikes and tanks. Soldiers guarded checkpoints all over Granville. Fighter patrols constantly circled overhead. He'd arrived just before dawn by surf boat. The Nazis were on the verge of completing their sea defences, but hadn't quite done so yet, and so it was still possible to slip a small boat in. Half a mile from the coast, the Prometheus had surfaced, and he'd rowed the rest of the way in. Once on the shore, he'd signalled to the submarine with his hand-lamp, then deflated the dinghy. Finally, he'd removed his waterproof clothing and buried them above the water line.

On the way into town that morning, he'd walked past fortress-like observation towers and gun emplacements. The beaches and cliffs were heavily mined and ringed round with barbed wire. He had been very lucky not to have been spotted.

His mission briefing was very clear. It had been hoped that the French Resistance would make contact here and they'd compare notes on Hartung. For some reason, they hadn't come. Intelligence reports placed Hartung at an airstrip two miles north of here. Chris would have to make his own way across the country.

It was six o'clock, and it was getting dark outside.

Reed had come back to his office after an hour in the file room, and was surprised to find the door ajar. He pushed it open. Forrester sat at her desk, still peering into the aerial photographs. Lynch must have gone home. She hadn't seen him; she had her back to him. He knew how old she was from her file, but still couldn't believe she was in her forties. He would have guessed mid-thirties at most. It must be something to do with living away from the pressures of civilization. His eyes drifted down from her thick, cropped hair – which was flecked with grey, he noticed for the first time – to her slender neck, which was a dark chocolate-brown. Strangely, she didn't look out of place in uniform. He announced his presence.

She turned, wearily. 'Hi, George.' Her attention returned to the photographs. Her accent was still utterly impossible to place, containing elements of South African and American as well as English.

'Captain Forrester, it's getting late.'

'Yes, I know, but there's still so much to do.'

'Permission to speak freely, Captain?'

'Granted.' She looked up from her work.

'You were right this afternoon, Captain. The admiral wasn't treating you as your rank deserves. If I have done so, then I offer my apologies. I like you, ma'am, and wouldn't want to upset you.' He had spent most of the day planning this speech.

It seemed to work. Roz smiled at him, and there was genuine warmth there. 'Thank you, Lieutenant. Apology accepted, but it's my fault. What I did this morning was unprofessional. It doesn't matter whether I was provoked or not.'

'Ma'am, I –'

'End of story, George. Look, do you mind walking me home? The tube closes at six and there's no way Kendrick will spare a staff car. I'm not sure I'd be able to find Paddington by myself.' George's heart raced, and he eagerly accepted. She stood, folding over a couple of sheets of paper, and placing the photographs in the safe. He reached across for Forrester's coat and gas mask.

'Captain, may I ask you a question?'

'As long as you don't expect an answer. Joke.'

'Ah, yes. I wanted to ask about that tribe you mentioned before. The Servobots.'

Roz broke eye contact and she found another piece of paper to turn over. 'Yeah, what about them?'

'Well, I've read a bit about the South African tribes, and I've not heard of them.'

Chris made his way carefully across the fields. The airstrip was meant to be a mile to the north of here, but very little was known about it. There were certainly German patrols, with dogs and torches, but they made a lot of noise and were easy enough to avoid. Visibility was poor now; fog had drifted in off the sea. It would be a lot easier if he'd been allowed to bring his IR goggles, but the Doctor had made it clear why he couldn't. If he was captured, or if he just dropped them, then the Germans might just work out how to duplicate the technology. The consequences could be horrendous: foot patrols would find it easier to pick up people, U-boats would be able to detect convoys, aerial reconnaissance would enter a whole new era. It wouldn't take the Nazis long to work out that they could link up IR sensors to an anti-aircraft battery or to put it in one of their planes. All of a sudden, it would become very easy to spot Allied aircraft, and all because he dropped his goggles.

Chris needed to rest. He'd hardly slept for twenty-four hours. He had to find somewhere safe to settle for the night. It was just possible to make out a building a couple of hundred yards away, black against the royal-blue sky. It might fit the bill. A car darted past him as he made his way forward. The building was a large brick barn. Fifty yards away was a collection of farm buildings: a farmhouse, a stable, some sort of chicken shed. All were blacked out. There was the sound of a dog barking in the middle distance, but it wasn't getting any closer. The animal was probably chained up.

Chris made his way round the sides of the barn until he found the door. It was unlocked. He prised open the door and stepped inside. It was pitch black. After a few moments fumbling around, Chris established that there was nothing in here but a few bales of hay. The door he had come through was the only way in. He rearranged a couple of the bales, setting up some cover.

He was just settling down when the door burst open, and a torch was shone in his face. He raised his hands to shield his eyes. Behind the light, he could make out one, no, two figures. He reached for his revolver, and was greeted by the sound of two guns being cocked. He decided against it.

The soldier on the door saluted Forrester and Reed as they left the War Office. Reed led the way across Whitehall, all the time nervously looking back at Roz, checking that she was still with him, asking if she was all right. His overwhelming urge to appear concerned and his dogged desire to be liked reminded her of Chris.

Even in wartime, the London streets were normally busy with buses, cars and horse-carts during the day, but now they were almost deserted. Barrage balloons jostled in the sky. It was still only twilight, but it seemed darker, as no street lighting was permitted. The Doctor had claimed that when the restrictions on car headlamps and street lighting had first been introduced, the number of accidents had increased so dramatically that more people died on the roads than in air-raids. The blackout had been relaxed a little since then.

This was the first time that Forrester had walked any distance through London. As they picked their way past ruined terraces and cratered roads, she suddenly realized where she was. They were walking through a wide public space, surrounded by huge old buildings. In the middle of the plaza was a huge pillar, standing alone. As an Adjudicator, she had walked these streets in the thirtieth century, and the layout of the place was hardly different. In her day, the Underdwellers called this place Trafflegarr Square, and they were walking towards Sintjaimsys. Those in the Overtowns didn't really distinguish. To them, all this area was Spaceport Five Undertown.

'This hasn't changed in a thousand years.'

'No. And it probably won't for another thousand,' Reed answered. Roz was about to explain, but thought better of it. As George said, the city was an old one. There was no reason why it should have changed that much. Individual houses and office blocks came and went, but the basic layout of the streets themselves stayed the same. It was amazing, though, that many of the buildings that were already centuries old at this time would still be standing in a millennium.

'Whereabouts do you live?' Roz asked, wondering whether she'd recognize Reed's house.

'I've got a flat in Mayfair, not far from here. I'm on this side of Hyde Park, you're on the other.'

Again, it was a name Roz recognized from her time.

From Reed's tone of voice, it was clear that Mayfair in this time was somewhat more prestigious than in hers.

There was someone blowing a whistle in the next street. Reed grabbed her by the arm. 'It's an air-raid. We have to get inside.'

'Will your flat do?'

Reed nodded grimly. 'It's a basement flat. We should have enough time, usually we get about ten minutes' warning. We'll have to hurry.'

Reed broke into a run, although Roz found it easy to keep up. He was already fishing in his pocket for his keys. They were running along a row of elegant terraces straight out of a Sherlock Holmes simcord. When Roz looked up, the sky had become a cathedral of light. Solid white beams criss-crossed the night sky, creating a rippling net in the heavens. A thousand years from now, people would pay good money to see a light-show like this. Hardly anyone saw this spectacle, though. Every night, millions of Londoners sat in their Anderson shelters, or in the Underground railway stations. Above ground, searchlight crews probed the sky for German bombers. If one beam intercepted a plane, half a dozen more would instantly be brought to bear. Bathed in light, the German planes would be easy targets for the anti-aircraft batteries.

Right on cue, a mile or so behind them, there was a burst of artillery fire. It wouldn't hit a plane. Over the last three months, half a million shells had been fired, but, on average, only one bomber a night was brought down. The British wouldn't admit it; but the guns were there to reassure their civilians, not as a practical way of defending them.

George ushered her down a flight of stone steps to his dark blue front door, warning her that there wasn't a railing any more. After a moment struggling with the lock, they were inside.

George's hallway smelt faintly of boiled vegetables. Roz was occupied with this thought while he took her coat, and hung it with his own behind the front door. It was dark, too. The blackout material was in place and the bulb had been removed to save electricity. George struck a match, lighting a candle. He handed it to Forrester, who examined it. Primitive technology, but effective enough. Reed had a candle of his own, and led her through into his front room. The front room consisted of a sofa, a threadbare rug and an unlit coal fire. In the corner, a big wireless sat on top of a bookcase stuffed with old hardback books. The place was kept spotlessly clean, but because the windows had been painted over with blackout paint, it was claustrophobic. Reed assured her that they ought to be safe in this room. He excused himself, taking his candle with him.

Roz placed her candle in a metal holder, and began exploring the room. Bernice would love this, she thought, it was just like exploring an excavated Egyptian burial chamber. The candlelight danced off the wall, casting pools of shadow. There was a portrait above the mantelpiece. The subject, an elderly man, bore a strong resemblance to George, but he was bearded and wore a military uniform that Roz knew came from a much earlier time than this. Edging forward, Roz bumped into a small coffee table, knocking the telephone off the hook. She carefully replaced the handset and continued her search. She examined the bookcase. A few scientific textbooks, a couple of spy novels. *The Language and Customs of South Africa.* She pulled the picture book down, and sat on the settee. The book fell open at a full-page photograph of 'a Xosa maiden'. The image was murky, printed on poor-quality paper. The girl was about fourteen or fifteen, and was Zulu, not Xhosa, as a cursory glance at the dress confirmed. Her skin was relatively light and her nose was not as flat as a typical African. Despite that, the grinning face of this 'Xosa maiden' bore an uncanny resemblance to Forrester's own graduation photograph. The girl in the picture was prettier. Roz read the caption – 'The costume consists mainly of a blanket, beads, wire bracelets and bands round the ankles. At home the blanket is usually dispensed with.' Her breasts were indeed covered, presumably so as not to offend the sensibility of the English reader.

'Oh, you've found it. I was going to show you.' George had come back with a tray of tea and toast. Roz held up the photograph.

'It seems to have fallen open at this page,' she said sardonically.

Reed blushed, but was unapologetic. 'I got this book for my tenth birthday. You know, for years I couldn't work out what she wore instead of the blanket. Is that how you dress at home?'

Only in your dreams, soldier-boy, Roz thought, but she replied, 'It would certainly turn a few heads in Paddington.'

'I meant at home in Africa,' Reed explained patiently.

'I wore the traditional dress once, at a costume party.'

'You take your *ikofu* black because of the *ukuzila*.' He handed her a mug of thick, black coffee.

'I take it black, because I like the taste, not because of any tribal taboo,' she snapped. *At least I think that's the reason.* She sipped her hot drink. Reed had lit her a cigarette, which she gratefully accepted.

'I pronounced the words right, then, Captain Forrester? I've been swotting up ever since I found out that you're a Xhosa.'

'You pronounced them right, George.' She leant a little closer. 'And call me Roz.'

Outside, the bombs were beginning to drop.

6

Kill All the Butterflies

On his nineteenth move, the Doctor, playing Black, placed his knight on C5, threatening Steinmann's bishop. The German had predicted this and all he needed to do was . . .

'I know about Emil Hartung, of course,' the Doctor said quietly. Steinmann looked up at him. On first impression, this Doctor resembled nothing more than a smelly old tramp. The trick was to look into his eyes, gaze beyond the shabby exterior into his labyrinthine, brilliant mind. There you would find true genius, allied with the cunning of a wild animal. The Doctor was an opponent to be reckoned with, in life as well as in chess. Even a bully like Wolff had seen that. This Doctor was proving a fascinating diversion from the business of war, and was the only chess player for over a decade who had come anywhere near to beating him. Steinmann turned his attention back to the board.

'And I know exactly what Hartung is building. Please send him my regards,' the Doctor finished. The words hung in the air for the moment, then the little man said cheerfully, 'There are two kinds of chess-players.' Steinmann looked up again, as the Doctor continued. 'Those who give up when they lose their Queen and those who carry on playing.'

Steinmann moved his bishop out of harm's way. 'An interesting theory, if a little simplistic. Which camp do you belong in, Herr Doktor?'

'Oh, I never lose my Queen. It was just an observation.'

The Doctor pressed his knight forward, capturing the white queen. Steinmann could hardly believe his eyes, and turned his full attention back to the game. 'Which camp are you in?' the Doctor asked sweetly, as he removed the white piece from the board.

Steinmann knocked his king over. The Doctor grinned.

'Doktor, I congratulate you. You have mastered chess,' Steinmann offered.

'No,' said the Doctor, 'it isn't possible to. There's always someone better, somewhere.'

'A fascinating philosophical point. There are more potential moves in the game of chess than there are atoms in the galaxy, did you know that? The number of moves is finite, though. One day, the solution will be found to every possible chess game. Chess is just a more complicated version of noughts and crosses, or draughts, and a good enough mathematician should be able to work it out.'

The Doctor pursed his lips. 'That's not true. You're right that there are strict rules and only a finite number of moves, but there is a random element to the game: the players themselves. You could never work out your opponent's thoughts, or know his memories. You couldn't predict when he'll cough or when he's bluffing.' Listening to the Doctor's answer, Steinmann found it possible to believe that the little man had tried to square the circle – he talked as if he'd played every possible game, and tried to win them all. Tried and failed. He had won this particular contest, though.

'So you have proved,' Steinmann muttered, sipping at his wine. 'You are right, of course. There is always another set of variables to take into account. It's like that British slogan, "Careless Talk Costs Lives": a London housewife gossiping on the bus might reveal some sensitive information, a spy could overhear and we could use it to win the war. Even with obsessive secrecy, information slips out.'

'There's nothing you can do about it,' said the Doctor gloomily, 'it's the nature of the universe. Congratulations.

You've discovered the Butterfly Effect eleven years early. Everything is interrelated: a butterfly flapping its wings in Granville might lead to a hurricane sweeping across Berlin. You can never predict all the consequences of an action. You can never control everything. We all have to muddle along as best we can.'

There is another way, thought Steinmann, we could kill all the butterflies. Or make them flap their wings when we order them to. Visions of a party rally swam before his eyes, twenty thousand arms surging skywards in salute. Control the universe, never allow yourself to be controlled by it.

'Would you like another game?' the German offered. The Doctor was already setting up the pieces.

Reed's chest rose and fell steadily beneath Forrester's head, hypnotizing her. He cradled her in his arms, one hand resting in the small of her back, the other on her thigh. There was an intoxicating scent in the air, a blend of cigar smoke, brandy and aftershave. She hadn't felt so relaxed since –

'Goddess!' She bolted upright. George Reed's eyes snapped open, catching her before she fell off the sofa. He looked as surprised as she felt. She stood uncertainly.

'There's nothing wrong. We're at my flat, remember?'

It all came flooding back. They'd talked, smoked and got a bit drunk. Then she'd fallen asleep. That's all. Situation under control.

'Yeah, sure. Sorry.' It was still pitch black in here, thanks to the blackout paint. It was chilly, too. England was so cold in this century. If she didn't know better, then she'd have suspected that this was because the British hadn't discovered fire yet. It was impossible to judge the time of day in here, but she could hear birdsong outside. Roz checked her wristwatch.

'It's twenty past eight!'

'Don't worry, we're only a quarter of an hour away from Whitehall. Less if I phone for a car.'

'No it's –' It's too late to get over to the TARDIS and

see if the Doctor has turned up today. 'Look, George, I'm sorry. I don't normally oversleep.'

'No. Look, I need a bit of a scrub. Er . . .' George was grinning like a schoolboy. He made some arcane hand-gesture over his chest and left. Roz frowned, trying to puzzle out this latest English ritual. Then she glanced down at her blouse, which had come unbuttoned in a couple of places. It must have happened overnight, because George had been a perfect gentleman when things had got a little more intimate last night. His loss. And don't you dare pretend you were drunk, Roslyn Forrester, because you are not even slightly hungover. She buttoned herself up, tucked the blouse back into her skirt and adjusted her petticoat. One of her stockings had come unhitched overnight. She did it back up. There was a knock, and George peeked round the door.

'The bathroom's free,' he said nervously.

'George, I enjoyed last night – I enjoy your company – but anything we do out of office hours can't affect our work, OK?'

'I understand, Roz. No office romance.'

'I'm not a romantic person, George, we better get that straight right now. And I'm not going to be here very long. If you ask me to marry you, then I'll bite your nose off, is that understood?'

George looked down at his feet. 'Understood, Captain.'

'Good boy.' Forrester went to freshen up.

Gunfire.

Frantically, Armand pulled the radio set from under the bed, looped the headphones over his ear and pinned up the aerial. He spoke in English. He had been chosen because he was the most fluent English-speaker left. Another burst of submachine-gun-fire, upstairs this time.

'Raven Calling London. Raven Calling London. Over.'

'Receiving you, Raven. Status Tomato. Over.' If he wasn't used to it, the surrealism of the conversation might have been comical. He hadn't much time. He dropped the codebook into the ashtray, then set it alight with a match.

'Tomato Compromised. Repeat: Tomato Compromised. Over.'

The door burst open. Shouts in German.

'Hugin. Munin. Hugin and Mun– '

Gunfire. Footsteps. The last page of the codebook curled and blackened.

'Please confirm, Raven.'

Gunshot.

'Your moustache makes you very distinctive.'

'Thank you.' Chris glowed with pride, stroking his top lip. Monique was the young daughter of Monsieur Gerard, the farmer who owned the barn. They had found him, but luckily they had wanted to identify him before shooting. After initial suspicions, they'd welcomed him in, made up a bed for him. Now they sat around the breakfast table. Monique had told him something of her family's history. Her mother, Monsieur Gerard's wife, had died in childbirth and his two sons had served on the Maginot Line. Monique was pretty, with long, black hair. She was about five foot six, and looked a little older than her fifteen years. Last year, she had been planning to join a religious order, a nunnery near Mont St Michel. The war had changed all that. Now, she helped her father at the farm because his sons and all the other farmhands had been killed or captured during the invasion. Chris would not have described her father as pretty, however. 'Hulking', perhaps. He had clearly been a farmer for the whole of his life. His face was lined, his huge hands were callused. He was forty-one, 'as old as the century', as he put it. He looked older.

'It is not a good thing to be distinctive these days, Christophe,' he mumbled.

'No?' Chris was disappointed.

'Don't worry, you might not have to shave it off.' Monique giggled. She handed him a glass of wine, and a hunk of bread.

Her father's voice was grave. 'Mr Cwej, I am glad you

have not forgotten our country, but you must understand that your presence here puts us at risk.'

'I'm quite willing to leave now, I – ' Chris replied hurriedly.

'Sir, I did not mean that. I want to help. I have no contact with the Resistance. I can do little more than save the best of my produce for my fellow countrymen and keep my eyes and ears open. I am willing to help you in my limited way.'

'Thank you, sir. I will avenge your sons.'

'Avenge?' The farmer chuckled. 'You make it sound so melodramatic. Michel and Luc were soldiers, defending their country. I sometimes wonder why people have this notion that wars are such an adventure. I fought in the last war, the Great War. I was fifteen, so eager to join up that I lied about my age. I learnt then that it wasn't a place for heroism, it was just war. I spent most of my time marching and waiting. Lying in cold ditches, not sure whether my friends were still alive, or when the enemy would attack. I wasn't able to sleep, and my latrine was a bucket in the corner of my quarters, which I shared with five other men. I've never seen a novel or a film where the hero did that! They miss out all those bits.' He paused to sip his wine and gave a little chuckle. 'So, Mr Cwej, what exciting mission brings you here?'

'I was making my way towards the airfield. I'm looking for Emil Hartung.'

'The racing driver?' asked the farmer, but his daughter was already speaking.

'Not the new base?' she enquired.

'The what?'

'My daughter means the new *fence*. I don't think there is a base there yet.'

'Where is this?'

'South-east of here, about two miles.'

'The British have no photographs of this base. Could you take me?'

Monsieur Gerard shrugged. 'It is the least I could do.

But I have to warn you that there isn't much to see. I will take you there this evening.'

As soon as they arrived at their office, George could tell that something was wrong.

Kendrick and Lynch had been joined by three more men. Two of them were RAF, the other wore a double-breasted blue suit. He was either a civil servant or MI5, he was too smartly dressed to be a boffin. All five were bent over a map of the English Channel. One of the RAF men was drawing on it with a thick red pen. Reed glanced at Roz, who flashed back a look of concern.

'What's the matter, sir?' he asked.

'It's a disaster, George. Forrester, could you come over here?' She was the shortest person present, and Kendrick was allowing her a better vantage point. George stood on the other side of the table. Surrounded by half a dozen drab Englishmen, Roz looked all the more exotic.

'What, precisely, is the problem?' she asked, apparently sensing Kendrick's new-found acceptance of her, and warily trying not to break the spell.

'We've lost the whole "Tomato" network.'

'The Channel Islands,' said Reed.

'Exactly. And some of France, the area around Granville. Jersey and Guernsey should be totally secure, the network was entirely made up of British citizens. But it looks like the collapse started in Guernsey.'

'When?' Forrester was businesslike, and Kendrick seemed to appreciate it. One of the RAF men spoke up.

'Just this morning. In one day, thirty of our people were rounded up. It happened so quickly, we couldn't even warn them.'

'. . . so the Germans have known about the network for a while,' concluded the civilian.

'Is there anyone left?'

'Not one. The last was apparently killed at 08.24 this morning while he was calling London. A member of the Raven cell in Granville.' There was consternation around the table. Reed looked down at the map, examining it

94

properly for the first time. The red lines traced the collapse of the network. The Germans had eliminated the spies in less than a day. They had known exactly where to strike. It was a clear message to London.

'That last thing we got was rather cryptic: "hoogin end mooning". It means nothing to any of us. It came from that Raven cell. It's certainly not French or German. It must be a codephrase.' He looked up, hopefully, but it meant nothing to Forrester either.

George's brow was furrowed. 'How is it spelt, sir?'

'Well,' he handed Reed a slip of paper, 'that is what our operator made of it. Even allowing for the French accent, it makes no sense.'

Everyone around the table tried mouthing the words.

'That middle word, it's probably either "und" or "and". It's not "et" is it?'

'So we're dealing with two things. "Hoogin" and "Mooning".'

'Are they names?'

'If they are, we don't have them on file. They are not place names, and they are not the names of people either.'

Reed, like most Englishmen, had little ability with foreign languages. 'Sir, doesn't *hugel* mean "hill" in German? Could *mooning* be the word for "mountain"?' There was a murmur round the table.

'Sorry, Lieutenant, the German for "mountain" is *berg*, as in iceberg,' said one of the RAF chaps. Reed found it difficult to hide his disappointment. The murmuring died down.

'Could it be a name. "Hugh Ghin" and er, "Moon Inn". A hotel?' offered Lynch.

Kendrick's disbelieving expression was sufficient answer. 'Perhaps it's chinese, Lynch, but I very much doubt it.'

'Just a suggestion, Admiral, but why don't we ask a German linguist?' Roz asked.

Kendrick shook his head. 'The network has been compromised. These words are obviously vitally important. They should not be breathed to anyone who isn't

95

around this table. Ray here is going to look through the files to see if the words have ever cropped up in reports before, but I'm pretty sure they haven't.' The civilian nodded thoughtfully.

'Sir, I understand the need for security, but someone else might know straight away what these words mean.'

'Forrester, we've lost our eyes and ears in a whole section of northern France. The Germans mustn't find out that we know about this message, so we can't risk telling anyone else. My hunch is that this has something to do with the superbomber that Lynch proposed. We were getting close, and the German's knew it.'

'Cwej,' Roz said suddenly. The others looked at her.

'Another mystery word. Is it Welsh?' said the civilian.

'It sounded more like Polish,' offered the other RAF man, who had a touch of a Welsh accent himself.

'Cwej's my partner. He's been sent into the middle of all this,' Roz explained, indicating the map.

'He's trying to make contact with Hartung,' said Kendrick. 'At the moment, he's the only operative we have in the Granville area, and he's maintaining radio silence. So we have only two things left: Cwej, and the cryptic message.'

Roz spoke. 'Sir, this message means nothing to us. We don't have any advantage.' A murmur of assent swept around the table. Kendrick caught the mood of the meeting.

'Forrester, you don't seem to understand the need for secrecy.'

Roz shifted. 'Gentlemen, at the moment we have a clue, but none of us can shed any light on it. What use is it? From the Germans' point of view, it doesn't matter whether we've heard the words or not, it matters whether we understand them.'

Kendrick had been listening carefully, and now he nodded. 'I think we can risk bringing in someone else. Those two words are not to be uttered outside these walls, but I want everyone in this room to focus their attention on them.'

Steinmann was a vegetarian, and he had brought his own personal chef up from Stuttgart, so the cuisine had been simply excellent. There was no shortage of fine wine here, either. Life in wartime was luxurious for some. Although the Doctor hadn't been allowed to leave the townhouse, he had to admit that he had been well catered for. Ulrilda had been assigned to him; she had provided food and drink on request, and had answered his simple questions. She had even managed to procure the latest issues of all the major German scientific journals, although he hadn't learnt much from them. She was a pleasant companion, although chess seemed a little beyond her grasp.

Now Steinmann had joined them in the first-floor room that had become the Doctor's study. It had a good view, a packed bookcase, even a gramophone. There was a limited selection of music, all composed by Germans. The Doctor had selected a Beethoven symphony. The music drifted across the room to where the Doctor stared out across the harbour. Ulrilda smiled at him when she knew Steinmann wasn't looking, and the Doctor gurned back at her. Ulrilda stifled a laugh.

The German officer sipped from his coffee cup. 'This is very civilized, isn't it, Herr Doktor?'

'On a microcosmic level, yes.' A column of tanks wound their way across the seafront.

'Again, you have a cosmic view. Just like the Nazis, my friend.' Steinmann paused before speaking again. 'Doktor, you tell me that you know what Hartung is building.' The Doctor opened his mouth to speak, but quickly shut it again. 'Would you like to meet him?'

The Doctor kept his expression neutral. 'Yes. I'd love to see how close he has got.'

'Close? My dear Doktor, both have been built already. What do you know of jet propulsion?'

'Enough to fill a series of books on the subject,' the Doctor said matter of factly.

'Is that why you came?' Steinmann had finished his coffee. Ulrilda hurried to refill his cup.

'Not specifically.'

'But you have seen the plans?'

'Which plans?' The Doctor was puzzled. Ulrilda had moved over to the Doctor and poured him a fresh coffee. Now she began adding sugar.

'Doktor, there is no need to pretend, you are among friends here. Three weeks ago, the SID managed to a acquire a set of plans.' Steinmann gestured around magnanimously, almost knocking his mug over.

'I knew nothing of this.' The Doctor thanked Ulrilda, who returned to her seat by the window.

'No? Doktor, I am prepared to concede that the plans are almost complete. It might not be enough for the British to build a whole engine for themselves, but they will know what Hartung has built. That, of course, is why we let them have the plans.'

'I still have no idea what you are talking about.'

Steinmann's face fell. 'You mean that, don't you?'

'I do,' the Doctor admitted, furrowing his brow.

'The SID sent you over here, but didn't tell you, an expert in the field, about the plans they had. It must be the single biggest coup in the history of espionage.'

'I never said that I worked for the British. I certainly didn't mention the Scientific Intelligence Division.'

'Oh, Doktor, if you know what the initials stand for, then you must be working for them.' Steinmann fixed him with those piercing eyes of his.

'An interesting theory, if a little simplistic. For one thing, *you* know what the initials stand for. Logically, that means that you work for the British.'

Steinmann laughed. 'Ha! I sometimes wonder whether I do, you know. I feel an affinity with good old Arthur Kendrick. We have so much in common, we have the same concerns, are experts in the same fields. We are doing the same job, we face the same problems, we just happen to be on different sides. You are a scientist. You must feel some camaraderie with the scientific community in Germany.'

'I think that the German scientists should have made a moral stand. Under the Nazis, science has been perverted.'

'Really? You don't believe that science is objective?'

'Of course not. Science is a tool, a way of modelling the universe. What a scientist chooses to model reflects his or her concerns.' The Doctor was losing track of where this conversation was heading.

Steinmann sipped at his coffee before answering. 'So you agree that the scientist himself is part of the object which he investigates? Science is part of culture, not a universal truth?'

'Yes, of course. So much scientific research on this planet is directed to building new weapons. You Germans are obsessed with chemistry because you lack raw materials and you want to create artificial oil and fabrics. The Americans do just the opposite and concentrate on mass production.'

'Doktor, that is what Max Planck, the director of the Kaiser Wilhelm Society says. The British and Americans mocked him for doing so. Once again, you agree with us. Doktor, I want you to see the true state of German science. If you have not been allowed to see the stolen plans, then you are obviously not valued by the British government. The Reich, though, welcomes men of talent, and is happy to reward them. Tomorrow morning, we'll go up to where Hartung is working. You'll have a chance to meet him. The British won't show you the plan. We'll show you the finished product. You'll be free to make up your own mind.'

'You have a knack for ending the day on a dramatic note,' observed the Doctor. 'Yesterday you asked me to become a Fascist, now you seem to be offering me a job on your design team.'

'Fascism is about the opportunity that tomorrow will –'

'And of course, I get a daily dose of Fascist dogma,' the Doctor added.

Steinmann was silenced, but after a moment he continued, 'Doktor, I have a proposal for you.'

'Another bombshell! I'm flattered by the offer of marriage, Herr Steinmann, you are a very handsome man, with undoubted prospects, but I'm afraid that I'm already – ' the Doctor wittered. Steinmann cut him dead.

'Herr Doktor. I am being serious. My proposal is this: I will show you the future, show you what Hartung has built. I will let that speak for itself. Actions speak so much louder than words. As I believe you observed on the beach, Hartung's work will win the war for the Reich. I offer you the chance to be part of that future. If you do not want to, you will be free to go. Do you accept?'

'As Goethe might have said, Herr Steinmann, we have a deal.'

'Do you know what the simplest, most effective form of torture is, Nurse Kitzel?'

Standartenführer Wolff was peering through a slot in the cell door. He was tall, broad-chested, blond: one of the few in the army who looked like the soldiers on the recruiting posters. At thirty-two, he was still unmarried. His eligibility was a frequent topic of conversation for the girls at the complex. They thought he must be very brave and dedicated to have reached such an exalted rank so young. Either that, or he knew someone high in the Party. Either reason made him a good potential husband. Kitzel, surprised that such a senior officer would deign to talk to her, tried to remember her training.

'Electric shock,' she declared finally. Wolff sneered, and didn't even turn to look at her.

'The very simplest torture is electric shock?'

'No, sir.' Kitzel deflated. Pause. 'The Chinese say that it is dripping water, sir.'

'Yes, but as they are subhumans, their opinion is not valuable. You don't know the answer, do you?'

'No, sir,' she admitted.

'The very simplest form of torture is sleep deprivation.'

It came flooding back. 'Prolonged sleep deprivation, or, to be precise, "dream deprivation" can quickly lead to personality changes: typically heightened irritability or paranoia. After three or four days the subject might well begin to hallucinate. This decline is characterized by a loss of all sense of time. After a week there is the risk of permanent mental illness, usually schizophrenia. The longest a person has been deprived of sleep, without the use of stimulants such as amphetamines, is sixteen days.' Kitzel fluttered her eyelids.

'Very good.' Wolff smiled. 'Now to see all that in practice. Our subject has been in custody since twenty past six yesterday morning. Just about thirty-six hours ago. Since that time, she has been deprived of food, drink and sleep. If your calculations are correct, then the prisoner should be beginning to show the first symptoms. Her name is Bernice Summerfield, but you are not to use it in front of her. If I do give you permission to speak, she is to be referred to simply as "the prisoner". Bring that beaker and that bag.'

Without waiting for an answer, Wolff unbolted the door and ushered Kitzel inside. A woman, a long-legged brunette in her mid-thirties, sat in the corner. The skin around her eyes was grey-rimmed, as though it had been bruised. The eyes themselves were brown, but dull.

'Stand.'

The prisoner shuffled to her feet. She was wearing a dress with a floral pattern and was barefoot. She swayed slightly as she stood.

'Water.' Kitzel handed Wolff the beaker. He took a sip, all the time watching the prisoner's reaction.

'*Lovely*,' he said, presumably an English word, Kitzel didn't speak much English. Finally, he handed the prisoner the water, which she drank eagerly.

'Where am I?' the prisoner asked, when she had finished.

'In a prison cell. Nurse Rosa Kitzel, may I introduce the prisoner?'

'Delighted to make your acquaintance,' the prisoner said weakly in German, but with a trace of sarcasm. What occupied Kitzel's attention more was the fact that Wolff knew her Christian name.

'Undress.'

'Yeah, right. Look, I know this psychological stuff is

meant to make me feel inferior, less secure, et cetera. In a culture with a nudity taboo, like yours, it probably works all the time, reinforcing both your male authority and the female prisoner's self-image as victim. Textbook stuff, well done for remembering your training and all that, but it won't work on me.' She had unbuttoned her dress, and now she stepped out of it. 'See? Perfectly relaxed about the whole *sans frock* deal. To be honest, it's having the opposite effect to the one intended: I'm just wondering whether you'd feel secure enough in your . . . masculinity . . . to do all this to a male prisoner. Where I come from we're a relatively uninhibited lot, and so it's pretty damn difficult to play on our inhibitions. To be honest with you,' she unclipped her bra and handed it to Kitzel, who blushed at the prisoner's shamelessness, 'I'm feeling queasy, I'm still hungover, my stomach's empty, I've not slept for three days, and I'm scared poohless just being here, because I know what the Nazis do to prisoners.' She pulled off her knickers, and handed them to Kitzel, before continuing, 'it's those things that you should be playing on. All you prove by torturing me is your mental inferiority. Oh, thanks for the water, by the way.'

Whatever the prisoner had said, there was undoubtedly a trace of anxiety in her voice. She stood erect now, trying to look defiant in her nakedness, but she couldn't disguise the paleness of her skin, or the toll that rationing had taken on her body. Her legs and arms were thin, her hair lank. She was tall, only a couple of inches shorter than Wolff, but the Standartenführer seemed so much larger. Her stomach and thighs were covered with bruises. Kitzel looked away, a little embarrassed.

Wolff took the parcel from her hands and passed it to the prisoner. 'Open it.'

She did as Wolff said, and pulled out the contents: a short-sleeved buttonless shirt, and a pair of trousers in the same thin material with an elasticated waistband. Both were in the same pattern, black stripes on white. A serial number, F319–350042, was printed on the left breast and up one of the trouser-legs. It was what the slave workers wore, the standard outfit for inmates of the Reich's prison camps. Before Kitzel's eyes, the last vestige of the prisoner's resolve vanished. Shaking, even paler than before, she put her uniform on. All the time she tried to speak, but nothing came from her mouth except an inhuman whimpering noise. Not wanting to think about it, Kitzel picked up the bag, and put the beaker and the woman's clothing in it. Wolff was speaking.

'Thank you for the tip, prisoner. Incidentally, you have been here less than two days, not three. I wonder if you remember what that means from your textbook? I will talk to you tomorrow morning, after we've shaved your scalp. Come on, Kitzel.'

The nurse saw the prisoner slump to the floor again. She was on the verge of tears, but was too weak to cry. Wolff left. Kitzel followed, closing the door behind her.

One hundred yards ahead was the ten-foot wire fence. Signs hung at regular intervals informed the locals in French and German that the fence was electrified. The young Canadian, Cwej, reached out, and would have touched it had Monsieur Gerard not slapped his hand down. Despite what he had said before, the young man was still acting as though this was a game.

'The fence is live, Mr Cwej, take my word for it, there is no need to check,' the farmer grunted.

'The base is behind that?' Chris asked.

'There is no base, Christophe. But the Germans have set up these defences. It is utterly forbidden to go in there. We'd better go back, there are foot patrols.'

Chris peered through the mesh, but could see only hills, grass and pine trees. Countryside, indistinguishable from the surroundings.

'There aren't any guard towers, though, there are no buildings at all. This is weird.'

'I think they must have something underground,' the farmer gestured uncertainly. 'To be honest, I have no idea what it might be.'

'Perhaps I could pretend to be a delivery man, or a . . .'

'No one goes in there,' the farmer said.

'Cooks and cleaners must.' Cwej had a wounded expression, but the farmer was telling the truth.

He continued. 'No locals. Not even the Germans from Granville. The guards come direct from Germany, on three-month postings. They are barracked inside the fences; as I say, they must have some underground facility. Obviously, the guards do leave here, they frequent the bars and brothels in Granville. But even they do not seem to know what is going on in the base. They have been ordered not to say a word of what they do. Three German soldiers have been court-martialled for their indiscretion. One was sent back to Berlin simply for admitting that this fence exists. The Germans themselves bring supplies here, from the town.'

'There must be clues. Are they army, Luftwaffe, SS?'

'All three. No navy personnel. No civilians.'

'That's very odd. The structure of the German army is very rigid. Albert Speer claimed that the Nazi state is really feudal. The various leaders all jealousy guard their power and their personal interests. They very rarely co-operate with each other.'

'If Speer said that, then he would have been shot!' Gerard exclaimed.

'Perhaps it was a different Albert Speer,' Cwej said hurriedly. 'Tell me anything else you know. They order food from the village? For how many people?'

'Not many ... one hundred, maybe?' The farmer shrugged.

'Tell me more about these lights.'

'There is very little to tell. The fence was set up seven months ago on what used to be farmland. The owner, a coward, fled during the invasion. I have heard that Todt workers were used to build something within the perimeter. The Germans used a group that had been building coastal defences, and made sure that none of the workers they selected spoke French. Those workers have not been seen since – that, my friend, is not unusual. Shortly afterwards, we began to see the lights.'

'And you've seen them yourself?'

'Yes. So has Monique. Never during the day, but they have appeared in the early evening, it doesn't have to be dark. The first time, I thought it was just a plane, but suddenly it vanished. Another time it was just travelling too fast to be a plane. I don't mean just speed, but the manoeuvres it was making.'

'When you say vanished –'

'I mean vanished. One moment it was in the sky, the next it just faded away,' Monsieur Gerard said impatiently. Cwej seemed quite at ease standing next to this fence, but just its faint buzzing made the farmer feel restless. They could discuss all this back at the farm.

'Is there any engine noise?'

'None whatsoever. And no vapour trails.'

'What?'

'Vapour trails. Sorry, do I have the wrong word? I mean the exhaust fumes from the engines.' Gerard looked around. There wasn't any sign of a patrol. To be honest, the Germans had built up a reputation for this place. No sane person would come anywhere near it. Why waste time and effort patrolling such a place?

'What do you think the object was?' Chris insisted.

'I just have no idea.'

'Me neither. Hey, perhaps we'll see one of those flying objects. I need to get inside that base.'

'People have tried. Look, Christophe, I can't come with you.'

'I wasn't asking you to. You've been very brave already.'

'My friend. There comes a point where bravery becomes stupidity. Have you not been listening? You can't just storm in there like Humphrey Bogart.' He could tell that he had finally got through to Cwej.

'Maybe you're right. I'll need to sleep on it.'

'Come back with me, monsieur.' Gerard touched him on the shoulder. Cwej nodded his head, but continued to peer through the fence for a moment longer, before setting off.

* * *

'Captain Forrester, Lieutenant Reed, can I have a word?'

They were just about to leave. Kendrick had caught them in reception. He had a document wallet underneath his arm. Although they were the only people within earshot, his voice was a whisper. Forrester chose to find it comical. Kendrick handed Reed the wallet.

'I'm taking you off raid analysis. I've got a new job for you. An absolute priority. You are the only two I can completely trust.'

'Sir, everyone in this building has been vetted,' Reed objected.

'I know that, Lieutenant, but the SID was thrown together quickly. If the Germans knew about us back at that early stage, which it looks like they did, then it would have been very easy to get one of their own men in. I fought alongside your father, George, there's no way that he'd have brought up a Fascist, and I know for a fact that you're not a Nazi, Captain Forrester.' He had looked her straight in the eye as he said that. At least it was a compliment of sorts.

Reed had been looking through the documents in the wallet. He passed them over to Roz. She shuffled through a number of transcripts and maps and came to a single photograph. Kendrick drew their attention to it.

'I must ask you to look out for this man, and to prepare a report on him. Five have photographed him in or around this building a number of times. They suspect that he might be the notorious spymaster von Wer. He, and any of his associates, are to be considered dangerous.' Roz turned the black and white photograph over.

It was the Doctor.

7

I Spy

Cwej grabbed the hand that brushed against his forehead. Monique squealed. He was awake in an instant.

'Monique, I'm sorry. I didn't hurt you?'

The girl was standing in front of his bedroom window, rubbing her wrist. 'No, Christophe.' She was wearing a cotton night-shirt. She clearly didn't realize how easily the sunlight streamed through the thin material.

'It's my training. We have to be alert, even while we sleep.'

'How heroic,' she exclaimed, her pain forgotten. 'I have washed your shirt for you.' She held it up for Chris to examine. It was actually still a little damp, but he was grateful anyway, and he told her so. She asked him what he was going to do that morning.

'I'm going back up to the base. I need to keep watch, find out what's going on in there.'

'I shall cook you breakfast.' Monique sat on the edge of the bed, and stroked his arm.

'That would be great. Thanks. I'll eat it when I come back from my jog.' Chris jumped out of bed.

'Please don't.'

Wolff watched the prisoner recoil as the hair clippers hovered over her head. Kitzel was holding them, and was reassuring Summerfield that this was for the sake of her own hygiene. Although it was a shame to lose that pretty brunette hair, in a public facility such as this, there was a risk of lice and other parasites. Summerfield had been almost hysterical when they had arrived, but had quietened down. Her extreme response was quite unusual, but not unheard of, in circumstances like this; they had been forced to secure her hands to her chair. She was desperately clinging on to some vestige of her individuality. Deprived of sleep, keeping possession of her hair must now seem to her like the most important thing in the world. It might be possible to use this belief to gain some leverage. Wolff held his hand up.

'Nurse Kitzel, there might be no need to do this.' The prisoner looked at him hopefully. Kitzel hesitated.

'Tell me what you did,' Wolff said softly.

'I killed Gerhard. I let all those people die,' Summerfield admitted.

'You witnessed that, Nurse Kitzel?'

'Yes, sir. Sir, who did she let die?' Wolff shrugged.

'On Smith Street,' the prisoner answered.

'Oh, yes, of course. I'd forgotten about them. Don't worry, prisoner, there won't be any need to repeat the exercise now that you've admitted your guilt.' Wolff smiled.

'Sir, shall I cut her hair?' Kitzel asked. The prisoner gasped.

Wolff paused for dramatic effect. He looked at Summerfield, who was silently begging with him.

'No,' he announced finally. Summerfield was looking at him with a pitiful expression of gratitude. At this second, she would have willingly given herself to him, betrayed her own mother, reeled off a list of her contacts and fellow agents. Summerfield would not forget what had just happened. She was his, now.

'One small thing, prisoner. How do you know the name of the dead soldier?'

Forrester had already gone.

George Reed had spent the night on the sofa, at his insistence. Forrester expressed her disappointment, claiming that she would 'find it impossible to get warm'. Reed recognized this as sarcasm. He remembered dreaming about Roz, but couldn't remember the details. He had woken at a quarter to eight, and had immediately knocked on the bedroom door. There had been no response. Remembering the morning before, when Roz had been so worried about oversleeping, he had decided to open the door – an easy decision to make. The room was dark, and musky with her scent. It had been terribly anticlimatic to learn that although the bed had been slept in, it was empty now. Reed stepped over, placing his hand on the mattress. It was still warm. The flat was tiny, and it only took Reed a minute to confirm his suspicion that the kitchen and bathroom were also empty.

Roz's bag was there. Had she forgotten it, or did this mean that she was planning to come back before she went into work? A horrible suspicion dawned on him. He unbuckled the handbag, feeling very guilty about doing so. It was fastidiously neat. Roz's ration book, identity papers, purse and security pass were all there. Apart from that, it was empty. The photographs weren't there.

Last night, after Kendrick had told them about von Wer the spy, Forrester had insisted that they go straight back up to their office. She had opened up the safe, taken out the aerial photographs of London and put them in her handbag. He had pointed out that the photographs weren't meant to leave the room, let alone the building. Roz had smiled that knowing smile of hers and pecked him on the cheek.

Now Roz had vanished and so had the photographs. The consequences if the Luftwaffe got hold of reliable information about their aerial bombardments didn't bear thinking about. They would know which of their targets they had and hadn't hit. They could make a good guess which areas were adequately defended and which weren't. They would be able to plan future raids with almost total accuracy. Kendrick was right: Forrester was not a Nazi spy. So what was going on?

* * *

With a whirr, the double doors automatically swung shut behind Roz.

It had taken a couple of weeks of getting used to, but nowadays she took it for granted that the console room of the TARDIS was impossibly large. Roz still hadn't worked out where the light that flooded the room came from. For a while, she had assumed that it must emanate from the large piece of machinery hanging from the ceiling over the hexagonal console. She had mentioned this to Chris, but he had quickly proved that she was wrong. He was unable to come up with a better solution, and Roz had let the subject drop. She was still a little disconcerted by the low humming that seemed to come from all around, its pitch unchanged wherever you were in the ship. She had never had any problem with the slight vibrations generated by a good old Terran warp engine. Roz suspected that whatever was making the noise was so advanced and alien that even if she managed to discover its source she wouldn't understand it. As if the designer of this room wanted to reassure guests that everything was perfectly normal, antique furniture and *objets d'art* had been left lying around: a hatstand in the corner, an ornate clock on a pedestal, a couple of leather armchairs. It merely emphasized the incomprehensibility of this place.

Roz stepped over to the console. The hundreds of readouts and indicators dotted around the half-dozen control panels flashed away to themselves, marking time. The crystalline column in the centre of the console was glowing. Strange patterns twinkled within it, and Forrester gazed into it, momentarily hypnotized. She broke off, and looked around for any sign that the Doctor had returned. His hat, jacket and umbrella were all missing from the hatstand. There didn't seem to be a note pinned up anywhere in the room. There wasn't a voice or text message left on the computer. Roz was heading towards the circular archway that led to the rest of the ship before the practical difficulties of exploring a semi-infinite space dawned on her. Besides, she had other things to do here, and had to be back at the SID for nine.

So, the Doctor hadn't been here yesterday and he hadn't waited around for her. That was one less thing to be guilty about, anyway. He was quite capable of looking after himself, wherever he was. Forrester wasn't so sure she could say that about Chris.

The Doctor sipped at his lemonade as the Mercedes limousine swept through the Brittany countryside. Steinmann was not travelling with him, and his driver was not a skilled conversationalist. The Doctor had little to do but sit back in his leather seat, drink his lemonade, and watch the scenery roll past. There was little sign here that there was a war on. The car passed the occasional German motorcycle patrol, but apart from that the fields and little farms looked much as they had done for centuries. The road here was little more than a dirt track. Odd that: the Germans tended to improve the roads leading to their bases. Perhaps they hadn't got around to it here yet. Perhaps they were taking him into the woods to be shot. The Doctor chuckled to himself. Well, they could try. The Doctor decided to occupy himself with a game of I-Spy. I spy, with my little eye, something beginning with 'W'.

'Woods,' he replied, pointing out the small copse to himself. The driver glanced in his rear-view mirror and the Doctor raised his hat in greeting. He wished that he knew where his umbrella had got to. He hoped it wasn't still lying alone on the beach at St Jaonnet. I spy with my little eye, something beginning with 'F'.

'Field,' he answered himself.

'R,' offered the driver.

'Pardon?'

'I spy something beginning with "R",' the driver admitted sheepishly.

'You play this game too?' The Doctor was impressed.

'I play this game with my children.'

'Ah . . .'

'That's right, "R".'

111

'Does it begin with "R" in German or English?'

The driver grinned. 'Both.'

The Doctor looked around. The driver had glanced to his left, into that cornfield where a flock of coal-black birds hovered.

'*Rabe*,' the Doctor concluded.

'Well done, Herr Doktor. I gave you too much of a clue, I think. Your turn.'

'I spy with my little eye, something beginning with "C".'

Chris watched the limousine hurtle past, catching a glimpse of the passenger in the back seat. No, it couldn't be . . .

'Where the hell were you?'

'Language, Lieutenant Reed, there's a lady present. Not only that, she outranks you.' Forrester was infuriatingly calm, and she wasn't even slightly defensive.

'Ma'am, do you have the photographs?'

'They are back in the safe.' George sighed with relief, but Forrester continued, 'I made copies.'

'Copies? Roz, Kendrick will have us shot! That isn't a figure of speech.' Watching Forrester now, though, Reed realized that he trusted her. Roz sensed this, and smiled reassuringly.

'Invite me out for lunch, George.'

'You're invited. We'll go to the Salted Almond on Piccadilly. I was going to ask you this morning, but you weren't there. What on Earth have you got planned?'

'I'll tell you over lunch.'

Wolff called for her.

Kitzel put down the magazine she was reading, and hurried over to the door as it opened. Wolff strode out of the room, wiping his hands on a towel.

'Attend to the prisoner, please, Nurse Kitzel, she seems to have broken her hand. I will be back shortly.'

Kitzel stepped warily into the cell. The room smelt of sweat and urine. Fraulein Summerfield sat crying. Her wrists and ankles were still secured to the chair with adhesive tape. Her right hand was limp. Kitzel examined it, wincing as she saw the swelling.

'D-Do you think this is fair?' the prisoner asked weakly. There was no sign of her earlier defiance.

No, thought Kitzel. 'Yes,' she said.

'You think that I deserve this?' The prisoner managed to sound astonished.

No one deserves to be treated like this. 'Yes, I do. Please keep still.'

She began to strap a splint around the prisoner's hand. It must have hurt, but the prisoner did not acknowledge the fact. The prisoner tried to cough, but her throat was too dry.

'You're an evil little bitch,' Summerfield finally managed.

'I'm a nurse, you're a murderess. Work out from that who's evil.' Kitzel wrapped a bandage firmly around the wounded hand.

'Look at me!' For the first time, Kitzel looked into the prisoner's face. Her right eye was black and swollen, there was a nasty cut on her forehead. Wolff had not given permission to treat these injuries. Kitzel looked away.

'There is no permanent damage,' Kitzel said, attempting to sound reassuring. 'I am done here.'

'Please don't go,' pleaded the prisoner, attempting to grab Kitzel's arm with her good hand. It was easy to brush her aside. It was even easier to leave the cell.

The Mercedes came to a halt outside the gates, and the driver turned off the engine. Two of the Germans manning the sentry post came forward. One meticulously checked the car, including underneath the chassis and inside the boot. The second checked the driver and the Doctor himself. He scrutinized the driver's identity papers, and already had a photograph of the Doctor attached to his clipboard, which he carefully compared to the man in the back seat.

'You may get out,' he barked finally.

The Doctor said his farewells to the driver and stepped from the car. The first guard had finished his scrutiny of the limousine, now he performed a quick body search on the Doctor. His pockets had been virtually emptied at Granville, although the guard managed to discover an apple core that had infiltrated the Doctor's jacket since then. The guard tossed it away, then nodded to his counterpart.

'Thank you, driver.' The engine roared into life again, the car executed a three-point turn and then sped off back to Granville. The Doctor glanced at the ground, trying to look casual. There were vehicle tracks in the mud leading into the base: motorbikes mostly, one or two cars. Nothing heavier had gone into the base, as far as he could see. A couple of armoured personnel carriers had arrived here, but the troops had been dropped off at the gate, as he had been.

'Open the gate.' A couple of guards scurried forward from just inside the perimeter and pulled the heavy gates back.

'Do I not get chauffeured in?' the Doctor asked cheekily. The guard ignored him. A young Leutnant was waiting for the Doctor inside the gate. He was about twenty-five, with cropped black hair. The officer saluted him. The Doctor didn't return the compliment.

'Herr Doktor, I am Leutnant Keller. Will you follow me, please?' Behind them, the gates were already being pulled shut.

'Where are we going?'

'Just to the end of this track.'

The Doctor peered into the distance. The dirt track carried on for two hundred yards or so, before curving around a hillock. Their destination was obscured by this, and by a cluster of pine trees in the middle distance. It was just possible to hear running water down there. A herd of cows stood rigidly thirty feet from them.

'This does not look like a military installation.'

'No.' Keller chuckled conspiratorially. They continued to walk along the track. The Doctor watched a couple of swallows chase each other towards the trees. He and Keller had walked past the cows. It seemed strangely in keeping with Nazi mentality to surround a nature walk with a ten-foot electric fence, but he fancied that there was more to this place than met the eye. There was something very odd, something he couldn't quite put his finger on. The Doctor glanced back at the herd of cows.

'Mind the cowpats,' joked the Leutnant. There weren't any. It was hardly the best joke in the world, and merely served to distract him from his train of thought. They were coming up towards the pine trees. A couple of guards were posted up in the tree, and they peered through the slits in the branches down at the Doctor and his escort making their way up the track. The couple in the next tree were keenly watching the sky. The Doctor fixed his attention ahead. The path had led to the end of a small valley. Strangely, the stream he had heard cut across it. He scuffed his shoe on the grass as it suddenly hardened.

Hang on.

The Doctor spun back to look at the pine trees. The concrete pine trees.

The Leutnant was laughing. 'It's good, isn't it?'

The Doctor was pretty sure that his expression must have betrayed something of his surprise. The trees were guard posts, shaped and painted to look like pine trees. They'd fooled him from fifteen feet away. Now he knew what he was looking for, he could see how there was a metal ladder bolted to the 'trunk' of the tree which led up inside the 'cone'. Twenty-five feet in the air, foot-wide slits allowed almost a 360-degree field of vision. Two German soldiers were posted in each 'tree'. How odd.

The Doctor bent down, rubbing the ground. It wasn't grass at all, it was tarmac.

'Green tarmac,' the Doctor mused. Keller was looking very pleased with himself. The Doctor twirled around.

'I'm standing in the middle of an invisible airbase,' he declared.

It was incredibly clever. These hillocks were almost

certainly buildings of some kind, covered over with earth, just like Saxon burial mounds. Judging from the size of some of them, over a hundred feet square, they could only be aircraft hangars. There were smaller protrusions – fuel tanks? The barracks and laboratories were probably below ground: they would be sheltered from aerial bombardment down there, as well as being totally camouflaged. If they were really testing jet engines here, then it would be ideal soundproofing, too, as long as it was properly ventilated. What the Doctor had thought was a cottage was actually a control tower. An aircraft control tower with a thatched roof.

'This installation doesn't look like anything of the sort from the air,' the Leutnant was saying. 'Normally, everything at an airstrip is laid out logically and neatly. We've broken up all those lines. Everything is either covered up or painted. We've left as much natural vegetation in place as we could, and supplemented it with the odd fake bush and concrete tree.'

'It's invisible from the air.'

'As you have discovered, it would be invisible from the ground if it wasn't for the fence. We need that, though, to stop the locals stumbling upon us. Again, the barrier is too thin to appear on aerial photographs.'

'You've deliberately left the route here as a dirt track.'

'It carries on out the other side of the base and leads to the sea eventually. The track runs straight across the runway.'

'The –?' The Doctor looked around. Yes, of course, the valley was a runway, a runway painted a mottled green. It was about two hundred feet long. He quickly made a series of calculations.

'You've been to Guernsey, yes? Did you see the Mirus batteries? We put some gun emplacements on the cliff tops there, and painted them to look like cottages. Crude compared to this. If you know about them, they are pretty easy to spot. The trick is not to tell the enemy about them.'

'Indeed,' murmured the Doctor. 'Just one thing. Why

do you keep a herd of cows inside the perimeter? It's a nice touch, but it could be dangerous: you'd have to keep them from wandering all over the runway and – ' Keller cut him short.

'Herr Doktor, the cows are concrete. Did you not realize?'

The Doctor shut up.

This time last year, the Salted Almond on the Trocadero had got into trouble for an advertisement it had placed in a couple of the national papers. Under the caption 'All Set For Blitz-Leave', there had been a picture of a dinner-jacketed waiter ushering a couple of bright young things to their table. In the foreground, a navy admiral entertained a pretty young woman in an elaborate ballgown and hat. In the background, a band played, and a beautiful dancer danced. The advertisement went on to offer an escape from the Blitz, a place where the privileged could while away the hours, safe from German bombs. At a time when the government were desperately trying to instil a sense of national unity and urging restraint, this picture summed up the fact that, for some, there had been few real sacrifices. The poor huddled together in the Tube stations, without even basic sanitation, let alone any real organization; the rich dined in top restaurants, and retreated to their country homes when night fell.

The advertisement had been withdrawn, but as Reed and Forrester entered the restaurant it was clear that down here nothing much had changed. This was still a place for the Establishment to shut out the war, and the scene was just the same as that shown in the picture. As the door was closed behind her, Roz realized that she had just stepped into another universe. Who needs a TARDIS? All you ever need is money. Her parents lived like this, barricaded in their palaces, blaming the poor for the problems of the galaxy.

The waiter showed them to their reserved seats. Roz had grown used to the sideways glances that a black woman got on the street in this period. Here, the people

117

stared. She looked back, hoping to convey just a fraction of the moral superiority that she felt. A few looked down at their plates, apparently ashamed. Mission accomplished.

Reed pulled a chair back for Roz, then sat down opposite her. He'd lived all his life in places like this.

'All right, what is going on?' His face wasn't really built for anger.

'It's lovely and warm in here, isn't it?'

'Tell me, Roz.' George sounded genuinely angry. Roz didn't want to push him too far. She produced the duplicate photographs that she had prepared using the facilities in the TARDIS. She had been careful to annotate everything by hand to make it look as if it was all her own work. There would be quite enough questions without the distraction of having to explain how she had managed to invent the computer.

'London, on the morning of March the second. That was the night you and Chris met me at that police box. The night before the library was hit, yes?'

Reed agreed, adding that Paddington and St Kit's hospital had also been hit that night.

'You said the Germans were lucky, remember, and that a lot of the planes came from the Channel Islands,' said Roz. 'Now, what would you say if I told you that the spotters and radar both said that there weren't many planes in the sky compared with other nights?'

'I would remind you that Kendrick had taken us off raid analysis because we weren't getting anywhere and told us to look out for von Wer.'

'Von Wer isn't a problem.'

'And how can you make that judgement?'

A mental image of the Doctor's gormless grin swam across Roz's consciousness. 'I just know, that's all,' she concluded.

Reed sighed.

'Look, Lieutenant, trust me on that one. Now, logically, if, on only one night, less planes cause more hits, something odd is going on.'

'You think the Germans used the superbomber?'

'I know they did. Now, I got up early this morning and plotted out what happened on that night. This.'

She handed him the analysis prepared by the TARDIS. Again, she had painstakingly copied it out in her own handwriting, rather than just making a hard copy. From the photographs, the computer had known where and when the damage took place. It was relatively simple for the computer to work out the yield of each bomb by measuring the damage each one caused. Knowing which planes were capable of dropping which bombs, and comparing this with radar data, it had been possible to match each bomb to each plane. In a matter of seconds, the computer had plotted the course of an eight-hour air-raid. Now, not even the TARDIS computer was perfect, especially when dealing with this sort of chaos. It had rejected its own first guess, because it hadn't quite managed to match up all the information. Its second attempt was a lot more convincing. The whole process took just seconds. Forrester had then needed nearly three-quarters of an hour to scribble out the report, and had nearly been late for work as a result.

Reed was poring over the data. 'Roz, what you've managed to do is impossible.'

'Yeah, well, six impossible things before breakfast and all that. Which reminds me, let's order, I haven't eaten yet.'

'So we're too late? They've already built super-bombers?'

'They only used the one. They used it early in the raid, really early, about seven. It flew in through Greenwich, swept across Bermondsey, the City and Regent's Park, arced back and took out Paddington, Soho and Southwark.'

'Without anyone spotting it, not even radar?'

'What's one plane in a raid that size? I imagine that the Germans used this raid as cover. They sent in the superbomber early, then obliterated the evidence in the later stages of the raid. Look, it could be twice the size of a Heinkel before any of our radar operators got suspicious. It might have flown in at an odd angle, and that would have reduced its RCS.'

'Gosh.' Reed was still working his way through her report. 'I suppose you found out what Hoogin and Mooning are too.'

'No.' The words hadn't been in either the TARDIS memory store or the data store. This worried her.

'We need to get this back to Kendrick.'

'Yes. I thought I might need someone else on side before I did. Thank you for trusting me, George. Now, let's eat, I'm starving.'

Niclauss saw the young woman standing at the side of the road. As he got closer and closer, she turned his way. She must have heard the sound of his engine.

He broke hard, skidding to a halt just in front of her. She was grinning broadly, impressed. She was young and very pretty, with long black hair.

'Can I help you, mademoiselle?' he said. She giggled and held out her hand.

'I can help you, brave soldier.' There was no doubt what sort of help she had in mind.

'I really have to get back to the . . . my job.' She looked so disappointed. He dismounted, and stepped towards her. She pouted, clearly realizing how arousing she looked with this expression.

Crack

'He looks so young,' Monique said.

Chris bent down, unbuttoning the Nazi's uniform. He hesitated. The soldier looked even younger than Monique, although Cwej knew that this couldn't be true. The age of conscription in the Reich wouldn't be lowered until the last few months of the war, when ten-year-old boys would be called on to defend Berlin.

'He wouldn't have felt anything. It's a standard move that snaps the spinal cord. My tutor claimed it was the quickest way to kill someone without making a noise. It certainly seems pretty efficient.'

Chris had undressed the corpse; now he began to strip. Monique seemed more interested in watching him than looking out for Germans until he reminded her. Chris pulled himself into the uniform, and rolled the body into the ditch at the roadside.

'It's a bit tight.'

'It is those muscles of yours, Christophe.' Despite himself, Chris blushed. She was examining the contents of the dead man's document case.

'He was taking a message to the base,' she exclaimed.

'Excellent! That's my passport in there. You had better go now, Monique. I'm going to rescue the Doctor,' he said, mounting the motorbike. He looked around to see how to start it. Monique leant forward, showing him the ignition. He gunned the engine.

'Good luck, Christophe. I have never kissed a man.' Cwej looked at her blankly. Monique hesitated, then launched herself forward, kissing him full on the lips. Chris didn't even try to resist until he ran out of breath, when he pulled back. He couldn't think of anything to say. Monique blew him a second kiss. He gunned the engine, and the motorbike pulled unsteadily away from her. Gaining confidence, he pulled down on the accelerator.

'There is no permanent damage, sir.'

'You hear that, prisoner? Nurse Kitzel says you are all right.'

A weak moan.

'Sir, may I ask why you are continuing this process?'

'Standard interrogation procedure.'

'But, sir, you aren't asking questions any longer. She has said who she is, admitted spying at the airstrip, she's explained how she managed to sneak past the coastal defences in a rowing boat. She's reeled off statistics about how many planes took off each night and you haven't even cross-checked them. Whenever you demand that she tells you who sent her, she just asks for a doctor.'

Mumble.

'She might have more information.'

'But, sir, you aren't asking her for it, just hurting her. She has a broken hand, a massive amount of bruising, she's lost blood, she's not eaten or slept for days, she's delirious now, or do you really think that she is an archaeologist from the future who has spent the last few years flying around all the planets in the heavens?'

'Thank you, Nurse Kitzel. Don't worry yourself, I think I have just about finished with her.'

The Doctor had been given a guided tour of the facilities, and now Keller had left him alone for a moment. As he suspected, the barracks were underground. It was relatively luxurious for an army base, spacious lounges, even a small gymnasium and a library. There were a number of offices. It was difficult to judge, but he doubted that there were more than about one hundred and fifty people here. Leutnant Keller had been happy to show him the living quarters, but seemed reluctant to show him the laboratories, the test rigs or the hangars. Steinmann wasn't here, and he hadn't been allowed anywhere near Hartung himself. Keller clearly had a scientific background, and the Doctor had been asking him leading questions, but hadn't gained much from the answers. Keller entered, carrying a sheaf of documents under one arm, a briefcase in the other.

'Here you are, Herr Doktor, something to keep you occupied.'

The Doctor flicked through the papers. 'The plans for the jet engine?'

'Correct, Doktor. So, what do you think?'

The Doctor put the blueprints down, and looked Keller in the eye. 'Well, I've only had a second or so to look through them, but I think that it's clear that you've not quite mastered the liquid oxygen and alcohol mix, which is understandable because you are used to working with diesel. I like the large axial-flow gas turbine, that should really give it some oomph. Fourteen thousand pounds of dry thrust, at least, that's ten times anything the British have managed. There must be a vast amount of vibration, I'd have thought. You've completely abandoned the centrifugal compressor, I see.'

Keller was almost speechless. 'Doktor, that is remarkable. You are a match for Hartung himself. I can see why Steinmann sent you here.'

'Talking of Hartung, when do I get to meet him?'

'In good time.' The young officer placed the briefcase on the table, and opened it up. Inside was a very large number of bank notes. 'Herr Doktor, here are one million Reichsmarks which I have been authorized to give you. A man of your talents is wasted in Britain. Here you will have a chance to work alongside the greatest scientific minds in the world. You will have unlimited resources, both personal and professional. All you have to do is sign this contract, then you will be rich, famous and part of the victory of the German Reich.' He held out a piece of neatly typed paper.

The Doctor read it aloud. 'I, Doctor dot dot dot, agree that . . .' ('If you could just fill your name in, and date it,' Keller suggested, handing the Doctor a fountain pen. The Doctor did so, pocketing the pen afterwards.) '. . . from today, er, March the fifth 1941, I shall become a loyal citizen of the German nation. I swear total allegiance to the authority of the Führer and the rule of German law. From today, I shall work exclusively for the Luftwaffe zbV. I shall from today follow unquestioningly the orders of the director of this group, at this time Oberst Oskar Steinmann. For the duration of the war, I shall work untiringly for the final victory of the Reich, and the total,' the Doctor hesitated over the next word, 'extermination of its enemies. I shall today become a full and paid-up member of the Nationalsozialistische Deutsche Arbeiterpartei, and I shall never deviate from its teaching. I renounce all previous associations with foreign powers, organizations and individuals. I am in full possession of my faculties and I am not signing this statement under duress.'

The Doctor read it back to himself, silently.

'I like this. No small print. No room for ambiguity. It all seems reasonable enough.' He took the pen and signed the contract at the bottom.

Interlude

The Doctor stepped out of the TARDIS. Now in his seventh incarnation – or so he claimed – he was a smallish, dark-haired man. He wore shabby brown check trousers, a brown sports jacket with a garish Fair Isle tanktop beneath, and a jaunty straw hat. He carried a long black umbrella with a plain cane handle.

'. . . eyepatches!' he finished.

A young woman followed him out. She was even shorter than the Doctor, with the skinny figure that could only have been achieved through regular exercise. Her hair was a cascading mop of red curls. She was Melanie Bush – Mel for short – and she had been travelling with the Doctor for a number of years now. She wore a cream trouser-suit, and she sported a floppy straw sun-hat.

She gave a mock groan. 'That joke is *terrible*.'

The Doctor was chucking to himself anyway. Mel looked around. They had landed in an oriental market-place – there were Arabs in flowing white robes and burnooses bustling around the stalls, haggling amongst themselves over peculiar artefacts. She could just make out a camel in the middle distance. No one seemed to have noticed the TARDIS arrive, or if they had they weren't paying it any attention. The air was thick and hazy.

'It is very hot, Doctor. I don't think you'll be needing that umbrella,' she observed.

'Ah well, it would be hot: this is Cairo. You did say you

125

fancied a holiday on Earth. What did you say? "I haven't been to Earth in ages." ' It was a passable imitation of her high-pitched tones. 'After Troxos 4, I thought that we both needed a little break from adventuring.'

'I've never been to Cairo before.' Mel looked around. She would certainly have no difficulty finding a souvenir of this trip – carpets, tapestries, sculptures, prints, pictures painted onto papyrus, a cornucopia of treasures. A couple of yards away, a Western tourist, a man, was discussing the price of an ivory elephant with a merchant. Mel was surprised by his clothes: he wasn't wearing the typical tourist gear of jeans and T-shirts, but an altogether more formal outfit, a dark pin-striped suit.

'What year is this?'

'Oh, it doesn't really matter – Cairo market looks exactly the same whatever year you land in. Just relax and soak up the atmosphere.' Mel shot him an enquiring look, and the Doctor looked around. 'Well, judging by that tourist and the relative level of air pollution, this must be the mid-nineteen-thirties.'

'The past! I've only ever been to the future before,' she said excitedly.

'Well, yes, it's the past from your point of view. From another perspective this is the future. For that tourist over there it's the present.'

Mel was already bouncing over to introduce herself. 'Hello there. I'm Melanie, and this,' the Doctor doffed his hat, 'is my . . . uncle, the Doctor.' Mel held her hand out, expecting a handshake. Instead, the gentleman lifted it gently to his mouth and kissed it. Mel grinned, and hoped she hadn't gone too doe-eyed. He was handsome, with thick black hair brushed back across his scalp and lacquered into place. He had penetrating dark eyes, and a lovely smile.

'Emil Hartung.' His voice was cultured, with the slight trace of a mid-European accent. 'Are you here to watch the race?'

Mel was about to tell him the truth when the Doctor stepped forward. 'Of course we are. Wouldn't miss it for

126

the world. The roar of the greasepaint, the thrill of the chase.'

Emil smiled, clearly a little bemused. He looked back at Mel who realized that he was still holding her hand.

'Will you be coming to the party tonight at the Grand Imperial?' he asked her.

'O-of course,' Mel said.

'Then I shall see you there.' A thought struck him. 'Would you and your uncle like to watch the speed trials this afternoon?'

Mel nodded enthusiastically. With that, he kissed her hand again and disappeared into the crowd.

Mel watched him go, then she turned to the Doctor who was looking smug. 'What have I just let us in for?' Mel moaned playfully.

'An adventure,' the Doctor said excitedly. 'Emil Hartung is a very famous racing driver.'

'I've never heard of him,' Mel noted.

'Well, he's a little before your time.'

'Is he married?' she asked casually.

'Ah, Mel. I didn't think he would be your type. Well, I'll be a Melanie's uncle.'

Mel blushed. 'That's not what I meant.'

The Doctor pinched her red cheek. 'He's one of the most eligible bachelors in the whole of Europe. He's a millionaire playboy – and it looks like you've caught his eye. Heaven knows why.'

'Do you think so?' Mel asked, before. 'Hey, wait a minute.'

The Doctor was chuckling. 'Come on, Mel.'

8

Taking Sides

'Inform Standartenführer Wolff that I have arrived.'

'At once, Oberst Steinmann.' The secretary pressed a switch on the intercom. Steinmann looked around. A great deal of construction work had been completed since he had last been here, a fortnight earlier. When finished, the complex would serve as a bomb-proof administrative centre, command post, prison and even a hospital. That was still a few months away yet but, when finished, the base would provide a concrete symbol of Nazi power. A modern medieval castle, complete with dungeons and torture chambers.

The secretary stood. 'I shall take you to Herr Wolff, sir.'

'It must be difficult to find your way around this place,' Steinmann joked.

The secretary took him seriously. 'No, sir, your architectural skill is unsurpassed. You have created an ordered – '

Steinmann cut the flattery short with a wave of his hand. He had designed this place, but was not proud of the fact. He hadn't the skill to create anything as beautiful as the townhouse in Granville. Lassurance – now, he was a genius. The corridor they were walking through had not been painted yet, and was drab and grey. However, there was no doubt that his subterranean building would last for ever. It had been built out of reinforced concrete precisely so that not even high explosive charges could dent it. After the war, when this place was no longer needed, and the Channel Islands were being run as a holiday camp by the KdF, it would prove impossible to demolish. At least it was underground, unlike all those watchtowers and gun emplacements on the coastline.

Wolff was sitting outside the cell block waiting for him. His huge frame seemed perfectly at home in the brutish place Steinmann had designed. They saluted one another. A blonde nurse was just bringing in a jug of coffee. She seemed unsure whether she ought to salute before or after she had put the tray down. Steinmann magnanimously told her not to worry about it. She poured him a cup of black coffee.

'You were right to bring the Doktor to me, Joachim,' Steinmann began, 'and he is just what we need. Who have you got in there?'

'That is the woman who killed the German soldier. Her name is Bernice Summerfield. She's a civilian, but she's from the mainland. I've questioned her and she told us everything she knows. She's delirious now. Kitzel here suggested we torture her with electric shocks, but I decided to be more humane.'

'Sir, that misrepresents my – ' An angry glance from Steinmann silenced the young nurse.

'Joachim, you couldn't be humane if you tried. I saw what you did to the Doctor. Thankfully, I've managed to salvage the situation. Show me this woman.' Kitzel scurried to the door, unbolting it.

Steinmann stepped inside. In the corner of the cell, an emaciated figure sat crouched, its eyes staring wildly, but not focused on anything in particular. Her face was bruised and cut. She seemed to have registered his presence. Awkwardly, she pulled herself upright. She was tall and skinny, and couldn't quite straighten herself. Her brunette hair was greasy and unkempt. She mumbled something. Steinmann inspected her. She had clearly not changed her clothes for some time; there was a urine stain running down her trouser-leg. Her feet were covered in cuts and her right hand was in a splint. Two of the fingernails on the other hand had been torn off. Steinmann instructed her to turn around and lifted up her shirt. As he had suspected, her back was covered in red weals where she had been whipped.

'Joachim! Get in here!' he shouted. Wolff appeared, framed in the doorway, arrogance written all over his face.

'Is there a problem, sir?'

'How can you have done this? I wouldn't treat a dog like this. What did you hope to achieve?' The prisoner was swaying slightly. Steinmann caught her before she fell.

'Nurse. Bathe this patient, then place her in another cell, one with a bed. Provide her with a light meal. I shall join you shortly.'

Kitzel hurried forward and relieved Steinmann of his load. The patient was mumbling something, and Steinmann had to concentrate to catch it. 'Doctor, Doctor, you saved me. I love you, Doctor.'

It had been staring him in the face. This woman was the Doctor's accomplice: while he was down on the beach, she had been on the clifftop. She would provide an additional incentive for the Doctor to co-operate with him, if an additional incentive should prove necessary.

'Joachim, this prisoner is valuable, and I am taking over the interrogation.' Once Summerfield had been led from the room, Steinmann continued. 'It is the declared policy of the Reich that we keep all spies we capture alive.'

'Summerfield is alive, sir. I remind you that she killed one of my men.'

'Would you have treated a man the same way? Did you really need to break the neck of that poor girl at the docks? Wipe that expression off your face: I've read your file. You are a sadist and a bully, but you focus your aggression on women. An unhappy childhood, perhaps?'

'Psychoanalysis!' spat Wolff. 'I expected better from you than Jewish science. You've done worse to prisoners, sir. Water treatment, the merry-go-round, the dentist's drill.'

Steinmann wasn't listening. 'That will be all, Standartenführer. I will question the prisoner myself when she is able to speak. Joachim, we *need* the Doktor, don't doubt that. Without his knowledge, everything we have planned might collapse around us.'

'I look forward to seeing you at work, sir.' Wolff remained defiant.

'You may attend the first session, but you will be leaving this afternoon.'

Wolff frowned. 'So soon? I had thought that – '

'You don't play chess, do you, Joachim? We have to think ahead. At the moment we have the advantage, but one lucky move from our opponents could decide this. They might find a chink in our armour; they might work out what Hartung has built. The Doktor did. I've neutralized him, for the moment, but we are still vulnerable.'

Wolff stood to attention. 'What are your orders?'

'We shall proceed with the plan.'

Kendrick read through the notes for a third time. Roz glanced nervously at Reed, but his attention was fixed on the admiral. For the first time, Forrester had her doubts about what she had done. Kendrick was an expert in the field of raid analysis, and in her book that made him superior to any machine, even the TARDIS computer. If he were to challenge her on a point of detail, then she might not be able to answer him. It would become clear very quickly that she hadn't written the report.

'This is incredible.' Kendrick whistled. In credible? Not credible?

'In what way, sir? she asked, trying to keep calm.

'You've cracked it, Captain Forrester. You've done it! I have to tell the Cabinet. You'll get the Victoria Cross for this, Forrester, and if you work another miracle and find von Wer, then they'll probably make you a peer of the realm!'

The Doctor was getting restless. Keller watched him as he paced the room. The Doctor was constantly moving. One minute he would be looking around, then he'd scrutinize the contents of the bookcase, before moving on to examine the ornaments on top of the fireplace.

'When do I meet Hartung?' the Doctor asked again.

'In good time. Doktor, please sit down.' The Doctor continued to prowl around.

There was a knock at the door and a young private came in. Keller didn't recognize him, although he was expecting a messenger sent from Oberst Steinmann. The soldier was tall and broad, with a thick moustache and cropped blond hair. Once inside, he just stood there.

'Salute when you enter the room,' Keller ordered. Instead, the private raised his pistol, an SS-issue Mauser with a long, bulbous silencer.

'No, Chris!' shouted the Doctor. Before Keller could react, the Doctor had flown past him, pulling down on the tall man's arm. There was a muffled shot. Keller felt a hot sensation in his leg: spreading, agonizing pain. The Doctor had turned away from the private, and was examining Keller's leg. He was saying something.

'Don't worry, it's hit your thigh-bone. It will hurt, and will take a while to heal, but you'll be all right.'

'Come on, Doctor,' insisted the big man, pulling the Doctor away. The Doctor shrugged apologetically, and disappeared.

'My cell hasn't got a window.'

'We're underground, Fraulein Summerfield. None of the rooms here have windows.'

Steinmann watched as the prisoner pondered this new information. Summerfield was more presentable now. She had bathed, eaten a meal, then slept for a couple of hours and was beginning to look human again. Now, she wore a fresh prison uniform and her shoulder-length hair had been brushed straight. Summerfield was an attractive woman, with high cheekbones and a full mouth. The cut on her forehead was covered with a sticking plaster. The bruising around her face would be there for a couple of days yet, though. Her hand might never heal properly, although the dressing had been changed.

Wolff was hovering behind him, and was clearly making both Summerfield and Kitzel nervous. Like it or not,

Steinmann thought, it was an indisputable fact that Wolff and he were two of a kind. How simple it would be to turn a blind eye to the laws of race, pretend that the Doctor, or the beautiful Miss Summerfield, were Aryans, too. Life is not like that. Such compromises could only weaken the resolve of the German people, deflect them from their destiny. There are no exceptions to a universal rule. Not just that, he thought; just looking at us, it is clear that he, Wolff and Kitzel, were a race apart. He looked at the prisoner again, and realized the contempt he felt for her and her kind.

'Start the tape-recorder, Kitzel. Prisoner F319–350042, I am Oberst Oskar Steinmann, Direktor of the regional Luftwaffe zbV.'

'I'm Professor Bernice Summerfield, no fixed abode. So, you're the nice cop, right? The acceptable face of Fascism?' Her tone was antagonistic, but she couldn't disguise her fear. Steinmann held the position of power here, and no amount of arrogant resolve would change that.

'I beg your pardon?'

'You know: nice cop/nasty cop. You get some bully to soften me up, then you come in and act all nice and I'm so grateful that I'll blab everything. It won't work, Oskar, I live with a nice cop and a nasty cop. I'm used to it.' She had a 'Home Counties' accent – the clipped, ever so slightly nasal tones spoken by the upper and middle class in the south-east of England.

Steinmann had little patience with insubordination. 'Ready her arm, Kitzel.'

Kitzel brushed the prisoner's forearm with a swab. Naturally enough Summerfield was alarmed. 'What are you doing?' Her sarcasm was clearly nothing more than a façade.

'When it come to my job, Professor Summerfield, I am not a nice man. You have killed a sixteen-year-old boy while spying for an enemy power. You have already exhausted my patience, and I do not intend to waste any more of my time.'

Kitzel jabbed Summerfield's arm with a hypodermic needle. The prisoner managed not to cry out.

'Thank you, nurse. How long does the drug need to take effect?'

'It should be effective now, sir,' Kitzel declared. Summerfield was glaring at the nurse with unrestrained hostility. There was no such thing as a 'truth drug', but simple relaxants like the one that they were using on Summerfield would loosen tongues, break down some mental barriers. He had tried a more civilized version of the same technique on the Doctor, trying to get the little man drunk. The Doctor's metabolism didn't seem to be affected. Normally he would try to relax his prisoner in some small way, offer her a cigarette, make a joke. He didn't feel any need to tread so softly with Summerfield.

'We shall begin. Are you married, Professor Summerfield?' The prisoner shook her head. Steinmann wrote this down.

'What is your religion?' he continued.

'I'm not religious.'

Steinmann noted this down. Interrogation of this nature always started with standard questions like this. Begin by establishing a few basic facts about the prisoner's life. Learn what makes her tick.

'Have you ever belonged to a political party or trade union?'

'No.'

Steinmann made a note of her answer. 'Are you proficient in any languages other than English and German?'

'Quite a few: French, Egyptian, Hebrew, Ancient and Modern Greek, Latin, most of the Martian dialects, Old English, Old Norse. I can get by in a number of others. There was quite a heavy linguistics component of my degree, and I've got the knack.' It wasn't a boast, if anything Summerfield was apologetic.

'What do you hold your degree in?'

'Archaeology.'

Steinmann looked up from his notebook. 'Really? A friend of mine, Hans Auerbach, is writing the history of

134

the islands. It will contain a catalogue of the prehistoric sites.'

'Yes, I've read it.'

Steinmann made a note of this lie, but didn't challenge Summerfield with it. Slips of the tongue, blatant lies, factual errors and the like could all be brought back into play later in the questioning, used to pull holes in an agent's cover story. All these inconsistencies would mount up and come back to haunt her. For the moment, he wanted to retain the prisoner's co-operation. So Steinmann continued the interrogation with a new question. 'Where did you acquire your degree?'

'It's none of your business,' the prisoner said curtly. It would be unprofitable to continue this line of questioning, Steinmann decided. She had seemed talkative, but the last question had put her on the defensive for some reason.

'When were you born?'

'The twenty-first of June.' This response was a little more promising. By carefully watching a subject's Adam's apple and eyelids, it was a simple matter to tell if they were lying. Summerfield was not.

'Which year?'

'I'd rather not say.'

'Are you shy about your age?' But she laughed at his suggestion: either the drug was having more of an effect, or she was genuinely beginning to relax. Whichever was the case, he ought to be able to get a few more answers now.

'No, no. I know I'm in my mid-thirties,' she was saying. 'If I had to name a figure I'd say thirty-three, but I'm not sure.' She was very strong-willed, still capable of holding back the whole truth.

'But you can tell me what year you were born?'

'No,' she said quietly. She seemed convinced she was right. She was also trying to keep her answers as short as possible. Forcing an interrogator to fight for every last bit of information was a standard technique used by captured agents. He had won many such battles of will in the past.

'My dear, you must know which year you were born.

135

1909? 1908?' He was trying to jog her memory. Odd that she could forget such information. It must be a side-effect of the sleep deprivation.

And then the words came pouring out. 'It would be quite difficult to give you the precise date the way you understand it. Time is a relative concept, and when humanity started flying around in sleeper ships, everything got mucked up. Once we had hyperdrive, and people started arriving places before they set off because they were travelling so fast, the whole thing became somewhat meaningless. The big corporations and most of the people on the Inner Worlds use their own local time, in which case the days and years aren't always the same length as Earth. Those of us bumming around the Outer Planets, or outside Human Space entirely, tend to use Terran Mean Time, simply for convenience. You see the problem? I could give you the date relative to Galactic Centre Adjusted, that would be about three-quarters of a century before the same date on Earth. In your terms, I'm from the mid-twenty-sixth century.'

Before she had finished Steinmann had asked, 'What is she babbling about, Joachim?'

'I have no idea.' The Standartenführer was bored, and would clearly rather be abusing the prisoner in some way.

'Sir, if I may speak?'

'Yes, Kitzel?'

'At the end of Standartenführer Wolff's interrogation, the prisoner claimed to be from the future. She is doing it again,' Kitzel said softly.

'It's not much of a cover story, is it?' Steinmann asked, exasperated.

'Sir, she has now made these claims on two separate occasions while under great stress. I'm not suggesting that she is right, but she might believe that she is telling the truth.' Kitzel spoke with some authority.

'She is mad? The British sent a madwoman to spy on us?' Wolff sneered, 'No, sir, she is just pretending. Trying to convince us she is feeble-minded.'

'I'd hardly do that, would I, Joachim?' the prisoner

136

snapped. 'I know what you gits do with the mentally handicapped.'

'Sir, these island populations are rife with inbreeding. This dulls the mental faculties. She might just be a simpleton. Perhaps she is not even involved.' Kitzel's suggestion seemed plausible enough.

'The descriptions of the murderess were somewhat confused,' Steinmann noted.

'Excuse me. Who's "she"? For that matter, what the hell sort of interrogator doesn't wait to hear what his prisoner has to say?' Summerfield asked. She sounded personally aggrieved by his behaviour.

'Professor Summerfield, under torture, you claimed before that you were an archaeologist from the future.'

Benny blanched. 'Did I? You didn't believe me, I take it.' She was sticking to this story, then.

'If you are from the future,' began Wolff sarcastically, 'how did you get here? Is there a double-decker bus that stops off in 1941? You rang the little bell and stepped off? All change here for Earth, Mars and the Moon!'

'No, if you must know, it's a police box. And, yes, I've been to all three of those places.'

Steinmann ignored her flippancy, allowing her to build up this peculiar cover-story. 'A what?'

'A police box. Yes, it's quite obscure, I know. Apparently the British police used them before they invented the walkie-talkie. The light on the top would flash whenever the police station had a message for one of their bobbies on the beat, and he'd know to phone them. People could phone the police from it, too, if they needed help. Cute, really.'

'And what exactly is a walkie-talkie?'

'Oh, sorry, you've not got them yet. Portable radios. They're about the same size as a packet of cigarettes.' Steinmann had been noting all this down.

'I see. When are these portable radios invented, then?'

'Oh, quite soon. The 1960s, I think. They had them in the '70s when I was there.'

'You've been to the future?'

137

'She was born there, remember?' Wolff reminded him.

'Quite right. 1976 was the past. Except, of course, that it wasn't the real 1976. At least not at first. I think it was at the end.' Summerfield was apparently working it out for herself as she spoke.

'So you travel around in a police box. How big is it? Bigger than a packet of cigarettes?'

Benny chuckled. 'It's about the size of a very big wardrobe. It would fit into this cell. Except you couldn't get it through the door.'

'What colour is it?'

'Blue. Dark blue.'

'And you live in there with the Doktor and . . . two policemen. No doubt the police box is the property of these policemen. No one else?'

'Well, there's the cat. Er, look, the Doctor owns the TARDIS, and it only looks like a police box.'

'It must be very crowded in there.'

'No, it's bigger on the inside than the outside.'

'Is it now?'

'It all sounds a bit silly now I say it out loud, I admit.'

She was beginning to see now that her strange story wouldn't hold up.

'You make it sound like Skidbladnir.'

Kitzel and Wolff both looked puzzled, until Summerfield said, 'He means Frey's magical ship in the Norse myths. It could contain all the gods, their horses and weapons while still fitting in Frey's pocket. The reason he brought it up is that a real archaeologist would probably be familiar with the myth.'

Summerfield was right of course, but she didn't realize how much she was revealing with her sarcastic response. It was a not-quite-successful attempt to appear unafraid, but it proved that she was still very much in charge of her faculties. Most importantly, it was clear that Summerfield thought she was more intelligent than he was. She was trying to play psychological games with him. Very well. Steinmann changed the subject. 'How does a "TARDIS" work?'

'I'm not sure about the technicalities. In layman's terms the TARDIS removes itself from Minkowski space, then integrates itself into a fifth dimension. It travels through something called the Vortex, a transdimensional spiral built by the Doctor's people which encompasses all points in space and time. Then, the TARDIS just reorientates itself at the other end, and re-establishes a plasmic real-world interface.'

Steinmann laid his pen down, and glared at her. When he spoke his voice was just a touch harsher than before. 'Professor Summerfield, I am a scientist. What you have just said is meaningless nonsense.'

'Is it? Damn. As I say, I take it for granted.' Summerfield shrugged apologetically.

Steinmann changed tack once more. 'Can you describe something more mundane? Something from the future?'

'No. I can't.' Her answers were curt again.

'Can't? Not won't?' Steinmann challenged.

'Don't get pedantic on me, Oskar. I'm from the future, but I can't tell you about it. It would risk affecting established history.'

Steinmann's eyes narrowed. 'If I were to learn the future, I might be able to change it?'

'Well, yes. If you took knowledge you had now back to the last war, you could have altered the outcome. You could have sent Heinkels and Dorniers against London, not Zeppelins. You could have sent Panzers into the British trenches.'

'You wouldn't need to do that,' suggested Steinmann. 'Just a few pieces of information would be enough: we could check our historical records, have a complete list of where the weak links in the Allied defences were in the last war, warn our people precisely where and when the enemy would attack. Even with only a few grains of random knowledge, we could draw conclusions about the future. If we knew the exchange rate between the dollar and the mark in – what year did you say? – 1976, or who holds the record for the fastest seaplane, or who the King of England is then we'd have a way through the chaos. We'd be able to negate the Butterfly Effect.'

'You know about that? Then you know why I can't tell you even the slightest detail about the future,' Summerfield said stubbornly. Wolff and Kitzel were watching this exchange.

'Sir, you are beginning to talk like this crazy woman,' Wolff said flatly.

'Shut up, Standardenführer. It's too late, Professor Summerfield. You talk of Inner Worlds and Outer Planets. You talk of Galactic Centre and Human Space. So, man has reached the stars?'

'Yes,' she admitted.

'So you've already described the future. Tell me something specific.'

'No, I can't.'

Steinmann leant over, and said gently, 'Have you ever been to my home city of Stuttgart?'

'Yes, when I was a child. I refuse to describe it.'

'So Stuttgart still exists in 1976 and it's still called that?'

'I'm not from . . . look. I'm not saying anything more.'

'But you have said so much. You see, I already have some knowledge of the future. I know for certain that Germany wins the war. So, I have another piece of knowledge about the future: the existence of *Der Tausendjährige Reich*! A millennium from now, the Reich will still be standing.'

Benny thought about that for a moment, then burst into laughter. 'Sorry, but I've seen Earth a thousand years from now. As a matter of fact, it's where the Doctor and I met Forrester and Cwej, the two policemen I was talking about. Their time was hardly perfect, but there wasn't a Nazi to be seen. In fact, when the Doctor told us we were coming here I had to tell them all about you. At this point I really do think I should mention that they knew all about Freud and Einstein. Fascism disappears as a political force in your lifetime, Oskar. This Reich doesn't even last a thousand weeks, let alone a thousand years. By 1976, to pick a year at random, the only people wearing the Nazi uniform were sad little blokes who couldn't get it up any other way. A few gangs of glue-sniffing thugs had the swastika tattooed on their foreheads, but they never learnt what it really stood for. They hung around on street corners, spitting and swearing, trying to shock their parents. They weren't up to anything other than petty vandalism and beating up immigrant women and children. In other words, Fascism ended just like it started. Your only legacy will be their hatred, their ignorance. You want to see what Nazism means, you just look at Wolff and Kitzel there: the men are sadists, the women just stand in the corner and simper. Neither of them are exactly mental giants, are they?'

Summerfield's eyes were wide now, full of passion. Wolff moved forward to hit her, hardly a refutation of her argument. Steinmann restrained him. Instead, the older man asked simply, 'How can we lose this war?'

'Ah. Don't try to trick me.'

'It was a straight question. How can we possibly lose? Are you suggesting that the British can ever beat us back to Berlin? They can't even stop us attacking their cities! The English are a mongrel race, corrupt, decadent, divided. You tell me of their "stiff upper lip", their "quiet resolve", their "Blitz spirit", their "tradition of democracy"? Just look at Guernsey, my dear, see how long those things lasted here. Not a single shot was fired. There isn't any organized resistance. Don't fool yourself that the Channel Islands are a special case, or that London and Manchester would resist any more than Paris or Lyons did. The sun has already set on the British Empire.

'You ask me to look at Kitzel and Wolff. I am glad to. Look at how tall Wolff his, how physically fit. Look at Kitzel's childbearing hips, her hourglass figure. Look at their clear complexions, their blue eyes, their golden hair. How can such a pure, such a beautiful race, possibly be defeated? I see two attractive young people, working for their country. They are my bloodline. Do you not see: the Reich unites us. It harnesses our skills, leads us to total victory. I am of the first Nazi generation, but already

141

the second is here, and they are stronger still. They, and the generation after that, learn in their schools of our science, our achievements. They learn of the failure of democracy. They learn to distrust the Jew, the Marxist, anyone who talks of equality while claiming to be set apart from lesser men. It is the twilight of the old age, elderly men like myself will soon give way to the *ubermenschen*, a glorious race of supermen. How can such people ever be defeated when the possibility of defeat does not even exist for them?

'That's why I know that you are lying, Summerfield. Not because you talk of men on the Moon and time travel. Not because you babble unscientific nonsense. These things you speak of are imaginative, but they are not impossible: half a century ago Lasswitz was writing about trips to Mars. Oberth and von Braun claimed ten years ago that they could build a "Moon Rocket". The Reich's scientists have already broken the sound barrier; I'm sure that we'll soon be travelling faster than light, and then even faster than time itself. I always knew that Einstein was a fraud. But so are you, my dear.' Steinmann paused. 'You can't be from the future. We Nazis are united by our heritage, and our destiny is in the stars! In the future, people such as you – the weak, the decadent, the liberal – have all been eradicated. Future history has already been written by men such as Hartung. Tomorrow belongs to us, not you. If you were really from the future, Miss Summerfield, you would be a Nazi.'

Roz Forrester threw another piece of bacon fat into the midst of the flock of pigeons swarming across the grass near her bench. She had needed a break and a cigarette.

The birds circled round the stringy rind, waiting their turn for a meal. As the pigeon with the rind in its beak bit into it, it tossed its head from side to side, carelessly hurling little scraps into the air, which other birds eagerly pounced on as they landed. The pigeons maintained a strict pecking order. Odd how that phrase had lasted in human language to her time, centuries after the last bird had become extinct. Every wild animal and plant species had disappeared from the Earth by the thirtieth century, except for humanity and the rat. Here, a thousand years earlier, the ecosystem was virtually intact. This Earth teemed with life: there was moss between the paving stones, flowers sprang up in the rubble of the bombsites, little brown birds nested in the trees.

There was a sense of certainty here, too, a sense of order. This was a time when everyone knew their place, from the King right down to the smallest pigeon. Other people might find that restrictive, but Roz could see the attraction of such a rigid system. There was order, and a sense of discipline. There was crime here, but it was so small-scale: a protection racket here, a burglary there. The criminals and the police force had a gentlemen's agreement that they didn't carry guns. There didn't seem to be a drugs problem. There weren't any rogue combat robots or gangs of evil mutants roaming the streets. She had to remind herself that this was the *Undertown*, the place that no right-thinking human would ever go. The chattering classes in her time kept asking: why not sterilize the whole area and start again from scratch? Half a dozen photon charges would do the trick. This past London was like a parallel world where the city was still beautiful, still proud of itself.

There were no *monsters* here. Nothing deformed with a horned snout would lumber round the next corner and ask her the time in haltering English. No slimy, green-skinned blob would menace her for spare change. In the thirtieth century, down in the Undertown, there was an alien beggar in every doorway, an alien crime lord behind every door. They were all *immigrants*, of course, they had come to Earth to take a human's job, or just to claim ILC allowance. Although there had been a number of incursions later on in this century, the first official, lasting, contact with an alien race wouldn't be made for one hundred and fifty years. Everyone here was purely human, with two eyes, one nose and one mouth, all in the correct place, and so it would remain for another century.

The Age of Legend was fast approaching, the time when her people overthrew their masters and went on to become examples of hope and justice for the entire world. A thousand years from now, South Africa was still there: a rock of stability in a chaotic world. Her family were still part of the ruling élite, their genetic material almost unchanged from the Xhosa in this century. The Forrester clan stood out in a world in which humanity had become racially homogenized. While other people's ancestors succumbed to cosmetic gene surgery, and the rest of the thirtieth century had been swept by the craze for body-beppling, she was *pure*.

The pigeons had finished feeding, and the whole flock were standing still, looking at her with their strange sideways glances. She threw her last piece of rind at them, stood and went back to work. It was beginning to rain.

'Have you seen the UFO?' Chris asked, checking his ammunition. They were nearing the exit of the accommodation block. They hadn't encountered any resistance.

'The what?' Two troops burst through the door in front of them, Sten guns blazing. The Doctor pulled his briefcase up, for cover, but Chris stood firm, oblivious to the bullets richocheting around him. Then he charged them.

'*Banzai!*' Chris whooped. He fired twice, hitting each of his targets in the chest. The Doctor ran over to them but could tell before he arrived that the men had died instantly.

'You killed them,' he whispered.

'Yeah,' grinned Chris, 'with my last two bullets. Neat, eh?'

The Doctor glared up at him. 'Those were people, Chris, this isn't a video game.'

'Look,' stammered Chris, 'I know that. But they would have killed us. This is war, Doctor.'

The Doctor laid his hand on Cwej's shoulder. 'Chris, I'm grateful that you came to rescue me. But there is always an alternative to violence. It's searching for that alternative that separates us from people like the Nazis.'

As the Doctor was speaking, Chris was bending down, picking up a couple of stick grenades and one of the Sten guns. 'Sometimes we need to fight for what we believe. That was the motto of my Lodge at Spaceport Nine Overtown: "Just fight for what's just",' said Chris. All the same, he hesitated, and decided not to take the weapons.

An alarm bell started ringing. The Doctor's head snapped up. 'We need to leave.'

'We're boxed in here,' said Chris. 'We need to head for the main gate.'

'That's the one place we can't go. They'll be expecting us, and they'll have all their guards there. They don't know where we are yet.'

'This base is tiny. We could easily blast our . . .' Chris's voice trailed out. '. . . find an alternative,' he finished.

'Quite,' the Doctor said. He thought for a moment. 'When we get outside, we need to follow the stream,' he announced finally.

The Doctor went first, looking around the fake landscape for any sign of movement. A squad of guards was running for the hangars and another group were already posted along the track to the main gate by the concrete trees. Tentatively, the Doctor and Chris stepped from the accommodation bunker.

'Because there's no way out of the base, their priority is to protect the high security areas. They know that we're not going anywhere. My guess is that they'll call in reinforcements from Granville.' The Doctor was striding confidently towards the stream. Chris followed. In his uniform, guards might think twice before shooting at him, and that was all he needed. He still had his mission.

'Doctor, we have to get Hartung now we're here. That's why the SID sent me over.'

'I'm not entirely sure that he's here. He might be in Guernsey, or even back in Granville,' the Doctor said.

'Yeah, British intelligence has seen him in both those places. The British don't know anything about this base, though. What do we do?' They had reached the stream and were following its course.

'Well, I'd love to have a look in those hangars, but they've doubled the guard on them, and that's just what we can see. They'll have done the same around Hartung. We need a breathing space, to work things out. We won't get it here, and we won't get it in Granville.'

'The farmhouse,' Chris realized. 'We could go to the Gerard farm. They looked after me last night.'

'We'd be putting them at risk,' the Doctor warned.

Chris shrugged. 'What else can we do?'

They had reached the fence. The stream vanished into a pipe, emerging on the other side of the barrier. Tantalizingly, fifty yards beyond was perfect cover: dense woodland. If they could reach that then they ought to be safe. The Doctor bent over.

'This drain is only six inches across; we can't get through.'

'The fence is electrified.'

The Doctor looked up at it. 'Yes, I thought it might be.'

'I've only got a knife. How do you get through an electric fence?'

'The traditional method involves a bicycle tyre, a partner and more than a little pot luck.'

Before the Doctor could elaborate, there was the sharp bark of a submachine gun. On the brow of an artificial hillock stood a Nazi soldier in the black uniform of the Waffen-SS. They had been warning shots, fired at the Doctor. Now he was yelling something at him in German.

'Are you all right, Leutnant?'

He thought that Cwej was a genuine soldier. Chris motioned that it was safe to come down, and made a threatening gesture towards the Doctor. His 'prisoner' played out his part, looking suitably terrified. The Nazi clambered down. As he reached ground level, Chris elbowed him in the solar plexus, then punched him hard in the jaw. The Nazi fell back, almost comically.

The Doctor blinked, bemused. He gazed at Chris for a second, then back at the fence. 'Yes. It's not perfect, but we don't have time for anything else. Lodge one of that man's grenades in the pipe.'

Chris did as the Doctor said, and they took cover. The grenade did its work, clearing the earth from the base, and even ripping the fence itself. The Doctor had broken cover and was heading that way before the smoke had cleared. Chris followed.

'It's still live,' the Doctor warned. Chris was careful not to touch the wire mesh, and was acutely conscious of the stream water lapping around his feet, but the gap was easily large enough for him to ease himself through.

There were dogs barking behind them. The Doctor clenched his fists in frustration. 'I forgot to replace the dog biscuits.' Chris looked blank, until the Doctor explained, 'I had a bag of biscuits in my jacket to slow down the dogs, but the Germans took them from me when they emptied my pockets. We'll have to hurry.'

Once they were on the other side, they ran upstream, water splashing around their trouser-legs. Here, in the water, both their footprints and their scent should be obscured. They were soon ploughing through the woodland. Chris was surprised how fast the Doctor could run. As the Doctor predicted, the Nazis had heard the explosion: Chris could hear the Alsatians behind him, almost at his heels, but the undergrowth was so thick that he couldn't see them.

9

Thought and Memory

They were meant to be looking for von Wer, the spymaster, but the search was proving fruitless. This didn't
surprise Roz, of course, because she knew that the Doctor
wasn't a German spy. What had surprised her was how
easy British Intelligence had found it to pin the blame on
the Doctor: they only had three sightings of him. The
surveillance reports were astonishingly mundane: the
Doctor walked down Oxford Street, the Doctor bought a
cup of tea and an iced bun, the Doctor caught a train at
Paddington Station. He had never been seen with anyone
else, he had never dropped anything suspicious into a
litter bin, something that might have been a dead-letter
drop. Despite that, and without any apparent reason, they
had linked him with a dozen known German agents and
three break-ins at defence establishments. The Doctor was
an enigma, and successive analysts had decided that he
was their problem. The more she looked at the 'evidence',
the more Roz was convinced that there wasn't a spymaster
at all. She continued to work on the 'problem', diligently
plotting his movements.

Watching Reed across the desk, as the afternoon wore
on, Forrester noticed that he was taking her for granted
now, something Roz found flattering. While he had never
behaved with anything other than impeccably good man-
ners, there had always been a distance between them. She
had been his Xosa Maiden, a dusky archetype from a
schoolbook deep in his unconscious mind; someone he'd

worshipped from afar from an early age, and had now come face to face with. Roz was uncomfortable being idolized. That gulf seemed to be narrowing. He accepted her on her own terms now, saw her as a person, a woman, a fellow officer.

Was she beginning to accept him, too? It had gone well beyond that. Looking at him now, as he jotted something down on a notepad, Roz realized that she could actually picture herself staying here with this man. The idea that she might live here with anyone – especially Reed – shocked her. Settling down had never occurred to her before, not with feLixi, not even with Fenn. She would turn a few heads, Roz mused, at a time when most English people had never seen a black woman. They could never have children, of course. How could she bring half-caste babies into this time? They would be true aliens: mottled hybrids formed by the grafting together of two genetic strains kept pure for centuries.

What on earth was so attractive about this rather dull Englishman? Roz had an innate distrust of psychoanalysis. She had let the undergrowth grow up around her own unconscious, actively discouraged missionary expeditions, and stuck up a few shrunken heads to warn off the more persistent explorers. Judge a person by their actions, not their potty training, that was her motto. She had been there too many times when the Freudroid at the Lodge had confidentially announced that the serial killer they were looking for was a solitary academic type in his mid-twenties who fancied his mother, only to discover later that the real killer was four times older and just liked killing people so she could brag about it in bars and on chat shows.

But she had to admit that she found George Reed and his leisurely world attractive. It was so uncomplicated a life. There was a clear distinction between good and evil. An emphasis on moral responsibility. Benevolence. Decency. Christ, they even let you smoke in their offices without giving you a lecture.

There was something familiar about George, with his

smooth, pale face, his neatly brushed hair and his precise accent. Deep in the dark continent that passed for Forrester's mind, was there a longing for an English Soldier? The English had always been a part of her culture. Chief Xhosa had led his tribe into the Transkei in the early sixteenth century. Less than forty years later, fewer years than Roz's own lifetime, the Europeans had arrived. It was they who had introduced Christianity, capitalism, even the idea of nationhood. Xhosa identity was defined by the English. In the nineteenth century, so close to 1941 that Roz could almost see it, her people had been split into two groups: those who opposed the British, and those that collaborated with them. You couldn't ignore them. Roz's ancestors? They'd collaborated. The Rarabe Xhosa had fought *with* the British in the Fifth Kaffir War, against all the other Xhosa tribes. Did that make her people any less 'pure'? Look at the English: culturally, racially, they were a mix of Celts, Anglo-Saxons, Vikings, Romans, West Indians, Indians, Jews and who knows what else. Learning from the English had paid off: it had been the Western-educated, reasonable Christian Xhosa who won their country's freedom, not the Zulu with their spears and fierce independence. The first name of her people's great liberator had been Nelson.

Roz wasn't being nostalgic; she wasn't going native; she was being practical. The Doctor had vanished. Bernice hadn't made contact. Cwej had been sent to his almost certain death. If the Doctor, Benny and Chris were all dead then she had two choices: stay here, or go back to her own time in the TARDIS. Benny had told her that the British won Earth War Two, four years from now. After that, life must have returned to normal. Roz was in her early forties now, so she could reasonably expect to live for another century, even given the primitive state of medicine here. She would live through the Age of Legend if she stayed; she could fight alongside her family, help build the future she knew was coming. Her fight for Justice would continue.

George returned her glance, and smiled. Roz smiled back.

The Doctor sniffed the air. 'Cordite. Shots have been fired here.'

Chris felt his stomach tighten. 'Monique and Monsieur Gerard?'

'There's no sign of them. There are heavy vehicle tracks outside, but they could have been made by a tractor.'

'We have to search.'

The Doctor nodded thoughtfully. 'Yes, we have to, but we can't be long. The patrol will almost certainly catch our scent again. Do you know your way around?'

'Yes,' Chris muttered. The kitchen looked just the same as it had when he was last here. The range was still warm. He had only been gone a couple of hours. What if he had led the Nazis here? What if he had killed the brave farmer and his daughter?

Chris headed upstairs, the Doctor remained in the kitchen, keeping watch. The farmhouse had four bedrooms, one for Monsieur Gerard, one for Monique, one for both of her dead brothers. Once on the landing, Chris opened up each of the doors in turn. He had slept in the one nearest to the top of the stairs. This had been Luc's room. It was untouched from this morning. Chris had not been into any of the other bedrooms before, but it became clear as he checked them that they were empty, too.

The last room he came to was Monique's. He paused at the doorway. The room was feminine, with frilly white netting and floral-printed wallpaper. It smelt of her perfume. There was a sparse dresser, a cluttered bedside cabinet. Monique had an old iron bed, with coral bedsheets. A doll had been carefully tucked into it. There was something else resting on the bed, something flat. A note? Chris stepped over to the bed. It was a sketch of him, drawn in pencil, from memory. A very good likeness, right down to the moustache.

He took it downstairs and showed the Doctor.

'She was a good artist,' the Doctor noted.

151

'What do you mean "was"?' Chris said accusingly.

The Doctor bit his lip. 'I'm sorry, a slip of the tongue. I haven't found any blood. They might have got away. We could check the barn and the chicken shed.'

Cwej shook his head. 'No, like you said before, we can't stay. At least the Nazis don't have this picture, so they won't be able to establish a link between me and Monique.' He folded the picture and slotted it into his tunic pocket.

'We'll go to Granville,' said the Doctor. 'Hartung might be there. It's probably where they've taken Monique and Monsieur Gerard. If not, at least Steinmann will be there.'

'Doctor, you're a bit conspicuous in those clothes.'

The Doctor patted the briefcase. 'Well, I've got plenty of money to spend on a new suit, but there's no gentleman's tailors for miles around. Do you think Monsieur Gerard would mind if I borrowed an outfit from him?'

'I doubt he'd mind, Doctor, but he's about as broad as you're tall.'

'Oh, that's not a problem, then, I'll just wear the clothes sideways. Isn't that what you humans call "cross-dressing"?'

'Er, no,' said Chris, unsure whether the Doctor was joking. He had a suggestion, but wasn't sure how the Doctor would take it. 'I do have a plan,' he began tentatively.

At ten to five, just as they were beginning to pack up for the night, Kendrick had phoned from Downing Street, and requested that Reed and Forrester remain at the SID until he returned. He had left no indication how long that would be, so they decided to sit and talk at their empty desks.

'What do you think that Hoogin and Mooning are, George?'

'Kendrick has told us to concentrate on finding von Wer,' he warned.

'Yes, but we're not getting anywhere with that, are we?'

'I was talking to Davis at lunchtime, and he's not got

anywhere with Hoogin and Mooning. Perhaps both are red herrings: it wouldn't be the first time.' George seemed entirely uninterested. The problem fascinated Roz, however. It seemed to be the only firm piece of evidence that the SID had. She needed to talk to someone about this suspicion.

'Let's assume they are code names for whatever Hartung is building,' she began.

'Reasonable enough,' Reed conceded. He didn't want to talk about this. He looked anxious, now, like a young boy who thought he was about to be caught scrumping apples. Kendrick had ordered him to think about other matters, and he didn't want to disobey.

'What do we know about other German code-names?' Roz continued, keeping her tone business-like.

'I'm not sure I can tell you.' Despite his reticence, she was managing to draw Reed into the problem.

'Why not?'

'Well, I'd have to give you a list of top secret German projects, then their codenames, then exactly why those names matched up with what the project was.' She could see the problem. Most intelligence organizations encountered the same difficulty: by definition they were dealing with secrets, and by definition, you couldn't go around telling too many people exactly what you did and didn't know. It led to compartmentalization. Small groups dealing with small problems, and no one able to see the big picture. Unfortunately, real life wasn't broken up into neat compartments. They knew that Hartung's group, officially a part of the Luftwaffe zbV, actually included members of the SS and regular army as well as the Luftwaffe itself. Reed obviously knew more than he was saying, here, and it might be important.

'Can you give me one example?' she asked reasonably.

George looked furtive. 'Don't you dare tell anyone about this: last year, one of the first jobs the SID had was to try and assess the German radar network. We knew that the Germans called a new system "Wotan", but we had no idea what it was, or even if it had anything to do with radar. Well, would could work out from the name that it was something important, so – '

'Hang on a second, you've lost me.'

George grinned, a pleasing sight. 'Wotan, or Odin, was the king of the Norse Gods. The top Nazi brass are obsessed with the Norse myths, believe it or not. Anyway, the very first piece of equipment the SID bought was a reference book about the Norse myths. And lo and behold, we found out that one of Wotan the God's characteristics was that he only had one eye. We managed to match up that with a single-beam radar guidance system we knew they were developing. One eye, one radar beam. So we found out what Wotan the Weapon was, just from the codename.'

Roz and Reed looked at each other for a second. The same idea had just occurred to them both. Reed hurried over to the bookcase, and pulled the book down. It was a handsome, leather-bound edition, and hadn't been touched for a year, since the Wotan incident he had just related. Reed thumbed his way through the index.

'I don't believe it . . .' he breathed, flicking his way through the book. He opened up the book, and handed it across to Roz.

There was a full-page engraving of Odin, seated on a magnificent throne. Odin was a man in his fifties, bearded, wearing an elaborate eagle helmet. He had an eye-patch over one eye, a spear in his hand, a magnificent ring on his finger. At his feet were two wolves, at his shoulders two black birds.

Roz read out some of the text. ' "Odin also commanded Hugin and Munin, two ravens perched upon his shoulders. Their names mean 'Thought' and 'Memory'. Every morning Odin sent them out, and they returned at nightfall, when they whispered the news of the whole earth to him. No one could catch these birds, and they could come and go as they pleased, as swift and as silent as their name might indicate. Through them, the All-father knew of all earthly happenings." '

Roz sat back. 'OK. So we have a clue. Next question: what does it mean?'

'Well, Hugin and Munin are birds. Aerial weapon. It's the superbomber.'

'They don't say "superbomber" to me, George. "Thought" and "Memory"? Why have two names?'

'Two types of bomber: heavy and light, long or short range,' George offered.

'What if this is a double bluff?' Roz said, suddenly suspicious.

'What do you mean?'

'Isn't it just a bit hokey that this German codename gives us this clue?'

'No, Roz. The beauty of working in counter-intelligence against the Germans is that they never learn from their mistakes. During our standard training we are told about a system the Germans had for passing messages at the last war. In 1916, there was a woman – I forget her name – but every day she'd cross a checkpoint. She said she was visiting her brother, and every single day she was searched, and no one ever found anything. The guards befriended her, and the search became a formality. One day, the officer in charge was talking to her and, conversationally, he asked what she had in her basket. "Just a few boiled eggs and some bread and butter," she said. He reached in, and plucked out one of the eggs.'

'I take it that this story is going somewhere?' murmured Roz irritably. Was George trying to lead her off the subject?

'Of course. Here's the point: the woman looked utterly terrified, and the officer couldn't work out why: all he'd done is pick up an egg. He checked it in his hand: not a mark on it. But she had made the man suspicious, so he examined the egg more thoroughly. He picked off the shell, and discovered little brown dots on the egg white. When these were magnified, they turned out to be a plan of the troop movements in the whole sector. The Germans had discovered that if they wrote in – oh, what's the name? – *acetic* acid on the shell of a soft-boiled egg, let

155

it dry and then boiled it, then the message would get absorbed, leaving no trace of it on the surface.

'Now the Germans knew that we discovered this, but they still carried on using the exact same method, without even the slightest variation. It seems to be a quirk of the German character: either a love of routine, or an unwillingness to admit they've been bettered. In the end, it was almost embarrassing: the army would constantly be arresting and executing these poor women, just because their superiors wouldn't change their system. And do you know what? They are *still* doing it! We've discovered German agents doing exactly the same thing three times already in this war.'

Roz frowned. 'OK. So it's a clue. So let's see what it means. What properties do Hugin and Munin have?'

'They are birds. There are two of them. They are fast and long-range. They have something to do with Odin, or Wotan. That's it. Powerful birds: a superbomber,' Reed concluded.

'They fly by day. They're used for spying. Thought and memory. They have magical properties,' Roz continued.

'Ah, the codenames are still a bit cryptic. Don't read *too* much into them,' Reed warned gently.

'George, this is not a bomber. Kendrick is wrong. Hartung has built two of them, and they are something new, something unique. And we have no idea what they might be.'

'Excuse me, sister, have you seen anyone suspicious? Two men, one dressed as a German officer; the other an older, smaller man in a linen suit?'

'Oh, no, Major,' the nun chuckled. 'You really are a big lad, aren't you? Not as big as my Kristian, here.' The nun giggled.

The major peered at her. The nun was short and middle-aged. She had a bulbous nose and thick eyebrows. Although plain, her eyes and mouth were kindly. There was a German officer escorting her, a man in his early twenties. He was tall, blond, with piercing blue eyes. He

156

was heavily built, like an athlete and he had a thick moustache.

'I do not recognize you, Leutnant. May I see your papers?'

The nun leaned forward. 'Young man, this is Kristian. I teach music at the local school, and Kristian looks after me.' She giggled again, then batted her eyelids at him.

Hastily, the Leutnant decided that the nun must be telling the truth. The Leutnant moved them on. It was getting dark.

In this light, Steinmann looked like the incarnation of evil. He was lit from beneath, the way that Dracula always was in horror films. It emphasized the arch of his eyebrows and the curve of his forehead. His distinguished nose became hooked, and his mouth even more cruel. His skin became grey and lifeless. The shadows made the sockets of his eyes look sunken, and his grey eyes glinted malevolently.

He lit himself a cigarette. He offered Benny one, but she refused.

'My right hand,' she said. 'I have no feeling there.'

Steinmann bent over to examine her hand. Delicately, he unwrapped the bandage and gently stroked the back of her hand. Finally, he took his cigarette from his mouth and stabbed it down just behind the knuckle of her middle finger.

Benny screamed.

'The feeling seems to have returned,' Steinmann observed.

When she had finished sobbing, he continued. 'Fraulein Summerfield, it's late in the day, and I have to get back to Granville tonight. Events are moving on. You are not a time traveller. That is a lie. Tell me the truth.' The shadows exaggerated every move of his face, distorting his features still further as he spoke. What he was saying was true. Her memories all seemed so real, but Steinmann must be right. If this Doctor existed, he would have rescued her by now. She wasn't sure that he could exist.

What was he meant to be? An immortal being who was capable of travelling through time and space. He didn't look the part. Actually, she found it difficult to remember what he looked like. She remembered that his voice was distinctive, but couldn't remember whether he was meant to have a Scottish or an Irish accent. It wasn't true, was it? None of it was true. She didn't live in a police box and she certainly couldn't speak Martian.

'I have told you everything that I know,' she insisted. Her hand was still throbbing.

She had retreated into a fantasy world, and now Steinmann was stripping away all the fantasy, all the science fiction, peeling away every one of her lies. She still had clear memories. Dreams of men goose-stepping, the drone of planes. Nazis in the bathroom. New Year's Eve: that German private who'd come into her room. She remembered his hot breath on her neck, his hand on her face. If it hadn't been for Gerhard and Kurt, then who knows what would have happened. Her bed at home was cold, cold and hard. There was a constant tang of cigarette smoke and rotten food in the air. The meat she ate was fatty, stringy, laced with salt so you couldn't tell it had gone off. The Royal Hotel was running out of soap, but still had plenty of carpet cleaner. Those were facts, facts that she could remember from real life. Her name wasn't Bernice, it was Celia. She remembered people calling her Celia. She couldn't remember anyone ever calling her Benny. It was such a ridiculous name anyway.

'Another injection.'

'You will kill her,' stated the nurse. Was that concern, or glee? Celia wasn't sure of anything any longer.

'That is of no concern. Perhaps we will learn the truth before she dies.'

Celia felt the jab, and thought that she could feel the drug flowing through her bloodstream, rooting out the truth. All the lies that had built up were dissolving away now. How much nicer it would be if she really was Benny, intrepid explorer and archaeologist. Someone who'd stand up to all this, quipping with supervillains. Someone special, who'd travelled further than anyone else, visited all those exciting ages in history. Battling evil, slaying the monster, but always back home by teatime. But it wasn't true. Her name was Celia and her job was to clean up after the Nazis, to beat their carpets and to scrub their toilets.

Another agonizing stab on the back of her hand.

'I hate you!' she heard herself shouting.

Celia had lived on Guernsey all her life. That explained why she couldn't picture London without her mind painting in glass skyscrapers on the skyline. She hadn't got a degree in archaeology. Deep down, she knew that much, and now she admitted it. Her whole life was a lie, it had been a lie ever since the day that her mother had died. What was her mother's name? What was her father called? What was her surname? She had no recollection, but she knew that her mother had been killed in an air-raid ... killed by the ... the word was a far and distant thing. Two syllables, harsh in the mouth. She couldn't recall the name, only what it symbolized. Evil. Something that had been there as long as she could remember. It was a byword for hatred and destruction. Death. They exterminated everything that wasn't like them. Indestructible monsters. Opportunists who attacked without warning, who ignored diplomacy. Divide and conquer. Invasion. They killed millions: they didn't distinguish between the military and civilians. Rows and rows of headstones. A planet full of graves. Remembrance Day. Lest we forget. Chanting their boastful slogans. Advance and attack, attack and destroy. Their right arms stiff, extended in a permanent salute. Power. Conquer and destroy. Genesis: an insane genius, wounded in the last war. Wanting the best for his people, knowing that they must change in this hostile environment, become harsher, more disciplined, more loyal. Change their very genetic make-up. Round up and destroy the enemy within. Their Nation must return to its former glory. Resurrection. War machines pouring from production lines. Advancing, guns blazing. Technical achievement. Scientists, working in laboratories, conceiving new terrors. They built all those weapons. Germ warfare. Powerful explosives. Their supreme ruler barking orders. I obey. Total war. Buildings shattering, bricks and concrete cracking and splintering. Racial purity. They ran slave camps, killed their prisoners for sport. Experimenting on the inmates. Twisted science. Permanent warfare. Master Plan. The future, with London in ruins. Destiny. Blond supermen, brutish subhuman servants. Their rightful place: the supreme beings of the universe. Planet, Doctor, not universe. Revelation. Halt! Stay where you are!

'I know! I know who you really are!' Bernice bawled, her throat dry. Darkness falling. She couldn't hear herself; she couldn't see where she was. Her hand was still burning with pain, but it seemed so far away, now. She knew the nurse was there, feeling for her pulse.

She slumped in her seat, her head lolling.

Kendrick entered the room. Reed and Forrester stood and saluted. It was just after six o'clock.

'At ease.' He faced Forrester, treating her as the senior officer in the room for the first time in a week. The admiral was smiling for the first time that Reed could recall. It suited Kendrick's lined face, giving it the air of a benevolent monarch. There was none of the weariness, none of the resignation that had weighed so heavily on him before. When he spoke, it had the ring of a royal proclamation.

'Captain, three hours ago I took your sterling work to the War Cabinet. It has convinced them. Tonight, Bomber Command will target Granville and the adjoining airfield. We'll blow Hartung, Steinmann and their superbomber right off the face of the Earth.'

Roz shifted in her seat as she spoke. 'But, sir, the reason that has never been done before is the danger to the French civilian population. Where next, Guernsey?'

There was no remorse in Kendrick's green eyes. 'The stakes are high. Captain Forrester, I understand your concerns, but if we don't take this action now then the whole course of the war will change. The sacrifice is necessary.' Something about his answer nagged at Roz's mind.

160

Goddess! He hadn't batted an eyelid when she'd mentioned Guernsey. She dare not accuse him here and now, but instinctively she knew that the War Cabinet had discussed the bombing of Guernsey if this raid wasn't a success. *They were going to bomb their own people.*

'Sir,' Reed began, 'there may be some evidence to suggest that there isn't a superbomber. We've found out what Hugin and Munin are.' He explained what they had discovered. Thought and Memory. A pair of birds that fly invisibly around the world. 'That doesn't sound like a short-range heavy bomber, sir.' Why was Reed agreeing with her now?

His conscience. Like her, Reed could picture the French civilians dying needlessly.

Kendrick considered the new information for a moment. 'No, they don't sound like bombers. But Hartung is still working from Granville. Destroying the town will destroy Hugin and Munin, too, whatever they are.'

'Sir, Granville is a civilian target,' Reed said forcefully.

'Lieutenant, this is total war. There are no civilian targets.' More quietly, 'George, I sympathize, but there is too much at stake.'

'I strongly recommend, sir, that we don't go ahead with the raid until we know precisely what we are dealing with,' Roz declared.

'My dear, the planes took off twenty minutes ago. They'll be in France in less than a quarter of an hour. An hour from now, Granville will have been removed from the map. After that, there will be nothing left of Hartung except . . . thought and memory.'

'That was impressive even for you, Doctor. You persuaded that man that you were a *nun*, of all things. That was the worst acting performance I have ever seen, and you got away with it!'

The Doctor gave a twirl, his borrowed habit spinning joyfully around him. He was almost certainly the least convincing nun the world had ever seen. 'Clothes maketh a man, Chris. Or woman. Think of it this way – what's easier to believe: that I am a nun, or that I'm a man pretending to be a nun? The human mind has a great capacity to ignore things that make life difficult for it. It much prefers to turn a blind eye, say it's someone else's problem, or that it's nothing to do with – ' The Doctor stopped in his tracks, his head cocked to one side.

'What's the matter . . .?' Chris began, but the Doctor ignored him. They were right in the middle of Granville's town square shortly before the curfew was due to begin, not a good place to stand around, especially in fancy dress. Chris tugged at the sleeve of the Doctor's habit, but before Chris could speak again, the air-raid sirens had started. Slightly higher in pitch than those in Britain, but unmistakable. Searchlights began probing the evening sky. In the distance, further up the coast, anti-aircraft guns were firing. The Doctor grabbed Chris's arm.

'It's the yellow alert. We haven't much time.'

The first bombs dropped in the harbour. The sea wall was breached, and over a dozen small boats were destroyed, along with a handful of storage sheds. At the same time, another plane attacked the coastal road, rendering a mile-long stretch impassable. British aerial reconnaissance had been focusing on the Granville area for some weeks, at the request of the SID. As a result, the RAF knew exactly which bridges to hit to cause maximum disruption to German damage control teams.

The main purpose of this first wave was to mark out targets more clearly. Flares were dropped in key areas, drifting down to the ground underneath their own minia-ture parachutes. Decoy flares were also dropped to cause confusion. A pair of larger targets, Granville's two pump-ing stations, were bombed, cutting off the town's water supplies. A bomb hit Granville's main fire station, but failed to go off. It hardly mattered, as the (mostly French) firemen were all huddled deep underneath the building, in their shelters.

As yet there had been no casualties. This changed when a fuel storage area on the outskirts of the town was hit,

killing thirty soldiers stationed there. A chain reaction
started, with each of the fuel tanks exploding in turn. The
fire burned for three days. In the centre of Granville, the
RAF missed the telephone exchange with their first three
efforts, the bombs exploding in nearby residential areas.
The fourth attack was successful. It took the Germans
ten minutes to restore communications with the outside
world.

'The church bells won't stop ringing. What does that
mean?' Chris asked.

'It means that the spire has been hit and the bell-ringing
mechanism has been damaged,' the Doctor answered pro-
saically.

They had been on high ground when the fuel dump had
exploded. From this distance – three miles, perhaps four
– the string of explosions had been spectacular, an incredible display of air power. The earth pounded with each
blast. Night was falling, but a new sun had risen in the
east, and the whole town was lit by the firelight. Cwej
could hear the jangling bells of fire tenders making their
way across town.

Chris glanced over at the Doctor. The little man was
fascinated by the events unfurling beneath them, apparently oblivious to any danger they might be in. A couple
of miles further up the coast to the north, there was a
long, reverberating crash.

'The airfield,' said the Doctor.

'The British don't know about it,' Chris observed.

'Not the camouflaged one, the normal one. They probably think that Hartung is there.' There was a series of
distant explosions from the direction the Doctor was
looking.

'Perhaps he is. Or was.'

Isolated points on the landscape below them began to
flare.

'They're beginning to target the town itself. There are
only two searchlights for the whole of Granville. As far
as I can tell, there are only three anti-aircraft batteries.'

'Without the searchlights, they'd be firing blind. Looks like the good guys will win this one.'

'The RAF have the advantage, certainly,' the Doctor said dryly. 'We need to get down there, try to find a clue to Hartung's whereabouts.'

A small group of bombers had separated from the main party five minutes before the start of the attack, while the squadrons were still over the English Channel. At the airfield, the first reports of the attack on the harbour were being radioed in. Fighter crews were scrambled, but the RAF bombers arrived seconds before the pilots reached their planes. Not a single fighter was launched, and both runways were carpet-bombed. Over two dozen trained Luftwaffe pilots and a whole squadron of Messerschmitt fighters were caught in the explosions.

The RAF were free to continue their raid unmolested. Fires had broken out by now in dozens of places all over the town. These lit the battlefield for the air force, allowing them a much clearer view. As yet, there wasn't any thick smoke to blot out the view.

It was time for the RAF to consolidate their position. It was time to drop the incendiaries. Thousands upon thousands of tiny devices were dropped, each one bursting into flame as it hit the ground. Before long, these little fires had joined up, and the whole of central Granville was ablaze. Fire tore through the shopping streets.

'Run, Chris, run!'

All around was choking black smoke. Chris could hear the Doctor's voice, but couldn't see him. The ground rocked with each detonation. The bombardment was concentrated a little way behind them, but the explosions came as rapid as machine-gun fire, and were getting nearer. The sky was filled with incendiaries, pouring over the town like a rainstorm.

The Doctor was suddenly standing in front of him.

'It's too heavy. We won't reach the townhouse. We need to get into a shelter,' he was saying. 'Follow me.'

Chris was a pilot, he'd fought in simulated combat missions. Down here, though, he found it impossible to find his bearings: the planes seemed to be coming from all directions at once. They roared overhead, almost impossibly low.

There were screams to their right. The Doctor stopped in mid-step. He looked back at Chris. They had to help.

Edging across the rubble, they found a man trapped under a chunk of masonry. Chris looked around, trying to see if the slab had come from a building or from the road itself. The Doctor motioned to him, and together they tried to move the slab away. After a moment, the little man let go.

'We're too late,' he said sadly.

Chris looked around. Why were there so many people on the streets? There were soldiers and firemen, but also civilians: a small crowd of men, women and children, all heading in one direction. As he watched some were blown off their feet, others were pelted with rubble. Why weren't they under cover?

'Doctor. They're heading for a public shelter!' he shouted over the clamour.

'It's our only chance!' replied the Doctor.

Together, they followed the stream of people.

The townhouse used by the Luftwaffe zbV as their regional headquarters had been completed in 1715. It was referred to by the experts as one of the finest of the early works of the architect Jean Lassurance. It had been ordered by a wealthy naval officer, and had taken eight months to build.

It was partially demolished when a two-thousand-pound bomb exploded in the street outside. The façade of the house shattered, as did all the glass. The statues on the roof fell through the rafters. Shrapnel and debris tore holes in the walls in the rooms that faced the sea. There was no time for a fire to start: twenty seconds after the first explosion, the RAF scored a direct hit, and the building was blown apart. It had been built before the age of high explosive, and so not even the wine cellars were safe. The walls were thrown outwards, the roof collapsing to the ground. Fire swept through the wreckage, consuming every piece of antique furniture, every book in the library, every painting and tapestry.

They dashed across the park, which exploded around them. Ahead was the entrance to the public shelter. A woman with a baby in her arms was at the entrance, being ushered in. Thirty feet from the entrance, Chris tripped, stumbling on the broken ground. The Doctor hesitated, then turned back to help pull the large man to his feet.

And then the shelter was hit.

It happened in slow motion. The plane swooping over their heads, deafening them. The black shape of a bomb the size of a car falling. Hurtling through the roof of the shelter, which splintered under the pressure. The searing flash, radiating outwards. The explosion deep below them. The violence as the shelter was blown apart. A storm of concrete, iron, brick and mud. Relief: I wasn't in there. The realization that everyone who had been in there was dead. Memories of the mother and her child.

The Doctor was shouting instructions to those who hadn't reached the shelter. Stay calm. Stay still. This park was safer than the streets: there was no risk here of collapsing walls or flying glass. The strongest men were to help cover the shelter with earth, put out the fire. Use the litter bins as buckets, fill them with water from the duckpond, use them to extinguish any incendiaries that dropped. No, there weren't any survivors down there. No, don't look.

The raid lasted a little under three hours. At half-past nine, the squadon leader ordered his group to break off. The mission had been a total success, the commander reported, he hadn't lost a single plane, every major target was confirmed destroyed. Granville was a dead city.

166

10

Blind Justice

Dampness on her face. Water.

Benny Summerfield was awake. Benny Summerfield was alive. Benny Summerfield was relieved. She opened her eyes and was surprised how quickly they focused. The nurse, Kitzel, was on the other side of the room, her back towards her. The nurse was hunched over something on the table. They were alone. Benny pulled herself upright. Hearing the movement, Kitzel looked over her shoulder, a wave of blonde hair falling over the epaulette of her uniform. The nurse had Slavic features and grey eyes. In other surroundings, in different clothes, she would be beautiful. She reminded Benny a little of an old friend from her early teens. She had been beautiful, too.

'You are awake?' Kitzel spoke in stilted English.

'I can tell you've got medical training.' Benny wasn't surprised when the nurse failed to recognize the sarcasm. They were in her cell. Where was that? An underground complex, Steinmann had said. There was a bed here, a chair, an empty bucket in the corner. The door was ever so slightly ajar.

'I have prepared you some food,' the nurse droned. She had brought over a metal tray with a steaming bowl of tomato soup and a hunk of bread. There was even a knob of butter on the side of the plate. Benny took it from her, resting the tray on her pillow.

'There isn't a spoon. I haven't anything to spread the butter with,' Benny snapped. The nurse passed the cutlery over, her face impassive. She stood, watching her prisoner. Benny sipped at her soup. It had been watered down, but it was still too rich for her palate after so many days without proper food. The hot food burnt her tongue and the taste stung the side of her mouth. She found the bread easier to digest, but could only nibble at it. It would be a while before she could hold down a full meal.

Pausing between bites, she made conversation. 'Do you know where the Doctor is?'

'You need medical attention?'

'No. My friend the Doctor. He must have been captured on the beach. If he was, he'd have been brought here.' The thought had only just occurred to her.

'You are the only prisoner in the complex.'

'Where else would prisoners be taken?' Benny was standing now, surprised how unfamiliar the soles of her feet felt with weight on them. She stretched her legs, arms and spine in turn.

'Criminals would all be in normal police cells.'

'What about military prisoners?' Benny began massaging her right shoulder, easing away some of the stiffness. Her left shoulder would have to wait: her right hand was still in a splint.

'There aren't any.'

'If there were?'

'Here at the complex.' Her eyes were watering. The woman was almost on the verge of tears.

'Nowhere else?' Benny insisted.

'Nowhere else. Even if he was dead he would have been brought here.' Benny's stomach lurched. She pitched over towards the slops bucket, her nose suddenly full of the smell of disinfectant and vomit. The Doctor couldn't be dead. The possibility didn't exist. There had been too many times before when she'd thought he was dead and he wasn't.

She straightened up. That wasn't exactly logic, was it? He hadn't rescued her. He knew what Nazis did to their prisoners. If he was alive he would have dropped everything and come running to save her in the nick of time.

Wouldn't he? She'd learnt that the Doctor's definition of 'a nick of time' occasionally left a bit to be desired, but by any calculation he should have rescued her by now. She remembered the single shot, now. He'd been on the beach when there was a shot. No burst of machine-gun fire. No Germans shouting warnings. A single shot. She hadn't seen the Doctor since.

Kitzel handed Benny a flannel to wipe her mouth.

'Nurse. I'm an archaeologist. On one of the first digs I went on, I discovered a great hoard of daggers. At least that's what I thought at first. It doesn't matter where this dig was, but the civilization we were excavating was meant to be pacifist. If these were daggers, then all previous notions of their culture would be overturned and I'd be famous. All this so early in my career. It turned out that it was just a cutlery drawer. One of the senior archaeologists took me to one side and said that there was something I had to remember, and I do, I remember the exact words: "The distinction between a dagger and an inoffensive knife blade is hard to draw and may never have been clear cut." '

Before Kitzel could react, Benny was holding the butter knife at her throat.

'Now, you're going to take me to the morgue. If we are challenged, you are going to stick up for me. If you don't, if you even speak, I cut your throat. Understood?'

Kitzel nodded, her mouth clamped shut.

The dust still hadn't settled when dawn came. Chris's eyes watered as he picked his way across the rubble. Bricks and shattered glass littered the streets. It was very quiet. Everything was dead. There was still an after-image here of the evening before, when this had been a small fishing town. Chris had walked up this street ten hours before, when old men had been playing boules in front of the town hall. Their ghosts were still there, persisting even after their town had gone. What struck Chris was a sense of *déjà vu*: he had seen this scene, or one very like it, in monochrome photographs of Blitz damage. The reality was only a little more colourful than the black and white pictures and the thick fog drifting in off the sea only added to the effect. With their fronts and roofs blown away, the buildings reminded Chris of giant doll's houses. The streets were full of debris, small fires still burning. A handful of rescue teams were toiling away. Every single window in the town had been shattered. The buildings looked like a row of people with their eyes gouged out.

Behind him, the sound of the Doctor's crunching footsteps stopped. Chris turned. The Doctor's expression was carefully neutral. Neither of them had slept last night. The Doctor was still carrying the briefcase containing the stolen plans.

'The townhouse,' he said. Yesterday, on the way into the town, the Doctor had pointed out the same building. Chris peered through the gloom, but couldn't see it at first. Then he saw that where the townhouse had once stood there were two vast craters and a single wall, three storeys tall decorated with a patchwork of wallpaper and wood panelling. The ground was covered in bricks, plaster and roof slates. There wasn't even enough to call it a ruin.

'How could they have done this?' Chris asked.

'The Germans do it every night. They've done it to London, Southampton, Bristol, Coventry, Manchester, Liverpool, Sheffield, Hull – '

'But how could they? I know the Nazis are evil, but most of these people were French,' Cwej insisted.

'We don't have time to discuss the morality of war: we need to find Hartung.' The Doctor turned a chunk of masonry over, scraped away at the rubble. Chris was about to speak again when the Doctor discovered something. The little man bent down. Chris moved forward to catch a glimpse, but the Doctor held him back. Using Chris for support, the Doctor pulled himself to his feet, then picked up his briefcase.

'Her name was Ulrilda Fegelein, from Falkenstein in Germany. She liked opera, she had a small collection of gramophone records. She told me a very rude joke about two sailors and a one-eyed goat, but she didn't understand it. Ulrilda liked her coffee black and strong, with two sugars. She wasn't old enough to vote when elections were abolished, but she would have voted for the Nazis given a chance. Did that make her evil?'

'Yes.' Chris was surprised by the certainty in his own voice. The Doctor looked shocked, but Chris continued, 'She had a choice. Everyone gets a choice. There is evil in the universe and there is injustice. The Nazis are evil. Everything they stand for must be wiped out, without mercy.'

The Doctor managed a thin smile. 'I left my home planet many years ago. I discovered things on my travels, things I never suspected: monsters and villains, death and disaster, ghosts and godlings, evil coalescing from the beginning of the universe. Dark forces. I've fought against them, beaten them back. Wiped them out, as you say. But I've always tried to show mercy.'

Chris was angry now. 'Sometimes mercy isn't appropriate. The British tried to bargain with the Nazis. They gave them the benefit of the doubt, they tried diplomacy. The Nazis took advantage of them, sliced away more and more territory. Used the time to build up their military. Appeasement doesn't always work. The Nazis are monsters.'

The Doctor looked up from his excavations. 'That's your perspective. That's my perspective. From a monster's point of view, though, things look rather different. I've always tried to listen to the monster's point of view. You'd be surprised how passionate, how eloquent, they can be.'

'Herr Doktor,' a German voice called out.

'Speak of the devil,' muttered the Doctor, who stood up and dusted himself down.

Chris followed the sound, and saw a Nazi officer stepping towards them through the fog. The man was of average height and build, and wore his uniform as though it were a Savile Row suit. As he got closer, Chris guessed that he must be in his late fifties: his thin white hair had receded to his crown, his face was lined and sunken.

'Oberst Oskar Steinmann,' the Doctor announced. The officer stopped in his tracks.

'Herr Doktor,' he responded formally, clicking his heels together. He sounded almost relieved, Chris noted with some surprise. He scanned the area, but the officer was alone.

'I am sorry, Oberst. I had no idea this raid was going to happen.'

'No, Doktor, I'm sure that you didn't,' Steinmann said softly. The Nazi pointed at Chris, who prepared for the worst, but Steinmann simply asked, 'I take it this man is not really one of my officers?' The remark baffled Chris until he remembered that he was still wearing a Nazi uniform.

The Doctor grinned. 'This is Christopher Cwej, a friend of mine.'

'The policeman,' Steinmann said pleasantly, offering his hand. Chris found himself shaking it.

The SID staff car raced through the fog towards Paddington station.

'So what do we know?' Roz asked. George only had one telephone, in the front room. Just before seven o'clock it had rung, waking them. When George returned to the bedroom, all he said was that they were needed at Paddington and that a staff car was on the way. They'd dressed and left the flat quickly.

'The transport police picked up a man half an hour ago. Scotland Yard were trailing a known German agent, a woman, on behalf of MI5. They've known about her for six months, but they didn't pick her up because we've always thought that she could lead us to bigger fish.'

'Von Wer?' Roz suggested, hesitantly.

'Well, Five don't know about von Wer,' Reed grinned. 'But they might just have arrested him.'

'So the arrested man made contact with the known spy?'

'Yes. They met and they exchanged a code phrase on one of the platforms of Paddington tube station. Neither of them realized that we had been following the woman. Both were arrested. His identity papers were forged.'

Roz nodded. It was straightforward enough. It didn't sound like the Doctor, either.

'Did the admiral mention the Granville raid?' Roz asked.

'He said it was too early to tell. Bomber Command claim one hundred per cent success, but they always do. If it's as foggy as this in Granville, we won't have got any aerial photographs this morning.' Reed was still sullen. When Kendrick had announced the decision to bombard Granville, George had been shocked. Walking back to his flat together afterwards, Roz had found that she was the one defending the decision. Even though there hadn't been an air-raid on London last night, they had been in no mood to go out on the town. They had sat together silently in George's front room. When she looked into his eyes, she could see raw feelings, the same emotions she felt herself: rage, frustration, a sense of injustice. One of the beliefs they held most dear had been betrayed by a superior officer. Roz had been through all this before. Reed hadn't. They had needed to do something positive together, something passionate and life-affirming. But now it was twelve hours later. Thousands of French civilians had died last night, business in London continued as normal.

The car threw itself round Marble Arch. They were ten, perhaps fifteen, minutes away.

Professor Summerfield was in front of Kitzel, the cutlery knife concealed up her left sleeve.

The young nurse struggled to remain calm. It was still very early in the morning, and there was no one around yet. She had already judged that escape would be impossible.

'How far is it to the morgue?' Summerfield demanded.

'It is the next door down,' Kitzel said quietly. Summerfield seemed at home in these featureless corridors. There was a spring in the older woman's step again, even though, as far as Kitzel understood, she now thought that one of her friends was dead. Perversely, the archaeologist seemed almost relaxed.

Summerfield glanced up at the sign. ' "LEICHENHAUS". The morgue?' Kitzel nodded. Summerfield pushed down the handle and stepped inside, holding open the door for Kitzel to follow.

The morgue was cool and brightly lit. Kitzel had never been in here before, but it was almost exactly the same as the morgue in the Cologne sanitorium where she had done her training. An autopsy table in the middle of the room, cold storage drawers on one wall, a basin and a row of lockers on another. The attendant, a little bespectacled man in his forties, stood as they came in.

'You've brought this one in prematurely, nurse. You want me to arrange something?' He leered at her. The young nurse recoiled. She had heard stories about this nasty little man, and she believed them.

'Bolt the door, Kitzel,' Summerfield ordered. Kitzel did as she asked. The attendant was suddenly worried.

'Who are you?'

'I'm the Professor, and this is my friend Kitzel,' Bernice announced.

'What's going on here?' He looked from Summerfield to Kitzel.

'Liberation,' said Summerfield simply.

There was a flash in the morgue attendant's hand, a lightning-swift response from Summerfield: a slashing motion, a yelp of pain and a clatter as something fell to the floor. The attendant clutched his wrist. Then Summerfield was poised on tiptoes, her knife in hand.

'In case you missed that, Kitzel,' Summerfield was explaining, 'he tried to pull a scalpel on me and I cut open his wrist. Hold this.' She tossed Kitzel the knife. Before the nurse could react, Summerfield had grasped the back of the terrified attendant's head and brought it down hard on the edge of the autopsy table. His legs buckled and he fell against the tiled floor. Kitzel felt the weight of the knife in her hand, and decided to lay it down.

'Is he dead?' Kitzel winced.

'Well, he's come to the right place if he is,' Summerfield said dismissively. Kitzel bent over. The attendant was still breathing. The nurse made him comfortable, examined his cut wrist and then glanced up at Summerfield, who was opening up one of the large army lockers. She dug around in the contents for a moment then pulled out a shapeless dark blue piece of cloth.

'It's my coat,' Summerfield explained, dusting off some of the dried mud. As she was doing that, something else in the locker caught her eye and she glanced back. Summerfield swallowed, and reached inside, pulling out a long black umbrella. Its handle was red bakelite, shaped to resemble a *fragezeichen*.

Summerfield was examining something sewn to the material. 'It's a little name-tag. It says "This is the property of Doctor – " – I can't read the name, it's covered by a patch of oil – "if lost please return to Portland Street Library, Paddington, London".'

'This is your friend's umbrella?'

'Yup,' said Summerfield absentmindedly, as she flicked through a set of notes on the clipboard. 'There are only two bodies here. Drawer 3 and Drawer 7. It doesn't say what date they arrived, it only says "March". One of them might be the Doctor. You'll have to help me.'

Summerfield moved over to Drawer 3, and tried to pull it open. Kitzel joined her. The drawer still wouldn't budge. They tried again, and Summerfield grunted some curse. Kitzel tapped the keyhole.

'There's a lock,' she said lightly. They caught each other's eye and smiled. Kitzel regained her composure as she realized what she was doing, but this only made Summerfield chuckle again. The older woman had already found the key on the floor by the attendant, and was slotting it into the lock. This time the drawer opened without resistance, sliding out and locking rigidly into place.

The body was that of a boy, about Kitzel's own age. Naked, with a shaved scalp, the corpse was pale and virtually hairless, except for a patch of light brown pubic hair. There was a large entry wound in his abdomen that had been cleaned up. The boy had been shot at point-blank range. His eyes had been closed. It was nothing she hadn't seen before; a lot of young men had died in this war, but it shocked her anyway. Summerfield was sitting down on the autopsy table.

'I'd forgotten. I forgot all about him.'

'This is your friend?' Kitzel had expected someone older.

'No, this is the man I killed. Gerhard.'

'You are feeling guilty, now?' she said reprovingly.

'I felt pretty damn guilty when I did it,' Summerfield snapped. Abruptly she stood, and pushed her hip against the drawer until it slammed shut. Gerhard vanished. Kitzel moved to Drawer 7 and unlocked it. Summerfield pulled it open. Together, they peered in.

The contents were twisted, blackened. So much so that it took Kitzel a moment to realize that the object had once been human, and wasn't some sculpture or tree trunk. It must have happened quickly: the skin had been carbonized. She glanced at the face. It was grinning, with pearl-white teeth. Its dark eyes were open. It smelt of roast pork. Kitzel was sick over it.

'It's no improvement, Kitzel, he still looks a mess.' Kitzel shot Summerfield a glance, and it was enough to make her blush and apologize.

'Is this your friend?' Kitzel asked, wiping her mouth. Summerfield shook her head, but checked the name-tag tied to what remained of the corpse's left foot.

'No,' she confirmed. 'Could you close it up?' Kitzel did as she asked, grateful that the burnt body was no longer in sight. As she did this, she heard Summerfield opening up a third drawer. The tall woman grasped Kitzel's shoulder.

'How tall are you, nurse?'

'Five feet, four inches.'

'Nearly six inches,' Summerfield cursed.

'What do you mean?'

176

The knife was suddenly jabbed between her ribs. 'I mean you're six inches too short. Where I come from, women are taller than they are here. You'll have to do. Strip.'

Kitzel hesitated, but not for very long. She had to step back to take off her jacket That done, she began unbuttoning her blouse. Kitzel watched as Summerfield looked across at the unconscious attendant. This would have been her last chance to resist, but Summerfield kept the knife poised above Kitzel's midriff. Kitzel watched as the taller woman scooped up the blouse and began to put it on over her prison uniform. Kitzel pulled down her skirt, and was beginning to unclip her bra before Summerfield motioned her to stop.

'I draw the line at second-hand underwear. Sit down.' Kitzel fell back, the drawer buckling under her weight. Summerfield had pulled off her uniform trousers and shrugged herself into the skirt. Kitzel glanced down at her arm, which was prickling with goose bumps. Not just from the cold. Summerfield leant over and patted Kitzel's wrist.

'I'll have the wristwatch, please,' she said. It was gold, an expensive present from her father on her sixteenth birthday. Kitzel undid it, and passed it over.

'Christ, is that the time?' the tall woman joked as she put it on. Kitzel didn't react.

'Do you think I'd pass muster?' Summerfield asked. The skirt was loose, but it was barely below her knee. The blouse fitted, just, but the jacket was pinched at the shoulders and was almost ridiculously short.

'No,' said Kitzel.

Summerfield laughed. 'At least you're honest. When I put the coat on it won't look quite as bad.' Summerfield reached over for the coat and umbrella.

'What happens now?' Kitzel said nervously, her arms crossed over her chest. It was cold in here.

'Now I pose as a Nazi nurse, march out of the base unchallenged and go to the docks. No guards will stop me, but I'll get wolf-whistled. Then, I convince a fisherman to take me to the mainland. He'll think I'm a Nazi, I'll point out that the uniform is obviously stolen and I've got two black eyes. I'll say that if he takes me I'll give him this wristwatch. He'll agree. I'll cross the Channel in his fishing boat, which will take about seven hours. I'll use that time to catch up on my sleep. I'll arrive in Dover at,' she checked the watch, 'about two-thirty this afternoon. Then I'll catch the 14.57 to Waterloo, I'll catch the tube and meet up with my friends at Portland Street. One final question, before I go: do you think these drawers are airtight?'

Before she could react, Summerfield's palm had shoved against Kitzel's shoulder, pushing her flat on her back. With her knee, Summerfield slammed the drawer shut. Kitzel felt herself slide backwards, watched the crack of light at her feet vanish and gasped for breath. She was facing the wrong way, there wasn't enough room to turn around. It was dark and cold. Was any air getting in? There wasn't a chink of light from the opening. If she screamed would she just use up her air? She heard the key turn in the lock of the drawer. A moment later, the door to the morgue slammed shut. She kicked out at the drawer door, but it didn't budge. Kitzel screamed.

'I can't believe that you're talking to him,' Chris said stubbornly. The Doctor checked that Steinmann was out of earshot. He was twenty yards away, busy talking to one of the survivors who had been pulled from the rubble.

'Would you prefer me to shoot him?' the Doctor asked quietly.

'Yes.'

The Doctor gave one of his sad, flickering smiles. 'What if I told you that Generalleutnant Oskar Steinmann was one of twenty-three Nazis tried at Nuremburg at the end of the war?'

'I'd say he was a war criminal.' To his credit, though, Chris paused. 'But I admit that if we were to kill him now we'd alter established history. What was his sentence?'

'Life imprisonment. He was released on medical grounds in 1969. He died in 1972, at the age of eighty-nine. A very nasty form of spine cancer.' The Doctor looked at the fifty-eight-year-old man standing a stone's throw from him, a man in the prime of his life.

Chris grunted approvingly. 'Well, at least the British won in the end.'

'Did they? I've seen a future in which the Nazis did, a future that wasn't all that different. Ten years from now a swastika flew over the Festival of Britain instead of a Union Flag. The king was called Edward, not George. Tiny changes.' The Doctor leant down sadly, and tried to rest his hands on his umbrella handle, before he remembered that he no longer had it. Instead he had to look Chris in the eye.

'You changed history back.' A statement, not a question.

'I changed history. Like I said, I made tiny changes, and ensured that the Allies won.' The Doctor checked Chris's reaction, watched him reach the next stage of the argument.

'But if you can do that, why can't you stop the war entirely? History's been mucked about so much, who knows what's true and what's false? And who cares, anyway? Six years of war. Everything from the Holocaust to Hiroshima, with Dresden along the way. Stop the war now, before any of those things.' Chris had that faraway look, that dangerous innocence.

'Chris, I have been doing this sort of thing for a long time. Believe it or not, I have occasionally considered my responsibilities. It has dawned on me that my actions have implications and ramifications. I am aware that I'm treading a slippery slope. I'm afraid that this isn't a school debating society, this is a war, so you'll have to take my word that there are certain standards of behaviour that we are expected to follow. All we are concerned with here is tracking down Hartung and finding out what he has built. We have to redress the balance, not tip it over. Trust me,' the Doctor insisted.

'Just follow your orders?'

'Just fight for what's just,' the Doctor said, smiling

179

sweetly. Chris nodded, thoughtfully. Steinmann was stepping back towards them.

The staff car arrived at Paddington at a quarter to eight, driving past the empty taxi rank to the small police hut. Roz noted with approval that the police presence here had been stepped up, two men on every door, watching the crowds. They got out of the car, Reed identifying them to the constable who came out to greet them. The policeman led the pair downstairs, past the echoing ticket hall.

'The male prisoner's in the manager's office, ma'am. You'll want to see him first, I take it?' Roz found it gratifying that the constable accepted her authority without question, and confirmed that they were only interested in the man. They walked over to the glass-panelled door, which opened as they arrived. A tall blond male stepped out, bursting into a run as he saw them approach. Reed moved to block him, but the larger man shouldered him out of the way and charged down the escalator, pushing passengers out of the way. Reed recovered quickly, but seemed dazed.

'After him, George! I'll follow in a second,' Roz yelled. Reed nodded, drawing his revolver. The constable who had brought them down followed the lieutenant. There was screaming from passengers on the escalator. Roz was already checking her ammunition, confirming that her gun was fully loaded. When that was done, she poked her head around the office door. Three policemen were picking themselves off the floor. One of them had a broken nose.

'I'm Captain Forrester, from the War Office. Who's in command?'

'I am, I'm Sergeant Hood. I'm in charge.'

Roz flashed her identity card. 'Wrong, Sergeant: I'm in charge. I want all the exists sealed off, I want the trains stopped. I'm right that none of you is armed?' They nodded, a little too bewildered for her liking. 'Okay. He's gone underground, not tried to get to the street. I want the police to evacuate the civilians from the station, and

180

I want them to be damn sure that they don't accidentally evacuate our target. Check every single man, woman and child.' One of the constables left to co-ordinate the evacuation.

'Where's the female prisoner?'

'She's with a couple of men from Five, sir . . . I mean ma'am,' piped up the man with a broken nose.

'Are you in a fit state to take a message?'

'Yes, ma'am.'

'Good man. You get her out of here and into a locked cell.'

'Yes, ma'am.' He scurried off.

The remaining policeman, Sergeant Hood, looked pained. 'Ma'am, do we have to stop the trains?'

Roz glared at him. 'No, Sergeant, we could let the target commute all over London. Do me a favour and stop them.'

The sergeant was already on the phone.

'When you've finished, call up reinforcements from the MPs. I'm going after the target.' The gun was in her hand; she'd already released the safety catch. Forrester left the office. She had only glimpsed the target, but had a good picture of him. He'd stand out in a crowd: he was tall, broad, blond. He looked like a Nazi. He had on a dark-blue blazer, with a badge on the pocket – a yachting club, or perhaps it was regimental. Beneath that he was wearing a pristine white shirt. He wore fawn slacks.

He'd gone down the escalator heading towards the Bakerloo Line. Forrester stepped on to the same escalator, standing still, letting it carry her down. There would be plenty of time later for running around. The target probably wasn't running, he'd only draw attention to himself doing that. Her adrenalin was there already. After twenty years as an Adjudicator, you might have thought that its effect would have lessened, but as always her senses had sharpened, and she was hyper-aware of her surroundings. The breeze that always ran through the Underground tunnels wafted up from below, tickling her face and stockinged legs. She could hear every sound, smell every scent. A steady stream of passengers was being led up the escalators by the police. Forrester scanned the crowd for her target but, as she suspected, he wasn't there.

She stepped from the escalator as it reached the bottom. Two directions, two identical tiled corridors. If he was right-handed and combat-trained, the target would instinctively head right. If he was human, he'd fight against the instinct and go left. She headed left. Roz began jogging along the corridor, gun held high. As she ran, she was drawing a mental map of the station, filling in her danger zones. This was going to be tricky: no hand-held communications, no bio-sensors, no surveillance cameras. On the plus side, there weren't any holographic decoys or transmat points, and the target was as blind as she was. The corridors were brightly lit: there wasn't much cover. Was the target armed? She presumed not – however lax the police search, they'd have found a firearm, and he wouldn't have had an opportunity to grab a gun from anyone except her and George. He might have a hostage. She doubted it, though: he was quite capable of getting away without a bargaining chip. This was a man capable of overpowering three policeman with his bare hands.

There were no maintenance hatches on the ceiling. There were a couple of access points on the floor, but they clearly hadn't been disturbed for a hundred years, let alone during the last five minutes. As you'd expect, the floor was covered in oily footprints of all shapes and sizes. Roz reached the end of the corridor. Pause. Check behind. Nothing. Look left, cover left. Nothing. Look right, cover right. Nothing. Choose. The sign says northbound or southbound. Head south. Right.

Roz checked her watch. It wasn't even ten to eight, yet. The target had been loose for three minutes, maximum. If he was making contact with a known London spy, it was probably because he wasn't familiar with the city, and needed help. If he wasn't used to London, he wouldn't know his way around Paddington station. He was running around looking for an exit, not heading for an exit he knew about. Her subconscious added a warning: that's a supposition, Forrester, not a fact. Care to stake your life on it?

To the left there was a door. Staff Only. She kicked it open, checking behind her. Stairs, spiralling up, the crashing of the door reverberating upwards. Check this level first. Nothing. Close the door behind her. Clear. Forrester mounted the first step, peering up. It was darker here and there wasn't a breeze. She clasped her revolver in both hands, held high, close to her head. Back against the wall. The staff used this to get around, so it must lead up to the surface, or perhaps the ticket hall. Maybe even to the main train station. If the target had found this door, he'd have found it ideal.

Footsteps above.

Tense, Roz listened. Footsteps coming down. Glimpse of fawn trouser leg. Roz swung her arms, clasped together around the butt of the revolver like a club, hitting him hard where it hurt. Target down. Aim.

The train driver with the gun at his temple whimpered something. Roz relaxed, but not much. This man was not the target: he was ten years too old and a foot and a half too short. She was already heading up the stairs before he managed to shout a complaint. So the station hadn't been fully evacuated. Had the target come this way? Damn, there was an easy way to find out which she'd managed to overlook. She headed back downstairs. The driver had struggled to his feet.

'You,' she demanded, 'did anyone come up past you?'

The driver shook his head, clearly terrified.

'OK. Where does that lead?' She pointed upwards.

'U-up to the ticket hall.'

'Not up to the main station?'

'No.'

'Good. Get up there, and tell Sergeant Hood that I want a policeman on the exit.'

The driver nodded and scrambled upstairs. Forrester stepped back down. The door was still closed, but she double-checked that no one else had come through. Then she eased open the door. Footsteps, running up the corridor towards her. Someone coming around the corner. Forrester levelled her gun, taking careful aim. A shape came hurtling round.

'Freeze!' she yelled. It was the target, and he didn't even hesitate. Neither did she. Forrester fired once, missed, the bullet shattering the tiling at the end of the corridor and ricocheted off. The target didn't break his stride until he reached her, and he grabbed her right wrist and slammed it against the wall. And again. Roz's grip on the revolver loosened and it clattered to the floor. The target bent down, moving for the gun, so Forrester kicked him very hard on the small of his back. He sprawled, but recovered quickly, rolling over onto his front. Forrester kicked the gun away from his reach, then crunched her heel on his hand, before stepping back. He didn't make a sound, but effortlessly pulled himself upright. Roz hit him very hard in the stomach. And again. He didn't flinch. Roz had been an Adjudicator for over twenty years, but until that moment had assumed that things like that only happened in the movies. Was this man human? She hesitated for a fraction of a second, unsure how to carry on. The target took full advantage of the lull, and delivered a savage blow just below her ribs. Roz tried very hard not to flinch, but couldn't stop herself from doubling up. She tried very hard not to cry out, but couldn't stop herself from yelping. She tried very hard to breathe, and found she couldn't manage that, either.

The gun. Roz dived for it, and succeeded in catching the target off-balance as he was about to reach it. Once again, the pistol flew from his grasp. Roz was upright. So was the target. They faced each other. He was a foot taller than her, and probably seventy pounds heavier. He was combat-trained. He was also over-confident. He under-estimated her, even though she was still standing. Roz realized that at some point in the last five seconds she had started breathing again. Reed and any other police or soldiers down here would have heard the shot. They'd be coming. Time was on her side. Amazingly, he straightened up, relaxing.

'Go on, you little black witch. Give it your best shot.'

'Are you sure?' Roz kept him talking while she worked on her strategy.

'One free punch. Show me what you're made of.' He oozed confidence. Who could blame him? Her arm loose against her side, Roz squeezed the first and index fingers of her right hand together, folding the other two fingers back. Her thumb held them flat against her palm.

'Are you absolutely sure?'

'You can't harm me, little nigger girl.'

Roz thrust her hand up to his face, her outstretched fingers thrusting straight into the target's right eye. She felt the jelly of his eyeball give way, she felt the retina detach beneath her fingertips, she felt droplets of blood splash against the back of her hand as his eyelid ripped. While he sank to the floor, screaming, clutching his face, she recovered the gun and placed it at the back of his head. Footsteps behind. Reed's voice. Followed by other policemen.

'That was only my second-best shot, sport.' Roz cocked the revolver. 'Care to try my best?'

'I've got him covered, Roz. Well done.' Reed was behind her. In front of her, a dozen Military Police and regular soldiers were edging forward, pistols and rifles aimed at the huge fallen figure. Roz stepped back, holstering her gun, wiping her fingers on her skirt.

The adrenalin kept on flowing.

'What's your name?' Reed was asking.

'I am Standartenführer Wolff, J.' He gave his serial number, then fell silent. Reed obviously recognized the name.

'You know him?' Roz asked.

'Joachim here is notorious. Try asking one of the French exiles about him.' One of the policemen had produced handcuffs, and was securing Wolff's hands behind his back. The huge man was offering no resistance. His right eye was a mess.

They led him away.

Interlude II

The flash powder ignited, the camera clicked.

Mel blinked a couple of times, but when she opened her eyes again, there was still a red after-image. They were standing just away from the pit lane, racing cars roaring past them on a practice run. The photographer, Jarvis, had wanted a picture of her with Emil, and they were happy to oblige. Jarvis asked Mel her name, then scurried off to find something else to photograph. Emil was laughing. 'You'll be a star, tomorrow – assuming the car starts.'

'The Doctor will find a way,' Mel assured him. They walked back over to the garage, where the Doctor was fiddling underneath the bonnet of Hartung's racing car.

'Try it now,' he suggested.

Emil did so and the car revved into life.

'You are a genius, Herr Doktor. My engineers just couldn't find the fault.' He grabbed the little man firmly by the hand.

'Well, yes, I am a genius,' the Doctor admitted modestly, wiping the oil from his hands, 'but I only started the car, you built it. It's a magnificent machine.'

'If you excuse me, Doktor, I have to put in a couple of practice laps.' Emil kissed Mel on the cheek and jumped into his car, which had been chugging quietly away to itself all this time. Emil dropped the handbrake and shot away.

'It doesn't look very safe. He's not even wearing a proper helmet.'

'It isn't. Dozens of drivers die every year. The sport is still pretty amateur, and there's certainly no regard for personal safety.'

Mel shot him an angry look; it wasn't what she wanted to hear.

'Relax, Mel. I've modified the brakes, improved the steering and reinforced the chassis a little. He might also find that his car has a little more pep than normal.'

'Isn't this interfering in history?' Mel asked as she watched the huge vehicle power off around the track, effortlessly passing his opponents.

'No.' The Doctor was still grinning broadly. 'I know for a fact that Emil Hartung wins the Cairo 500 tomorrow, and he couldn't very well do that unless his car started.' He winked conspiratorially.

11

Peace In Our Time

They were alone together in the manager's office at Paddington. George Reed had just finished phoning his report through to the SID.

He wrapped his arms around Roz, and they held each other. Roz's heartbeat might have slowed, but her eyes were full of fire and she remained poised, ready to pounce. It had been twenty minutes since Wolff was led away, but she still hadn't calmed down. He caught just a hint of her scent, the same jungle musk as the night before. He leant over, kissing her softly on the nape of the neck, where she liked it.

Last night her ebony skin had been invisible in the darkness. After they had finished their brandy, Roz had held his hand and led Reed to his own bed. Unable to see her, he had traced an elaborate tactile map of her body with his fingertips as they lay alongside each other. In turn, Roz had done the same, caressing him with long black fingers, exploring him. They had talked, and that had been just as intimate. He'd listened to her low, sonorous voice, uncovered some of her secrets, learnt about her family and their expectations. How she was a disappointment to them, and to herself. They talked of empires and wars and making history. All the time they had pressed themselves as close together as they could be, never wanting to lose each other. At last they had exhausted themselves mentally and physically and they fell asleep curled around one another.

They'd made a difference this morning. So much of this war had been fought at a distance. Not for centuries had generals led their troops into battle, except in stories; Reed knew that. Even in the last war, though, they had been forced to ride through the blasted wastelands and ruined towns of France. Reed had been to Granville with his family as a young man. He remembered the bullet-riddled buildings, all that levelled ground. You couldn't see those details on aerial photographs. You couldn't see the people picking through the wreckage. War became a comparison of casualty statistics, a list of dead men's names.

Just one look at Wolff's face, though, was enough to remind a soldier that they were fighting evil, hate-filled men. Men that had to be destroyed, whatever the cost. He still didn't agree with the Cabinet's decision, but he understood now why it had to be made.

Reed stood straighter, becoming more formal. Roz did the same, and now they were soldiers again, not lovers. 'Kendrick says that there's no point us going in this morning,' he reported. 'There are hardly any photographs from Granville, because of the fog. Initial estimates put the dead at fifteen hundred; we know the airfield there was completely wiped out. That's all they really need to know. It's going to take a couple of hours to clean up Wolff's eye. He expects us back at midday. I think he's guilty about getting us out of bed.'

Roz raised an eyebrow. 'He knows about us?'

'Heavens, no. I meant that he woke us up this morning.' Reed stepped back, releasing his hold on her. He had been caught off-guard. 'I would never tell anyone. Your reputation is safe with me.'

She smiled. 'George, I'm from a different civilization, one that's more open about sex.'

He blushed at the word. 'Well, here, we're not. People here aren't meant to do ... what we did last night until after they're married.'

'Look, that wasn't your first time, was it?' Roz rested her hand on her hip, shifting her weight onto the other foot. Whether she realized it or not, George found her posture more arousing than indignant.

'N-no,' he admitted, not wanting to think about anyone else. As Reed spoke, Roz reached into her pocket for her packet of cigarettes. She handed him one and took one for herself. Reed found his lighter and lit them.

Roz inhaled before speaking. 'Thought not. And it wasn't mine. We don't need anyone else to tell us that last night was special. Some people wait until they are married, and perhaps they gain something from waiting.' She exhaled a column of rich grey smoke. 'I can respect that. We've made a different decision – I don't regret it, I don't think you do either. Let's not pretend otherwise.'

'You are right, of course. I certainly don't regret it.' Reed laughed nervously.

'You're like me, George. I can be a team player, but I guard my privacy, too. I'm not normally an intimate person. With you, I am. I don't know why: I usually go for older men – or so I've been told – and you're young enough to be my son. Goddess, you are almost young enough to be *Cwej*. Let's not ruin it by trying to explain why.'

'Roz,' Reed began, stubbing out his cigarette, 'does this mean that I can tell Kendrick about us after all?'

Roz clearly found the prospect as daunting as he did. 'If the subject comes up in conversation,' she deadpanned.

George had decided. He knelt down, awkwardly. 'Is there something wrong with your knee, George?' Roz said. 'It had better be your knee,' she muttered to herself.

Reed looked up at her. She towered over him, an expression of concern on her lined face. 'Roz, I know you told me that you would bite my nose off – after what you did to Wolff this morning, I believe that you might literally do that – but will you marry me? Not for anyone else's sake. Just for ours.'

And to his intense relief, she broke into a wide smile.

'One thousand, four hundred and fifty dead. The figure would have been a great deal higher without your help.'

'I doubt it,' the Doctor said. He was distracted by the piece of paper Steinmann had handed him. He passed it on to Chris, who saw that it was a preliminary report listing the names of German officers who had died. Over thirty in total. Hartung wasn't on the list. Did he count as a civilian? Was he a casualty? Had he even been here? There was no mention of the Gerards. Chris had already realized that he couldn't ask Steinmann directly about Monsieur Gerard and Monique without implicating them.

'The town wasn't prepared. We've learnt our lesson the hard way.'

They were sitting on what had once been a pavement, outside what had once been a café. They drank coffee wearing tin hats, surrounded by ruined shops, schools and churches. They rested their cups on a makeshift 'table', the Doctor's briefcase resting on a tripod of breeze blocks. It was nearly dusk, now. The rescue teams had unearthed all the survivors and cleared the cellars of roasted corpses. Now the team members, men and women, army and civilians, sat in the pale early evening sun, eating their dinner. Everything was covered in a thin powder of grey dust – concrete dust, probably. Steinmann seemed ten years older than when they had first met. He looked like a tired old man.

'Why?' Steinmann asked, gesturing around.

'To end the war,' the Doctor said simply. 'They are fighting for peace. Murdering and destroying to protect their most deeply held principles. Spending every penny on bombs and bullets so that their people can be prosperous. Like your people.'

Steinmann sipped at his coffee. 'My people don't . . .' he began, but couldn't finish the sentence. His eyes were watering. 'We are fighting for what we believe in,' he concluded finally.

'Yes. So are the British and so am I. If you fight, though, people get hurt. People die.'

'Hartung's discoveries will minimize casualties. What he has built is so terrifying that it will end war for ever,' the German officer stated. The Doctor snorted derisively.

'Herr Steinmann,' began Chris gently, 'you fought in the last war. You rose through the ranks from a conscripted private, ending up as a Leutnant. An impressive achievement by any standard. Do you know what the British called that war?'

' "The War to End All Wars",' Steinmann noted. The Doctor was nodding approvingly.

'The English thought that their Civil War was the same, that the Napoleonic War had settled things once and for all. Bismarck felt that there would never be a European war again. So did Chamberlain. No matter how terrible the weapon, it will be used, no matter how terrible the consequences will be, wars start,' the little man said.

'This is different. One demonstration is all that is needed. Once the British have seen our capability, they will surrender.' Steinmann glanced at his watch. 'There is only one way to convince you Doctor, and that is to show you. We shall leave at once.'

Steinmann stood. Chris looked at the Doctor, who was picking up his briefcase.

Wolff sat silently, handcuffed to the chair, head down.

Roz watched him from the darkened room behind the concealed mirror. Kendrick stood to one side of her, concentrating on his captive's expression. George Reed, her . . . whatever the word was for *possible fiancé*, had just entered the room, carrying a file. She was surprised how much she'd missed him. They'd bought an engagement ring on the way back to his flat, on the strict understanding that she hadn't accepted yet. Roz had tried it on in the shop, and held the emerald up to the light. The little Jewish goldsmith had smiled a knowing smile. Reed had bought the ring, and Roz chose to wear it on the way home, to see if it suited her. She was still wearing it.

'It's definitely him?' Kendrick asked.

Reed held out a photograph from the file. 'It's him.'

Roz only needed to glance at the picture for confirmation. None of them had doubted it.

Roz stubbed out her cigarette. 'How do we proceed?'

Kendrick hadn't taken his eyes off the prisoner. 'Joachim Wolff is an evil man. He killed two hundred at Mallesan, gave the orders to have them rounded up in a church and machine-gunned. Apparently, he did something similar in Guernsey four days ago. I want every last piece of knowledge he has. I want him to confess to every single one of his sins. Captain Forrester, he deserved to have his eye removed.'

The prisoner slowly looked up, staring straight at them for a moment. What remained of his right eye was covered with a simple felt eyepatch. Roz hadn't realized that they couldn't regrow eyes in the twentieth century. She didn't feel sorry for him. He couldn't see them, of course, he didn't know they were there, but all three shuddered.

'I didn't remove his eye, I just poked it very hard with my fingernail. If I'd wanted to remove it, I'd have used my thumb, in the corner of the eye.'

'When did he arrive in London?' Reed asked, not wanting to continue that particular line of conversation.

'We don't know. The first sign of him was at Paddington. We have reliable reports that he was personally responsible for the elimination of the Tomato network. So he was still in Guernsey on the fourth. Why's he here?'

'Guernsey? He's connected with Hartung?'

'He's connected with Hartung. He knows everything about the superbomber.' Kendrick held up a sheaf of papers. 'The police found these on the woman he made contact with. Raid analysis from the night of March the first. The night the superbomber was used. She was going to pass them on to him. Any idea why she couldn't just radio the information across?'

Roz had already wondered about that. 'No. How did he get to London?'

'We have no idea. As far as we know, he simply materialized on Paddington station at eight o'clock this morning.'

'Sir, they could have perfected the Gruber-Schneider Devic–' Kendrick silenced Reed with a glare.

'Hartung has nothing to do with that. Fergus says they are still over three years away from a prototype. We'll worry about that little problem when we get to it. This is something quite different.' Kendrick returned to his scrutiny of the prisoner.

Reed nodded, but was clearly frustrated. Roz knew better than to enquire. A state secret, one for another day. 'Well, how did he get through? You can't just boat in, jump on a train and get off in London.'

'He could have flown in,' Roz suggested.

Kendrick shook his head. 'Last night was quiet over London. If he had flown in we'd have picked it up on radar.' The admiral straightened. 'I'll begin the questioning. Reed, accompany me. I think Captain Forrester's presence might be counter-productive. Keep watch, please, Captain.'

Roz nodded. The two men made their way round into the cell. Wolff pulled himself to attention as they came into the room. Roz plugged in her headphones and switched on the intercom and tape-recorder. Wolff gave his name and his rank. He was a Protestant, a member of the Nazi party – not a huge surprise – and had no special medical requirements. The interrogation was taking place in German, and although Roz could understand it, Reed was clearly having difficulties. She smiled to herself.

'How is your eye?' Kendrick asked.

Wolff didn't answer him. Kendrick began to speak, but Wolff interrupted. 'What is the time, please?'

'It is four o'clock on the afternoon of March the sixth.'

'You are Admiral Arthur Kendrick of the Scientific Intelligence Division. You have a direct telephone link to the War Cabinet, and to the Prime Minister himself.'

Kendrick nodded.

'I wish to make a statement. You will wish to relay it to Downing Street.'

Kendrick relaxed ever so slightly. 'I make no promise about that. Go ahead.'

'I am Standartenführer Joachim Wolff, assigned to the Luftwaffe zbV. I am speaking on behalf of certain senior elements of the German government and the military. When you hear my message, you will understand why this statement has not come through the normal channels. If asked, the German authorities will deny my existence.

'My statement is this: "It is a tragedy that the Germans and the British, Aryan blood brothers, are fighting one another. Far too many brave men have died on both sides, and the conflict can only escalate. We have a common enemy: the scale of the Bolshevik threat posed by Russia cannot be overstated. The Reich is willing to sign a treaty with the United Kingdom immediately to end hostilities. The British will be allowed a free hand in the control of their empire. Likewise, all the territories and colonies lost to Germany under the terms of the Versailles Treaty will be returned. Neither side would surrender, or offer reparations and neither side would meddle in the internal affairs of the other. Naval, air and military power would be regulated by a series of treaties. Exact levels would be decided later, but would not be unfavourable to the British. In the event of a Russian attack on German- or British-held territories, the other country would come to immediate military assistance. These are the major points. There are some minor details: Iraq must be evacuated; France would become a demilitarized area; the British must conclude an armistice with Italy." '

Kendrick sat back, astonished by this. It was a little while before he spoke. 'As you say, Herr Wolff, this is not exactly the proper diplomatic channel –'

Reed interrupted his superior. 'Mr Wolff, if you intended to deliver a message to the authorities, why did you attempt to escape from the police when they arrested you?'

'The police would not listen. Even if they had, they would not have the access to the Cabinet that the admiral here does.'

Kendrick straightened. 'Your claims are . . . wide-ranging. Why on Earth should we believe them?'

'The balance of power has been tipped, Admiral. The Germans are now in a position to win this war.'

'With what Hartung has built? Hugin and Munin?'

'If you know of them, you know the truth of my words. Several weeks ago, certain documents were leaked to you: selected blueprints of Hartung's device. Now, you only have incomplete plans of the propulsion system, but will know from them that the technology involved is many years in advance of yours.'

'We can fight it,' George piped up.

'No, Herr Reed, you can't. The Reich expected this response. The offer remains open for another twenty-four hours. At six o'clock this evening we shall use Hartung's weapon on one of the cities on your south coast. That city shall be systematically wiped out. Your analysis of the attack tomorrow morning will conclude that something new and dreadful was used. Something that no amount of forewarning, preparation or defensive action could stop.' Was he talking about a *nuke*? Forrester wondered. She quickly rejected the idea. It would be a 'new and dreadful' weapon all right, but nuclear weapons weren't exactly 'systematic'. And why pick a target on the south coast? – however primitive their understanding of atomic theory, they'd know about fall-out.

Kendrick was already standing. he stared straight through the mirror at Forrester. 'Get me Downing Street!'

Roz picked up the handset and got through just as Kendrick arrived in the room. He grabbed the handset from her. 'This is Kendrick. Cromwell. Repeat, Cromwell.' He replaced the receiver. Kendrick had just warned the Cabinet that Britain was about to be invaded.

'He wasn't lying, was he, sir?'

'He's over-confident.'

'But was he lying?'

Kendrick looked her straight in the eye. 'No.'

'Doctor. I've just thought of something.'

'Go on.' They were sitting in the back of a Mercedes, heading for the secret airbase. Steinmann's car was in front of them. Chris shifted slightly to face the Doctor.

'You said that according to the history books, Stein-mann doesn't die for years and years.'

'True.' Behind the Doctor's head the countryside slid past.

'What happens to Hartung?' Chris whispered.

'Hartung is a shadowy, mysterious figure. Once he retires from racing, in '36, he becomes a recluse. There are no photos of him after the Cairo race, his last public appearance. He never married. He dedicated himself to the Reich,' the Doctor said quietly.

'When did he die?'

The Doctor tried to scratch his head, but his hat got in the way. 'That's a mystery that's never solved. A secret buried deep in the Reich's archives. The information only ever appeared on a single sheet of paper. At the end of the war, that scrap of paper was taken to the Kremlin along with every other piece of information about Emil Hartung and his project: every surviving blueprint, note-book and diary. The documents were sealed in the deep-est, darkest vault in the Soviet Union and sat there untouched for almost forty years. In September 1984 the vault was opened on the direct orders of Konstantin Cher-nenko. Certain technological developments coming to light in the United States worried the Soviets. Their own scientists couldn't match recent American discoveries. You can't have an arms race if there's only one runner.' The Doctor grinned, removing his hat and scratching his head. 'Hartung's work was in the same area. The vault was unlocked, the bolts were drawn back. The heavy door swung open for the first time in thirty-nine years. It was empty. Unable to match America in this and other areas, the Soviet Union collapsed soon afterwards.' The Doctor kept his expression neutral as he unfolded a scrap of yellowing paper. He pretended to read it. 'Hartung dies in March 1941.'

Chris nodded. 'We kill him.'

The Doctor's expression was grim as he replaced his hat. 'We finish this. Tonight.'

'It's alien, isn't it? Whatever's in those hangars?' Chris offered.

'In your terms,' the Doctor said softly.

'A crashed spacecraft? He's using alien technology from a UFO that made planetfall in Germany. Or perhaps one that has been buried here in France for centuries that they've only just uncovered. The Nazis found the ship, they set their top scientist to work analysing it. They've organized a massive cover-up. Now he's built something centuries in advance of what they should have here and they've been testing it. Something big.'

The Doctor pointed ahead. They had arrived at the main gate of the secret airbase. 'The truth is in there.'

They stepped from the car. The guards searched them, but found nothing. Finally, they were ushered through the main gate. Steinmann was waiting for them.

'Is Hartung here?' asked Christ.

'I promised to show you what we are building,' said Steinmann non-committally. They had walked past the concrete cows, past the concrete pine trees, down the green tarmac of the runway. They reached one of the long, almost square, hills. Chris saw now that one end of this barrow was flat, a wide corrugated metal door, painted to look like grass. This door was edging open. Inside, neon lights were flickering on. The Doctor was consulting his watch. As the door inched open, Chris saw a word painted onto the concrete floor inside the hanger, thick white letters like road markings.

MUNIN

'The Norse for "Memory",' noted the Doctor thoughtfully.

Chris guessed that Munin was sixty feet long, and that its wingspan was just under twice that. The main fuselage was simply the shape of a cigar tube. The wings were flat, narrow, isosceles triangles mounted halfway along the length. Most striking was the colour, a mottled blue/grey/black, lighter underneath than on top. The cockpit canopy was lozenge-shaped, and coated in gold film. It was impossible to see into the cockpit itself. Although it was advanced for the time there was nothing alien about it.

A handful of technicians scurried around the plane. Rusty orange scaffolding encased one side of the fuselage and technicians were inspecting the exposed fuel system. Steinmann dismissed them, and they marched from the hangar. The three men were alone together, now.

'It's just an aircraft!' Chris exclaimed. 'An ordinary aircraft. It looks a bit like a U2 spy plane.'

'The first U2 was unveiled at Groom Lake, Nevada on July fourteenth 1955. Fourteen years from now. This plane is similar,' noted the Doctor. He sounded almost relieved.

'Look where they've put the engine,' Chris said. The plane had a single jet engine, running straight along the top of the fuselage.

'Fascinating!' the Doctor exclaimed. 'I had expected that the planes would be of a flying wing design, with the engines mounted above the wing. This dorsal-mounted engine would be impossible to detect using ground-based radar.'

'There is another type?' enquired Steinmann.

'No,' the Doctor assured him quickly, 'but that's the key, isn't it? This plane is invisible.'

'That thing's got a shroud?' Chris snorted. Munin was anything but invisible. Theoretically it was possible to bend light waves around an object, but the technology required was almost impossible to maintain, even in Chris's time. It required knowledge of force fields, gravitronics, computer management systems and lasers. It was incredibly energy intensive. If Hartung could build force fields and lasers, why bother with making his plane invisible? He could make it invulnerable instead – that would be a weapon worth having. The Doctor was shaking his head.

'Have a closer look,' the German invited. The Doctor stepped forward, reaching up as high as he could and brushing his hand along the nosecone. Chris followed his example. The surface was irregular, uneven. Tiny little pyramids of black rubber covered the plane. The surface had then been coated in some rough paint.

'Munin is covered in a revolutionary new carbon foam,' Steinmann announced.

'It acts as a Jaumann absorber,' the Doctor remarked, poking it experimentally.

Chris struggled to remember what the jargon meant. 'You've lined the walls of your hangar with it, too,' he noted, not wanting to be left out.

'Very observant. As well as absorbing light and radar energy, the material makes almost perfect soundproofing.'

'Hartung has built the first radar-invisible plane. A stealth bomber.'

Chris looked again. It certainly had primitive stealth characteristics. The plane had no sharp edges: the wing surfaces and tips were rounded, the tail was almost pear-shaped. The plane's outer surface was free of any scoops or ridges. The air intakes were as small as they could be and there were no protruding antennae. There was virtually nothing to bounce a radar beam off: no breaks in the skin, no right angles, no wing fences. He hadn't seen the back of the plane yet, but he imagined that the heat emissions were controlled in some way.

'Not just radar-invisible, Doktor. Look closer.' Steinmann indicated the side of the plane.

The Doctor peered up. 'Yehudi lights!'

'I beg your pardon?' Steinmann said. Chris was puzzled too, and the Doctor was only too happy to explain.

'That's what the Americans call them. They would normally be used to light up engine intakes and other places where shadows build up, but here they are arranged all over the surface of the plane. The exact colour of a camouflaged plane isn't that important, believe it or not, it's all to do with its shape and the way light falls on it. The human mind can be tricked into thinking that a flying object isn't a plane if it is lit in an unusual way and makes the silhouette look odd. Remarkable.'

Chris wasn't impressed. 'It's not terribly advanced, is it?'

The Doctor had that faraway look again. 'Ten years ago aeroplanes were built out of balsa wood and canvas. Any plane in production now could outperform them.'

Chris could easily have tracked Munin using a gravity displacement sensor, or a mass detector. Hartung, of course, wouldn't even suspect that such equipment existed. In twenty years' time, any reasonably competent operator could have spotted the plane using radar, but Munin was certainly stealthy enough to slip past the primitive radar they had in 1941. In a war where everyone was using state-of-the-art technology, being only a couple of years more advanced than your enemy made all the difference. Some Adjudicator instinct buzzed a warning.

'How long does it take to design and build a plane like this?' he found himself asking.

Steinmann was only too happy to tell him. 'First, we work out what sort of planes we need. We work out the exact operational requirements: how many pilots it will have, how fast it will fly, the range of the plane, its rate of climb, its service ceiling, its bomb load, its armament –'

'We get the message,' the Doctor said distractedly. He had wandered over to the exposed flank of the plane and was toying with his abacus. Despite the Doctor's indifference, Chris had a hunch that he was on to something and was interested in what Steinmann had to say.

'It usually takes six months to draw up the exact specification for a large aircraft like this. We send out the requirements to the various aviation companies for competitive tender. The companies work out whether they can build the plane, how long it would take if they did, and they tell us what the unit cost would be. Nine or ten months later, the Luftwaffe decide which company has put in the best bid.'

There was a new sound, a *clack* coming from the inspection platform. Chris saw the Doctor up there, opening up his briefcase. The Doctor retrieved large sheaves of paper from it: blueprints. He struggled with them for a moment,

201

trying to unfold them. Steinmann was still speaking. 'Then comes the hard part: the prototype. It took over two and a half years to build Hugin and her sister Munin, here. A whole host of problems had to be solved, from perfecting the revolutionary new jet engine to working out the exact positioning of the controls.' The Nazi's voice receded as he stepped over to the Doctor. The little man had his arms wide, trying to stop the blueprints escaping from his grasp. He had even managed to tie a knot in one of the sheets. Steinmann helped to straighten out the papers. The Doctor examined them intently for a moment. Steinmann frowned, and tried to turn the plans the right way up. In the resulting struggle, a couple of the blueprints escaped, drifting down from the platform to the oily hangar floor. Steinmann gave up; instead he turned his attention back to Chris, and grasped the safety railing like a vicar at a pulpit. The sermon continued.

'Then we begin the air trials: our top pilots test the plane for its handling, performance and suitability. The trials of this magnificent plane were completed at the end of February. Air trials take about sixteen months. Then, normally, production begins on a squadron of aircraft and they are tested in action. We see how easy it will be to construct and operate the planes. Typically, this takes another two years, perhaps two and a half. Then, the Luftwaffe decide how many planes they actually need. Another year.'

Chris had been doing some mental arithmetic. Steinmann was now so far away that he felt he had to shout. 'That's about eight years in total. The British have by far the best radar technology in the world. They are – what? – two or three years ahead of the Germans. But not even the British network is that good. The Chain Home network is still being set up. You can't possibly have started building this radar-invisible plane eight years ago – there wasn't any radar back then!'

'In wartime, the need is more urgent so we cut corners. We don't ask the aircraft companies what they want to build, we tell them. We build two prototypes: a simple measure that halves the trial period. This particular aircraft is a special case, it will –'

'What's that doing there?' the Doctor grumbled, interrupting. Steinmann just smiled, and bent over to see what had caught the Doctor's eye. 'Heat sink,' he whispered. The Doctor looked up at the Nazi officer for a moment, bemused, then checked his plans. Apparently satisfied, he returned to his investigations.

Steinmann continued. 'Munin is a special case, and it will never be mass-produced. At a unit cost of three million Reichsmarks, we couldn't afford to. Not that we need many. I have calculated that five of these planes would be enough for the British invasion. They could wipe out every radar station, every airstrip and every major bridge in the south of England before the British even knew we were in the air.'

'It still doesn't add up,' objected Chris, who had joined the odd pair on the inspection platform. The Doctor had all but disappeared into the workings of the aircraft now. Chris continued. 'Hartung's a genius. A hardworking genius. You've thrown resources at him, given him everything he wants. But even working flat out on an unlimited budget you couldn't build this plane fast enough.'

'Construction took just under four and a half years. It started in November 1936. It was completed on 28 February this year. I don't understand your objection. We have managed to design and build new fighters in under three years.' Steinmann shifted uncomfortably.

'No, listen. The first ever radar test was only a couple of years ago at Daventry. That was –' Chris struggled for the date.

' – February the twenty-sixth 1935,' supplied the Doctor, who had emerged from the depths, his clothes spotless. He made a show of wiping his hands on his handkerchief.

'There you go. Over a year before Hartung began work,' Steinmann assured Chris. Cwej was not impressed.

'That wasn't when the British had radar, that was the first time that a radar echo was ever detected. It wasn't until the summer that anyone proposed a coastal network of radar stations. Britain's got its own boffins, and they worked flat out, but the first station wasn't completed until the summer of 1937. By then, even if you hadn't cut corners, you must have started to build the prototype. How can you possibly have built counter-measures before the device you are trying to counter has been built? It's like building anti-tank guns before the invention of the tank! The German government wasn't going to throw millions of marks away on a pie-in-the-sky scheme like this rubber plane in 1936. They had quite enough to spend their money on.'

'Hartung convinced them,' Steinmann said simply.

Chris was sceptical. 'How?'

'He claimed that he had been told. A vision of the future, of Nazi destiny.' He hissed the last words, like an invocation. Chris glanced over at the Doctor to check his reaction, but the little man was still deep in study.

'The Doktor has been uncharacteristically silent,' Steinmann observed coldly.

The Doctor looked up from the blueprints at the mention of his name. 'Where is Hugin?'

'In the other hangar.'

The Doctor was examining the plans again. 'In one piece?'

'Why, of course.' But his Adam's apple rose and fell ever so slightly, and his tone was just a little too defensive.

'He's lying,' concluded Chris.

'I know he is. Didn't your mother ever tell you that lying was naughty, Oberst Oskar?' Steinmann's face was a picture of indignation. The Doctor rounded on him. 'Hugin blew up just before midnight on March the first above a small cove in St Jaonnet on Guernsey. If you remember, Herr Wolff met me there the morning afterwards. I recovered a small piece.' He flicked his wrist and a twisted scrap of metal appeared in his hand. The Doctor held it up to a point on the fuselage. 'Component F-989A,' he concluded, pointing to the corresponding place on the blueprints.

'Very good. Would you care to explain why the plane exploded?'

The Doctor hesitated. 'I'm not sure about that bit.'

'No, neither are we. I thought you might know.' There were footsteps behind them. Chris turned and saw a pair of Luftwaffe pilots stepping towards them. They wore full flight suits.

'What's going on?' Chris asked. The Doctor suddenly looked worried.

Steinmann smiled. 'These officers are about to launch an attack on Southampton in Munin. The town will be razed to the ground. The British government have been informed, but will not be able to stop the attack.'

The pilots began mounting the platform. Chris looked over to the Doctor. 'I thought you were pledged to peace, Herr Steinmann,' the little man said softly. 'You saw what happened in Granville. Yet now, later the very same day, you are willing to do exactly the same.'

'We have offered peace to the British. If they choose not to accept our offer, then we shall destroy them, and have peace that way. This is a demonstration of our power.'

Chris watched helplessly as the pilots began closing up the inspection hatch. His mind was racing. 'Doctor. I've worked it out. How Hartung built it.'

The Doctor was standing back, the blueprints clenched in his hand. 'Really? Do you still think it's a UFO?'

'No, it's terrestrial, but Hartung was obviously fore-warned about radar. Someone's gone back in time and told him.' The Doctor didn't answer; instead he buried his nose in the plans. Steinmann had a gleam in his eye.

'*Der Tausendjährige Reich!*' he declared, clenching his fist.

'*Gesundheit,*' offered the Doctor.

'The tiniest piece of information,' Steinmann whispered. He grasped the Doctor's upper arms, almost lifting him into the air. 'When is the time barrier broken?' he demanded. Chris moved forward to protect the Doctor, but Steinmann had already let go of the little man. The Doctor was readjusting his collar, getting his breath back.

'How long is a piece of string?' the Doctor answered finally.

Steinmann removed his revolver from its holster, flicked off the safety catch, and levelled it at the Doctor's forehead. Chris glanced across at the pilots. They were not large men and they weren't armed, but he and the Doctor were outnumbered. Chris stepped back, not wanting to provoke anyone.

'There's nothing you can do, Doktor. Nazi scientists from the future have invented a time machine. They sent Emil Hartung a message. Vital technical information about radar: how it worked, when the British would have it, how to counter it. Not too much, but enough.'

'Is that what Hartung told you?' said the Doctor, genuinely curious.

'Hartung never confided the exact source of his information. It doesn't matter, now. You are watching history in the making, the moment of victory that Hartung promised. For over four years we have been planning this moment, and now it is complete. *Sieg Heil!*'

The pilots had completed their tasks. They joined in the salute.

'You know your mission?' Steinmann asked, not taking his eye, or aim, off the Doctor.

'Yes, Oberst Steinmann.'

'Go to it.' The pilots saluted again.

'It's not over yet. The Doctor will think of something,' Chris declared. The first pilot was mounting the steps. Steinmann shook his head.

'The Doktor? Christopher, the Doktor is dead.' He squeezed the trigger.

Click.
Click.
Click.
Click.
Click.
Click.

The Doctor smiled thinly. 'I took the precaution of removing the bullets about an hour and a half ago, while we were having coffee.'

Steinmann glanced down at the gun. It was the lapse in concentration that Chris had been waiting for. He batted the revolver from Steinmann's hand, then rounded on the two pilots. He easily swatted one over the side of the platform, grabbing the other one before he could escape. A blow to the back of the neck rendered him unconscious. Steinmann stepped back.

'What was that about inevitable Nazi victory?' asked the Doctor innocently.

'You are surrounded. There's no way that you'll get out of here.'

Chris glanced back at the hangar door. Steinmann was right: they had been lucky the last time they escaped from this base. They might not be as lucky this time.

'There's no way out,' Chris concluded.

'Never overlook the obvious,' the Doctor smiled.

Steinmann's face fell. 'You can't be suggesting . . .'

The Doctor was still smiling. 'Chris, could you fly this plane?'

'Of course.' Belatedly, Chris realized what the Doctor had just asked. 'You don't mean . . .'

'Begin pre-flight checks. We're leaving.' The Doctor patted Munin's side.

12

Planning for the Future

The Doctor slammed his palm against the large red button next to the door. Alarm bells started to ring all around him and the hangar door began edging open. He jogged back to Munin. Chris had pushed the inspection platform away from the plane, then tied Steinmann's wrists to the scaffolding with a length of hosepipe. The Nazi officer glared at the Doctor.

'You'll never get away.' Even now, Steinmann was defiant.

'Where's Hartung?' the Doctor demanded, his voice low.

'Guernsey,' Steinmann stated. The Doctor was puzzled; he hadn't expected the answer to be quite so forthcoming. However, he didn't have enough time to worry about it. He raised his hat to Steinmann and left, pulling the chocks away from underneath the plane.

Chris was strapped into the pilot's seat, a leather face-mask fastened around his chin. The Doctor dropped into the co-pilot's chair, slotting his briefcase alongside the seat.

'Why haven't you started the engine yet?' the Doctor demanded.

'It's dorsal-mounted. Both pilots have to be inside first.' The Doctor nodded thoughtfully. Chris was already sealing the canopy.

'When we arrived, I timed how long it took to open the door: we've got about ten seconds to go.'

'It's OK, I've completed the pre-flight checks: the plane is fully fuelled, the bomb bay is full.'

Chris was already flicking switches. Behind them, there was a judder and the engine didn't roar into life. A masterful display of soundproofing. The seats and instruments began rattling.

'The sound is absorbed into the fuselage, where some of it becomes kinetic energy,' observed the Doctor. 'So Munin is a bit of a boneshaker, I'm afraid.

'I think I've just bitten my tongue,' Chris mumbled. The young man released a lever and the plane began edging forward.

The Doctor was scanning the co-pilot's instrument panel. He flicked a few switches. 'Variable Illumination Grid activated.'

'Where are we heading to?'

'Hartung: he's in Guernsey. I know the way. Can I help at all?' He looked out the window. Steinmann had worked his way free and was running towards the plane.

'The co-pilot's job in this sort of plane is to navigate, keep an eye out for trouble and to drop the bombs. Sit back and enjoy the ride.'

The Doctor smiled, his teeth rattling. Chris loosened the throttle and adjusted the rudder pedals – or whatever it was that jet pilots did on these occasions; it had been so long. The plane nosed out of the hangar and began taxiing out on to the runway. A column of guards was setting up a blockade, but they had obviously been told not to shoot at the plane. As the engine began firing faster, the rattling was smoothing out to a jarring vibration.

'Are the antigrav controls back there?' asked Chris.

The Doctor shook his head. 'We're a little too early for that.'

'I'll just have to improvise, then,'

The plane lurched skywards, in a manoeuvre that violated a number of the laws of motion. The Doctor's stomachs lurched. The ground spun on some alien axis beneath them, sloshed up alongside, and then proceeded to throw itself past them at several hundred miles an hour.

'Yahoo!' Chris hollered. The Doctor would have jumped out of his seat had he not been securely strapped into it. It was a good job that he was, because Chris took it upon himself to do a loop the loop. Gravity and the horizon took a little while to settle down.

'Is the plane easy to fly?' the Doctor asked casually.

'Sure. It's just like driving that motorbike I stole.' The answer did not inspire confidence in the Doctor. Then again, he ruminated, in the twenties and early thirties the Germans had been forbidden to manufacture fighter aircraft. Many aviation companies had been forced to branch out and built motorbikes and cars instead. For many centuries afterwards the BMW logo had been a stylized propeller blade, a symbol of this heritage. Chris seemed to have an affinity with machinery, especially fast and dangerous machinery. On their travels together, Chris had often managed to gravitate towards the local flying machines, and he'd been able to fly all of them so far.

'Which way, Doctor?' Chris was asking.

The Doctor thought for a moment, making a show of peering out of the canopy. 'Dead ahead,' he declared finally.

Benny watched the Kent countryside run by, the rocking of the train lulling her into a gentle doze, despite her aching hand. The sun shone through the compartment window, warming one side of her face. It was mid-March, so it would be cooler outside. The landscape was one of rolling meadows bordered by hedgerows, gradually becoming more and more urbanized as they got closer to London. This was the early electrical age: the first few electricity pylons and telegraph lines now ran through the fields and every so often it was possible to make out a radio mast in the distance. Mostly, though, the landscape was still made up of apple orchards and fields of hops. The trees were just coming into bud; the land was renewing itself after a harsh winter.

Every so often the train would slow down and come to a stop in a tiny village. The names of the stations had all been removed, presumably to confuse any Nazi train-spotters in the event of an invasion. All the towns looked the same anyway: pretty affairs with village greens, crammed full of brick houses with large gardens and tiny corner shops. There was an air of tranquillity here, something entirely missing from Guernsey, even though the two places looked superficially similar.

'Excuse me, madam.' An inspector leant over her, wanting to see her ticket. He used the form of address reserved for married women who ought to be at home looking after the children. Trains were unofficially reserved for military use, and unnecessary civilian travel was frowned upon.

Benny reached into her pocket. 'What time is it, please?' she asked.

'Nearly five o'clock, madam. Soon be there: we're coming up to Orpington.'

She had stopped off in Canterbury, picked up money, a ration book and identity papers from the house at Allen Road. While the building looked the same as it always did, perhaps a little less overgrown, it felt so different without anyone else there. She hadn't wanted to stay, and knew that she had to get to London. She wrote a note and pinned it up on the noticeboard in the kitchen.

Dear Doctor (past or present) – It is now just before four o'clock on the afternoon of 6 March 1941. If it isn't too much trouble, please come and rescue me. (signed) Bernice Summerfield XXX.
PS: There's no milk. Please bring some with you.

He hadn't come. A quick search revealed that while one wardrobe in an otherwise bare room was full of fur coats – real dead animal fur! – and mothballs, there was no clothing stored anywhere else in the house. She had found a pair of sunglasses, which covered up the bruising around her eyes. A gold brooch and wide-buckled belt discovered in a shoebox full of electrical components softened the effect of her uniform blouse and skirt, and she'd bought a new pair of shoes in the town on the way back to the station. It had added about an hour to her travel time, but everything else was going to plan.

The inspector clipped her ticket, and handed the stub back to her. She tried to take it from him, but found it difficult to focus.

'Are you all right, madam?' He clearly thought she was drunk. If only.

The train began slowing down. Rather more disturbing, so did the inspector's voice.

There was a flash on the sea beneath them.

'Pull hard right!' blurted the Doctor. Chris did as he said, the plane banking. Almost as he did so, an artillery shell hurled past them. A second or so later, its sound caught up with it.

'German frigate.' Chris saw it now. It was quite a small vessel, but it had brought at least three anti-aircraft guns to bear. At this distance it looked like a model, surrounded by little puffs of smoke.

'They've called in reinforcements,' the Doctor noted quietly. He had been monitoring German radio transmissions. 'What I want to know is, how they can see us?'

'Transponder?' Chris wondered.

'Too early for that. It might be something similar, though. Of course . . .' The Doctor began looking around his instrument panel. 'Have you got a screwdriver?' he asked.

Chris hadn't. The Doctor began picking at the panel with his fingernails. 'There must be a test signal – if you think about it, that's the only way that the Germans could track the plane during their air trials. You can't clock the speed of a plane if you can't see it or track it on radar. The radio signal has either been left on, or they can activate it remotely. This plane isn't invisible if you know exactly where to look.'

The Doctor had prised off a piece of metal. He began

212

tugging wires out and sparking them together. 'The Americans in the 1980s and '90s used to paint their stealth planes luminous orange during test flights,' the Doctor was saying cheerily, as the acrid smell of burning wire began wafting across the cockpit. The Doctor continued. 'Ironic really – they were radar invisible, but you could see them for miles and miles.'

Another panel came away in his hands.

'Careful,' Chris warned. If he shorted out anything important, they'd be dead. The Doctor didn't hesitate, and began poking around at the wiring.

'Fly!' he ordered. 'We should be able to outrun them.'

Roz looked out of the window. It was getting dark, so it must be coming up to six o'clock. George was off on a secret mission somewhere, and she was alone in the room. They had come back from the interrogation room with a sense of fatalism. All it seemed that they could do was to wait for the German attack. The attack that was due around now.

Air-raid sirens had been sounded along the whole of the south coast, and millions of citizens were huddled in their shelters awaiting their fate. The RAF had every available plane in the air; the radar operators had been warned. The listening stations were monitoring every known military frequency. On the ground, watchers had been posted, barrage balloons had been set up. Firemen and ARP wardens stood ready. Searchlight beams swung across the evening sky, thousands of anti-aircraft batteries stood ready.

Roz didn't think it would be enough.

Steinmann sat in the control tower of the secret airbase.

Keller was scribbling down a telephone message. The young officer was on crutches, shot by Lieutenant Cwej. Steinmann snatched the sheet from him as Keller brought it over. The test signal had ceased transmission. The frig-ate Vidar reported losing visual contact with the plane shortly afterwards. No air patrols had intercepted them. The Doctor had worked it out.

Steinmann crumpled the paper and dropped it to the floor. 'The air patrols are to widen their search.'

'But, sir, they'll enter British air-space.'

Steinmann didn't answer.

Benny clambered over the bombsite. She didn't know how old she was any more. It hadn't really mattered before – if anyone asked she'd probably have lied.

Her mother had been thirty-one when she had died, and Benny was definitely older than that. A weird feeling – a child older than her mother. It was a landmark she'd passed without realizing it. She pictured her mother as a middle-aged lady, grey hair tied up into a bun, her eyes still warm and kind. It hadn't happened that way. Benny couldn't remember what colour her mother's eyes had been, not for certain, and she didn't have any photographs. With a time machine of course, it would be possible to go back and see her again, just one last hug before . . .

Benny found herself sobbing, bent double.

Everything was ruined. Underneath her hands were scraps of paper, chipped pieces of brick, what had once been a library. How could anyone bomb a library? How could anyone bomb mothers and daughters?

Above her, something loomed. False perspective, no way of judging size. Blue. Square and solid. Humming softly, as though it were living.

The rules change with time travel, don't they?

What was it they used to say a few decades from now – *you can't uninvent the Bomb*. It was the reason given for stockpiling nuclear weapons – an excuse that had held until the Southport Incident. Well, she *could* uninvent the atom bomb, assassinate all the war criminals before they did anything nasty, show the people here how to build a cheap solar cell and save the panda from extinction. Would humanity be grateful, would they use these miracles to begin a new life on a clean, safe planet? No, they'd carry on as they always had: fighting in the mud like children. A thousand years from now, they'd still be murdering and enslaving, whether they called themselves Nazis or Christians or British.

Why did the Doctor bother? These weren't even his own people. Why not just explore the wonders of the Universe, why not spend time amongst civilized, peaceful people? Why did he let humans ruin it? Why didn't he wipe us out when we first came down from the trees? Good old-fashioned problem control. Get the Doctor to put us all to sleep.

The world was closing in on her.

Guernsey was visible now, a coastline on the horizon. It had taken them longer to get there than they had expected.

'That's odd,' the Doctor said. 'I just can't find their transmissions on any of the German frequencies.'

'Has the big air-raid taken place yet?' Chris wondered aloud.

'Which air-raid?' The Doctor was puzzled.

'You know, the one that Picasso drew about. I saw the painting once on a simtour of an Overcity Seven art gallery. It looked like a transmat accident at a dairy farm.'

'You're thinking of Guernica,' the Doctor assured him. Then, suddenly, 'Bandits, twelve o'clock low.'

Half a dozen black dots were heading in their direction, over the sea.

'Steinmann must have phoned through to Guernsey,' the Doctor muttered. 'I'll try to find their frequency.'

The squadron was slow to react to them. Chris began working through his options. 'This plane isn't armed, is it?'

'No.' He hadn't thought so: the operational requirements for this plane required speed and stealth, so Hartung had kept armament and armour down to a minimum. It wouldn't be a problem: air to air combat wasn't a precise science yet, and it ought to be possible to scatter the squadron by flying straight at them. Chris increased his speed. It would take them a while to regroup. They were still on a collision course. The Hun squadron leader was determined.

'It's logic really,' the Doctor was saying. 'How can you shoot down a plane that you can't see?'

They can't see us.

The planes were one hundred feet away; they were heading towards Munin with a combined speed of a thousand miles an hour.

'They can't see us!' Chris shouted, pulling the stick hard down. If they can't see Munin, they won't dodge out of the way.

Munin pulled up, but it was too late. One of the other planes had banked down, to avoid him, catching the wing of his colleague. There was a mid-air explosion, that caught a couple of the others, and forced another down. They had been flying low over the sea, and had nowhere to go.

The Doctor was staring back; Chris kept his eye fixed on his instruments.

'They've all gone, haven't they?' Cwej asked quietly.

'All but one. That wasn't the worst of it. Chris, those planes were Spitfires.'

A young Leutnant, one that Steinmann recognized from Guernsey, was at the door. He watched the lad talk to Keller. It must be a message for him. Sure enough, the two men came over and the Leutnant saluted him.

'Oberst Steinmann, we have found a bag near the crash site. Hauptsturmführer Rosner thinks you will want to see the contents.'

He handed over two hardback books. Steinmann examined them: the titles were in English: *Diary* and *Advice for Young Ladies*. Intrigued by why Rosner would think them important, he opened up the first book.

Being the Latest Volume in The Diaries Of Professor Bernice Summerfield. If lost, please return to The House, Allen Road, Canterbury, England, Northern Hemisphere, Earth, Sol Three, the Mutter's Spiral, the

*Universe. Sorry I can't be more specific, I've forgotten
the postcode – please refer to sketch.*

The little picture underneath included a stylized map of
the solar system with big arrows pointing to Earth, a
passable line drawing of a naked man and woman, along
with various pieces of astronomical data.

Steinmann began flicking through. Summerfield's neat
handwriting filled about half the pages. Every so often an
accomplished sketch, a rough map or a diagram would
break up the text. Many pages had little sticky notes
overlaid on them – presumably Professor Summerfield
went back over her diaries regularly and ensured they
were accurate. The last thirty or so pages contained pictures of German uniforms and sketch maps of Guernsey.
Steinmann turned back through the book. Her earlier
illustrations were more fanciful: there were pictures of
trolls straight from a pantomime and sinister insect-like
war machines. There were also people, of course, but
people in a variety of bizarre costumes most of whom
carried toy guns.

He checked the other volume. This was a proper,
printed book. Codes, semaphores, call-signs. It was all
standard material for field agents – material that Summerfield ought to have destroyed before capture.

One chapter was more substantial. Steinmann began
reading at a random point.

*The British had been outflanked by the Germans in
the Pindus Mountains and were forced to withdraw.
Four days later, on 23 April, the evacuation of Greece
began.*

Steinmann chuckled, remembering the . . .

The Germans hadn't defeated the British in Greece.
They hadn't even invaded. Was this a record of the last
war? No – two pages earlier was the Fall of Tobruk,
two pages before that the invasion of Romania. At the
beginning of the chapter, the terms of the Treaty of

Versailles were recounted (along with an intriguing note in the margin: 'I did *warn* them'). The chapter was long and ended with:

> on 9 May 1945 Field Marshal Keitel and Marshal Georgi K Zhukov signed the documents of German unconditional surrender. The Reich was totally destroyed.

Steinmann hesitated. The book was obviously an ingenious fake. Propaganda. Science fiction. He turned back a dozen or so pages.

The telephone hadn't completed its first ring when Reed snatched it up. He listened for a moment, jotted down what was said and then replaced the receiver. Forrester was watching him, a worried expression on her face.

'A Spitfire squadron has just been destroyed over the Channel. Amber Three.'

Roz pointed it out on the map with a long, black finger. The patrol had been ten miles off the Isle of Wight, flying at only two thousand feet. Six aircraft.

'Do we have an estimated speed and bearing?' If she knew those, Roz could work out where it was heading and when it would get there.

'No, but it was flying at least as fast as our planes. The surviving pilot says that they were attacked by an object travelling at high speed, which only appeared at the last moment. It was within the Chain Home perimeter. So the radar operators should have been able to detect it.'

'Of course . . .' Roz breathed. Her mind raced: the first analysis made by the TARDIS computer. The one that had been rejected. The phone was ringing again.

George listened, then put the handset back. 'Radar reports massive build-up of fighters over the Channel.'

The phone started ringing again.

'Hugin and Munin. I know what they are. George, trust me.' She kissed him on the cheek, grabbed her coat, and ran out of the door. Reed had no choice but to let her go. He picked up the telephone.

'George, this is Kendrick. I'm at Downing Street. The War Cabinet have been meeting. In the face of the threat from Hartung's weapon, they feel that there is no choice.'

'We're accepting the German offer?' Reed frowned.

'No, George. We attack Guernsey tonight. If the bomber wasn't at Granville, it must be there. The attack will be concentrated on military targets. Bomber Command will require our latest report, along with photos. Take them over. They want to be in the air as soon as possible.'

George thought about the order, then, 'No, sir. There must be another way.'

'Lieutenant, you have had over a week to think of one. The decision was not an easy one to make. Obey the order, George.'

'No, sir, I can't. You'll have to find something else.' Reed replaced the handset gently.

Next door, Lynch's phone started to ring.

The low hum of the TARDIS: a sound she hadn't heard for along time. For the first time in three months, Benny had an incentive to open her eyes. She was in the brightly lit medical room, lying on the bed. Some exotic piece of medical hardware sat next to her, warbling away to itself. A tabby cat was sitting on one of the stools. It looked up from whatever it was doing.

'Wolsey? Did you drag me in here?' Benny drawled woozily. Wolsey hopped over to the bed and allowed her to stroke him.

'Typical. She thanks the cat.'

Benny peered to the source of the voice. Roz Forrester was sitting on the other stool, a portable medical scanner in her hand. She was wearing the uniform of an Earth War Two British Army captain. Her face was set in that permanent scowl of hers, but there was something different, something Benny couldn't quite put her finger on.

'You've got a rosy glow!' Benny declared finally. 'In

fact, you're looking positively radiant. I do believe that the frowning Adjudicator is actually happy.'

Roz's expression didn't change. 'I'm just pleased to see you,' she said flatly. Benny and Wolsey looked at each other conspiratorially.

'Are Buster Keaton and Buster Crabbe around?'

'Not to my knowledge,' Roz said uncomprehendingly.

'The Doctor and Chris,' Benny explained.

'They're not here either.'

Benny moved to sit up, but found it hard to work up the energy. Instead, she glanced over to the readouts of the medical unit, barely managing to focus. A number of vividly coloured lines ran along the bottom of the viewplate.

'Roz, are you sure that you've got this thing monitoring me and not the cat?'

Roz read from a printout. 'You're suffering from malnutrition, protein deficiency and what little blood you have left has a low iron content. I gave you a top-up – flooded your system with as many nutrients, vitamins and minerals as the machine would let me. That's after I pumped all the weird hallucinogens, amphetamines and relaxants out. I pumped your stomach. Benny, you were covered in bruises and welts, even a couple of minor burns – I've done what I can.' Roz glanced down to jog her memory. 'That dizziness you're feeling and that metallic taste at the back of your throat, well, you've got twice the recommended dose of painkillers and antibiotics in your bloodstream. I've reset your hand, and regrown your fingernails.' Benny looked down, waving the fingers of her right hand experimentally. They weren't even stiff. Ironic really, because every other part of her body ached.

'Anything permanent?'

Roz shook her head. 'It's too early to say. Some of the scars on your back and shoulder-blades are going to be there for a while. Are you ready to make a sitrep?'

Benny pretended that she was trying to remember. 'Space In Time Relative . . . no, I give up.'

'You know damn well what a sitrep is.'

Benny swung her legs over the side of the bed. Her bruises had gone a strange grey colour, presumably some side-effect of the medicine. She could feel a draught coming from somewhere. 'No, sorry, I seem to have forgotten all my inelegant cop jargon. Perhaps if you spoke English? A simple "What's happening, Professor?" would suffice. "Please" would be even better.'

'Bernice, I don't have time, I really do have other things to be doing. Who did this to you?'

'Nazis,' Benny said distractedly. She had just realized that the hospital gown she was wearing was backless. She didn't particularly want Cwej to see her like this. Luckily, he wasn't here. Hadn't Forrester said that? Roz was tapping her foot impatiently.

'Care to be more specific?'

'Standartenführer Joachim Wolff, Luftwaffe zbV. I forget his serial number.' Standing up and speaking at the same time required more concentration than Benny could muster.

'We've got him.' Roz clenched her fist. 'I'll kill him this time.'

'What? Here in London? We are still in London? Where's Chris? What do you mean you've got Wolff? What do you mean this time? Have you seen the Doctor? Why haven't you got time? Hang on. Er . . . sitrep?'

'The Germans have launched their invasion. We've been warned that they are about to attack a city. Hartung's invisible bomber is in the air, it's sweeping aside everything in its path and I need to know anything you –'

'What do you mean the Germans are invading? How long was I out? No, cancel those questions. The Germans didn't invade. Off the top of my head – and I'll admit I'm still a bit spaced out – the Germans never, ever invaded Britain. Ever.'

'That's an interesting theoretical standpoint to hold. It is rather undermined by the fact that they are about to wipe out a whole city with an exotic new weapon and we can't do anything about it,' Roz said impatiently.

Benny was trying to catch up. 'Hang on, a couple of sentences ago did you say "Hartung"?'

'Yes.' Roz was clearly getting restless.

'As in "HARTUNG, E."?' Benny had found her stolen skirt and blouse in a pile on the floor. She thought about wearing them, then decided not to. She picked up the Doctor's umbrella and was too busy thinking about him to hear what Roz said next.

'Emil Hartung, racing driver turned military genius. What's your point?'

'I need to see the Doctor,' Benny said, grasping the umbrella handle resolutely.

'Bernice, no offence, but if the Doctor was around, do you think that I'd be standing here talking to you?'

'No, this is serious.' Benny began hobbling towards the exit, using the umbrella for support.

'You surprise me.' Roz hurried over to Benny, draping a silk kimono over her patient's shoulders, before opening the door.

Benny was still trying to piece together what was happening as she stepped into the corridor. 'You reek of cigarettes, you know that? Roz, hang on a moment. If the Doctor's not here, where is he?'

Forrester picked up a grey holdall that had been sitting just outside the door, and slung it over her shoulder. 'I don't know. I've not seen him since March the second. The last time I saw him, he told us to keep our eyes out for anything big, then he vanished and didn't say where he was going. Look, if you're OK now, I really need to get going, the defence of the realm is at stake, and so on.'

They were in the corridor now. They were quite a way from Benny's bedroom, but one of the wardrobe rooms was just two doors down. Benny tried to remember which way.

'Us? Where *is* Chris?'

'He's gone, too. The army sent him on a suicide mission to northern France.'

'I know the feeling.' They had reached the door to the wardrobe room. Forrester pushed it open for her. Just inside was a wicker chair, and Benny took the opportunity to sit down. Roz was looking around – she almost certainly hadn't been in here before, it wasn't her sort of thing. Rows upon rows of clothes stretched out: maze-like racks of elegant dresses, exotic lingerie, daring ballgowns, frilly blouses, skirts, jackets and hats of every size, shape and colour. Every form of female attire from the sensible to the downright saucy. Benny had often wondered when this collection had been acquired and why the Doctor had the inclination to collect women's clothing from a thousand worlds. Forrester stood by the door, uninterested. Roz was clearly a woman who wasn't in touch with her feminine side.

'What are you looking for?' Roz asked.

'I thought perhaps something like Ingrid Bergman in *Casablanca*.'

'What's that mean in English?'

Benny didn't attempt to explain, just to describe: 'A tailored wool suit, dusty pink. A jacket with big square pockets and round buttons. The skirt has to be cut just beneath the knee. That's going to be the tricky bit: I doubt you've noticed this, but most of the ones in the TARDIS stores are far too short. A white cotton blouse with a' – she indicated her collar bone – 'floppy collar. A matching hat, with a broad brim. Silk stockings and cashmere scarf, both white.'

Roz nodded and set off. She would be a while, but didn't question Benny's orders, or even challenge her authority, despite all that fuss earlier about being in a hurry. Travelling with the Doctor, that sort of blind obedience would probably get her killed. Benny leant over and peeked inside Forrester's holdall.

'So that wasn't Guernsey, it was the Isle of Wight?' Chris said disbelievingly.

'Yes,' the Doctor said, shifting uncomfortably. Munin was shooting over Berkshire, now, at a little under the speed of sound.

'I thought you knew the way!'

'Well, obviously I didn't,' the Doctor said irritably.

'Do we turn around and get Hartung?'

The Doctor folded his arms and refused to speak. Chris decided to change tack. 'Doctor. There's something I've been meaning to ask: you said before that Hugin blew up.'

The Doctor seemed happy to explain. 'Yes. I heard a rumour that on March the first there had been a mysterious explosion above the bay at St Jaonnet. I sent Benny to investigate it. She retrieved a fragment, and I went with her to the crash site the next morning to examine the wreckage.'

'Where is she now?'

The Doctor consulted his watch. 'Benny is in Canterbury. We got split up, but she sent me a note to say she was safe. She's at the house in Allen Road.'

'So how did the British sabotage Hugin?'

'What?' The Doctor scowled. Something on the ground below had just caught his attention, and he was clearly annoyed to be distracted. 'The British don't know anything about Hartung's little project – that's one of the reasons I'm here. They couldn't even see it, let alone sabotage it.'

'Well, Hugin didn't blow *itself* up.'

The Doctor went very pale indeed, and scrabbled for his briefcase.

'What do I do?' said Chris, trying to remain calm. There were safer places to be than in an untested jet aircraft with a history of mysteriously exploding.

The Doctor was running his finger along a diagram of the fuel system. 'I don't know, it might be nothing. Oh no. Oh my giddy aunt. Oh, great jumping gobstoppers.'

That didn't sound promising.

'There's a design fault in the reserve fuel tank – in an effort to reduce hot emissions, a lot of the heat from the engine is dumped into the fuel. That can be done perfectly safely, as long as you can regulate the temperature of the fuel. Here, though, the temperature keeps building up, and as the tank empties, it reaches flashpoint.'

'So the plane we've stolen, and are now flying over the outskirts of London, is essentially an undetectable, very large, very fast giant bomb and there's nothing we can do about it?'

The Doctor was banging the palm of his hand against his forehead, as if he might dislodge the solution to their predicament. Finally, he looked up. 'Essentially, yes.'

Chris regarded himself as a polite person, so the volume and scatalogical precision of the expletive he shrieked out came as quite a surprise to him.

Even the Doctor blushed, and Chris apologized.

'I think I may have miscalculated,' said the Doctor, blinking.

The crosshairs appeared right between the cat's eyes, the gunsight framed his fluffy little face. Oblivious, he padded across the control room towards his basket, completely unaware that he was being tracked across the room by a trained killer.

Roz stopped pointing the stungun at Wolsey and checked the powerpack. Fully charged: enough for about a dozen shots at maximum intensity. She tucked the gun into her uniform jacket. Not even she could miss with a weapon that fired in a forty-five-degree arc. The light-weight pistol was meant for riot control; it could bring down a small crowd of gravball hooligans with a single shot. 'Stungun', of course, was something of a euphemism – the citizens of Spaceport Overcity Five had always been wary of arming their police, and much preferred them to carry 'stunguns' than 'neural paralysis inducers'. This weapon was keyed to her thumbprint, which meant that it had a rather awkward firing position. More awkward for anyone else who tried to use it. Forrester watched Benny tapping experimentally at the console.

'Are you sure that you can fly this thing?' Roz asked nervously. Every time Benny hit a button there was a disconcerting electronic squeak or buzz. They were probably already on the other side of the galaxy. Benny was dressed up now as Ingmar Knopf, or whoever. She was again wearing her sunglasses to disguise the bruising around her eyes, and looked very elegant for someone who ought to be in intensive care.

'To be honest, no. If I work out how to fly it, that'll be a bonus. I do know that the Doctor is linked to the TARDIS, somehow. I'm trying to see if the ship can home in on him. If we can't get to him, at least we'll know where he is.'

It was a good plan, in theory at least.

'Could we find Chris the same way?' Roz asked tentatively, not wanting to get her hopes up.

'I've been thinking about that. It might be possible to search northern France for someone with beppled genetic material. Damn – it's overriding me!'

Benny slammed her fist down on the console. Just as Roz was opening her mouth to speak, the scanner shutters opened and the screen flickered into life. It was a map of the south coast, running up to London. A green dot was hurtling across the image. A single word flashed red at the bottom of the screen.

INCOMING

Benny's jaw had dropped.

'It's travelling at just over seven hundred miles an hour.' That was roughly twice as fast as the typical aircraft of the period. A stream of weird alien script ran across the screen, and the scale of the map increased. Now they were looking at southern England, northern France and the Channel Islands. Benny could read the symbols.

'The incoming object was launched from a site just outside Granville.' As she said the name, the town's location flashed on the map and a flightpath began filling itself in. 'An extrapolation of its current trajectory suggests that it will hit Whitehall in about sixteen minutes.'

Roz remained calm. 'Why is the TARDIS telling us all this?'

'I think she's trying to warn us about the bomber.' Benny reached across and flicked a switch. 'I've set it to automatic flight and put the ship on second-stage defensive alert. If the TARDIS is about to be destroyed she'll dematerialize and land somewhere safe.' Roz looked worried until Benny assured her, 'The ship returns when the danger has passed.'

Forrester had pulled down the door lever and hoisted the holdall over her shoulder.

'Where are you going?' Benny demanded.

'We've got a quarter of an hour. I've got to warn them.'

'If that's what it looks like ... Stay here – you'll be safe.'

But Roz didn't look back and the door closed behind her, shutting her out. It was dark outside, colder than she had been expecting. Church bells were ringing all over London: the signal that the invasion had begun. She needed to find a phone.

There was an unearthly grinding, surging sound behind her. Roz turned.

The TARDIS had dematerialized.

13

Ground Zero

Chris couldn't read German, but he didn't need to: the needle on the temperature gauge was quivering up past the orange zone and into the red. On a more optimistic note, everything else was fine: there was still plenty of fuel, and Munin was a beautiful plane to fly. Chris had even got used to the bone-jarring vibrations that pulsed through the fuselage. It was a pity that the plane was only minutes away from exploding, really.

'We haven't got much longer, Doctor,' Chris told him, as calmly as he could.

The Doctor had been mulling over the problem for the last couple of minutes. He had ordered Chris to keep the plane in the air while he considered their options. They hadn't got parachutes (and they couldn't leave the plane anyway, not now it was flying over London); a mid-air repair job was out of the question.

'Doctor, we could eject the fuel,' Chris declared. He was already reaching for the control.

The Doctor's face lit up. 'That's it! No, not ejecting it. Just the opposite.'

Chris's hand hovered over the control panel. 'We can't refuel, and why would we want to? Surely the more fuel there was on board, the more there was to explode?'

'Pump fuel into the reserve tank from the main tank – I'll explain, but we haven't got time,' the Doctor insisted.

'But the problem's in the reserve tank –'

'Do it!' the Doctor shouted. Chris began flicking

switches. Behind them, the rhythmic oscillation of the fuel pump started up, and they could even hear the fuel as it began sloshing around.

'It takes two things to start a fire,' the Doctor noted sagely. 'You need an inflammable material – and the jet fuel is certainly that – but you also need oxygen. Filling up the tank with fuel forces out all the oxygen. No oxygen, no fire.'

'That's brilliant,' Chris declared.

'We can't push our luck as we're over London now so we'll have to –'

'– Land in the nearest available open space. There are plenty of parks. If all else fails, we can ditch into the Thames. Don't worry, Doctor, I've done this sort of thing before.'

Chris was already scanning the skyline.

The central column rose and fell, rose and fell. Everything seemed to be progressing normally. Bernice was a little annoyed that after several years travelling with the Doctor she couldn't remember any of the routine that he went through when the TARDIS was in flight. She'd been content to watch him fuss around the console, press a button here, pull a lever there. It was a good job that he'd shown her how to open the door, or she'd be stuck inside for ever.

Benny was too tired to feel any panic – whatever else was about to happen, she personally was in no immediate danger inside the TARDIS. There were so many safety systems that she felt quite safe, and anything capable of destroying the ship would be either a) so devastatingly awful that it would be mercifully quick or b) so incomprehensible that she'd be too fascinated by what was going on to worry about it. That was the plan, anyway.

The scanner had turned itself off, and Benny was unable to interpret the navigational data flowing across the readouts. Every so often the console would make a reassuring beeping noise. Benny stepped back for a moment. Was it her imagination or was the column slowing down? Before her eyes it ground to a halt, and there was a resonant chime deep beneath the floor. The TARDIS had landed. The whole journey had taken a little under three minutes.

Benny ran her eyes over the instruments. The environment outside was cool, there was atmospheric moisture, but the gravity and radiation readings were perfectly acceptable. She thought she remembered the Doctor saying once that if it wasn't safe to go outside, then the TARDIS wouldn't let them open the door. Or was she making that up? It was the sort of thing he said, anyway. If it wasn't true, it jolly well ought to be. Benny crossed her fingers and pulled down on the door lever. The heavy double-doors swung open.

She stepped out into the gloom and onto wet grass. There were church bells ringing in the distance, from every direction. The TARDIS had landed in a public park, flat grassland with trees screening off the city. The odd statue was dotted here and there. Ducks bobbed up and down on an expanse of lake. The London skyline was silhouetted by searchlight beams across the sky. The TARDIS had moved across the city, and it looked as though it was still 1941. Benny knew enough about London to be able to work out where she was by finding a couple of landmarks. She began to triangulate her position. If that building behind her and to the right was Admiralty Arch, then . . .

Something huge, silent and almost invisible loomed ten feet overhead, swooping low, coming in to land. Instinctively, Benny pulled back, bumping into the side of the TARDIS which disorientated her for a second or two. When she recovered, she tried to make sense of the shape. This would be a tricky task – in normal circumstances, there wouldn't be any giant bats flying over London in 1941, but with the Doctor around there might well be. There was a disc of fire – an afterburner or an eye? Great black, flat wings. Tyres ploughed into the soft mud, churning it up. The evil-looking object skidded slightly, but ground to a halt not fifty yards away. It was a plane, almost invisible in the twilight. There was something spooky about it – the way the light fell on it perhaps, the eerie lack of sound. Benny wasn't really an expert on the war planes of the period, but it looked oddly out of place. She realized she had seen something like it before, glimpsed for a second before it exploded over St Jaonnet. If this was the TARDIS's idea of safety, than it really needed its Dictionary Disk looking at.

This plane hadn't exploded. The cockpit canopy was pulling back. Benny thought about getting back inside the TARDIS, but decided against it. She needed to find out what was going on.

A huge figure in military uniform came bounding over. Before she had time to panic, she realized that it was Chris Cwej dressed in Nazi uniform. One of her more lurid dreams come true, she mused.

'Benny!' he whooped, lifting her up and hugging her.

It took a moment to recover her breath. Finally, she managed to say, 'Chris what's that thing above your mouth?'

Chris probed his top lip anxiously. 'It's my moustache,' he concluded.

'It looks stupid.'

She'd forgotten how funny she found it watching his face fall. God, it was good to be acting childish again. She hugged him, nuzzled her head in that broad chest of his.

'Come here, you hulking great fashion victim, you.'

'At least I'm not wearing sunglasses at night,' Chris sulked.

Benny broke off her embrace. 'I've got my reasons. Have you seen the Doctor?'

Chris pointed back the way he had come. 'He was in the plane with me. He muttered something about unfinished business.'

'That's him all right.' Benny peered across the park. 'I can't see him.' She began stumbling towards the plane.

'He also said we had to stay back.'

'Oh, come on.'

Chris followed her.

* * *

231

The Doctor had just managed to prise open the bomb-bay door when he head the sound of pistols being cocked behind him.

'Hands in the air.'

The Doctor raised his hands high above his head and turned to face the gentleman who had addressed him. He was a British admiral aged about sixty, with lines around his eyes. The Doctor couldn't put a name to the face, but the officer clearly recognized him. Behind him were a number of troops, all armed.

'Doctor von Wer!' the admiral declared.

'Doctor who?' he scowled. There was only one thing worse than being recognized by an opponent, and that was being mistaken for someone else. The soldiers were moving to encircle him. Now he had moved, the Doctor's view of the TARDIS was blocked by the plane. There wasn't a clear escape route.

'He doesn't sound German, sir,' said a young army lieutenant at the admiral's side.

'Step away from the plane,' the admiral ordered.

The Doctor slowly edged back. A couple of the men ducked past him and began clambering up to Munin's cockpit. He couldn't let them get too close a look at Munin – much as he would love to give the Allies some advantage in this war, they couldn't be allowed access to stealth technology. The British state-of-the-art counter-measure against radar at this time was dropping short strips of tin foil from the planes. It scattered radar beams, causing hundreds of confusing echoes, and it was actually pretty effective, but the technology was not exactly in Hartung's league.

'Which one is this, Hugin or Munin?' the officer asked.

'This one is Munin. May I ask who you are, please?'

'I am Admiral Kendrick of the –'

'– Scientific Intelligence Division,' finished the Doctor. 'Of course, I'm so sorry I didn't recognize you sooner. That chap up there is George Reed, isn't he? We almost met once.'

Lieutenant Reed jumped down from the plane. 'There's

no sign of damage, sir, no sign of a forced landing. We did find this.' He held up the briefcase. The Doctor blanched.

'Ah yes, that's mine, if I could just . . .' the Doctor moved to take it from the young lieutenant, who snatched it away from his grasp. A couple of the troops moved in to restrain the Doctor. Reed laid the case on the ground and opened it up. The Doctor licked his lips nervously.

'Admiral, there's a fortune here in Reichsmarks.' Reed had clearly never seen so much money before. He rummaged underneath the pile of banknotes. 'There's also a set of blueprints. And this. Sorry, sir, it's in German, do you mind?'

Kendrick took the sheet of paper from him and began scanning it.

'Well, if my business here is concluded, I'll be off, then,' said the Doctor cheerfully. 'I can see you've got a lot on your plate and –'

' "From today, March the fifth 1941, I shall become a loyal citizen of the German nation, I swear total allegiance to the authority of the Führer and the rule of German law. From today, I shall work exclusively for the Luftwaffe zbV . . . I shall work untiringly for the final victory of the Reich, and the total extermination of its enemies . . . I renounce all previous associations with foreign powers, organizations and individuals. I am in full possession of my faculties and I am not signing this statement under duress." I believe that's what is known as a signed confession.'

The Doctor blinked. 'There's a perfectly simple and innocent explanation for this.' The Doctor paused for a moment, collecting his thoughts. 'The million Reichsmarks are . . . I have the blueprints because . . . er, the contract was . . . Herr Kendrick, I was working to –'

'*Herr* Kendrick?' Reed shouted incredulously. The young lieutenant would have hit the Doctor had the admiral not intervened.

'Out of the frying plane into the fire,' the Doctor observed. Reed grabbed his arms and pinned them against his back. Another man handcuffed him.

233

'Lieutenant, stay here with a couple of the men and guard Munin. I'll take this traitor back to HQ and interrogate him.'

There was a strange dark shape behind the trees in St James's Park. Roz decided that a barrage balloon had been punctured and had drifted back down to earth. The staff car screeched to a halt.

'What's the matter, Harry?' Roz's pistol was ready in her hand.

'Ma'am, it's Lieutenant Reed.'

Roz looked out of the windscreen. Almost impossible to see in the darkness, George was waving them down.

Roz pushed open her window.

'Where have you been?' Reed demanded.

She tapped her holdall. 'I've got something that'll be able to track the invisible plane. We haven't got long.'

Reed pointed over to the park. 'We've found it – it's landed here.'

She checked her watch. Her sixteen minutes had expired. 'Landed?'

Reed nodded. Roz leapt out of the car. A few drops of rain were beginning to fall; there was going to be quite a shower. Together, they ran across to the park to where George's men were guarding the plane. Even close up, Munin was only an outline. Roz ran her hand across the surface of the plane, which was still warm.

There was a commotion behind them.

Roz heard Chris's voice. 'Don't shoot, I am a British officer.' Chris was dragged forward by a couple of the men. He was wearing an unfamiliar green-grey uniform, but looked well. After four days keeping a lid on her feelings, Roz was surprised by how relieved she was to see him.

We found this Hun, sir,' one of the men said.

Benny stepped forward, looking out of place in her movie-star outfit.

'I'm Professor Bernice Summerfield, these are my friends Christopher Cwej and Roslyn Forrester. Lieutenant, there's been a mistake – these people may look strange, but they are on your side.'

Reed stepped forward, and couldn't keep his eyes off Benny. 'I know. I work with Cwej and I'm engaged to Roz.'

Chris and Benny looked at each other.

'No, really, he is,' Roz insisted, 'look at the ring.'

The British soldiers had let go of Chris, and Reed grasped his hand and welcomed him back. A second later and Reed was briefing Cwej and Forrester, leading them a little way away from Benny. The archaeologist tiptoed after them. 'We've arrested von Wer. He flew in on this.'

'But that's how the Doct–' Roz jabbed her heel down hard on Chris's foot.

'The Von Wer from the photograph?' she asked.

'The very same. It looks like you were wrong for once. We caught him underneath this plane, carrying a set of plans, a million Reichsmarks and a signed confession. Kendrick's taken him to SID HQ.'

Benny had already guessed. Roz caught her eye and nodded.

'Anything else?' Forrester asked.

Reed nodded grimly. 'They're going to bomb Guernsey.'

'No!' Benny shouted.

Reed whirled to face her. 'I don't like it myself, Miss Summers, but the Cabinet don't have any choice.'

Chris grasped his shoulder. 'They are trying to bomb the airstrip where this was built?'

'Yes.'

'It's not in Guernsey. We need to find Kendrick.' Reed stared at him for a moment, then the two men ran off together towards Whitehall.

Benny faced Roz. 'And we have to find the Doctor.'

'He's at SID HQ.'

'Where's that?'

Roz grinned. 'It's where those two are jogging to. Just under a mile away.'

Benny groaned. 'Couldn't we grab a taxi?'

Roz nodded. 'I've got a staff car waiting.'

* * *

Reed and Cwej caught up with Kendrick as he was about to step into his office. The admiral was beaming, and he ushered them both into the room. It was the first time that Chris had been here. The office was small and the oak-panelling and blackout curtain over the window made it even more claustrophobic. As with every other room in the building, maps and reports littered every surface. A scale model of a battleship took pride of place on the desk.

'It's good to see you back, Lieutenant.' Kendrick shook Chris's hand. The two lieutenants were still out of breath from their run. Chris couldn't waste any more time, though.

'Sir, I have heard from Lieutenant Reed that you intend to bomb Guernsey tonight. Hartung isn't based there; the Luftwaffe have a camouflaged airstrip just outside Granville.'

'We bombed the –'

'Sir, this is a different airstrip, one that you don't know about.'

Reed had found a map, and he brought it over. 'Show us, Cwej,' the lieutenant suggested.

Chris ran his finger over the map. The Gerard farm was marked on it. It was easy enough to trace the escape route he and the Doctor had used – back from the farm, through the wood, along the stream. On this map, an old one from before the war, there was still a farm on the site of the camouflaged airstrip. The country lane leading from Granville to this farm was marked. Chris estimated the position and drew a circle around it, carefully avoiding the Gerards' land.

'Send the bombers there, three miles or so to the south. There are no ground defences – they don't need them if no one knows that they are there. Everything is underground, though.'

Kendrick tapped the map. 'We've not even had a whiff of this from our agents in France, Cwej.'

Chris was insistent. 'I broke into the base on two occasions, sir. The Nazis had been testing Hugin and

Munin there for months. You've received reports about mysterious flying objects. You know that Hartung is in the area.'

'For God's sake, Admiral, call Bomber Command before the raid on Guernsey,' urged Reed.

Kendrick picked up the phone.

'Open up the door,' Forrester ordered.

The young private did as she asked. Roz followed Benny into the cell. The Doctor was sitting at the end of his bed, in the lotus position. He was stirring a mug of tea.

'Look at that,' said the Doctor crossly, holding up the spoon. 'What use is only one spoon? Oh, Benny! You found my umbrella.' He took it from her, hugging it joyfully.

'Hartung is dead,' said Benny softly. 'I saw his body in the morgue. He died on March the second at St Jaonnet.'

'When Hugin exploded,' the Doctor muttered under his breath. 'But . . .'

It was the first time that Roz could ever remember the Doctor looking surprised. It disconcerted her.

'So this has all been for nothing, hasn't it?' Benny suggested.

The Doctor put down the mug. He was deep in thought.

'Look at me, Doctor,' Benny insisted. She pulled down her sunglasses. Her bruising was still horrific, and both Roz and the Doctor winced. 'Hartung managed to blow himself up without any help from you.'

'I thought you were safe,' the Doctor said weakly.

'Hang on, though, Bernice,' Roz said. 'Without the Doctor and Chris, the Germans would still have Munin and the plans to build more.'

'Benny's right,' the Doctor said solemnly. 'Hartung was unique. Fifteen years ahead of his time – he was the only person in the world who could have worked out how to build Munin from . . .' The Doctor paused, before saying, 'Without his genius, the Germans won't be able to carry on with his work. A brilliant mind . . .' He trailed off sadly.

'This Nazi was a friend of yours, was he?' Roz joked.

The Doctor studiously turned his attention back to his mug of tea.

Benny's eyes narrowed. 'He was. It was you, wasn't it?'

Roz frowned. 'What are you talking about – the Doctor giving state secrets to the Nazis? He walked up to a top Nazi scientist and told him all about Chain Home, and how to reduce his plane's RCS? Somehow I doubt it.'

Benny was unrepentant. 'I'm right, aren't I? You sneaky little git. There isn't any supervillain, or alien incursion. There's no giant rubber hamster from before the dawn of time. It's just you.'

'It was a mistake, a miscalculation, that's all.'

'Care to tell us about it?' Roz said, suddenly suspicious.

'I met him in Cairo back in January 1936, at a race meeting. He was clearly a very intelligent man, and glad of such company, for once, so I –'

'– told him all about radar and how to build stealth planes.'

'No.' The Doctor was clearly hurt. 'You humans are quite capable of inventing weapons all by your –'

'You're hardly in a position to lecture us, are you?'

'No.' The Doctor looked down at his feet like a naughty schoolboy.

'So what happened?'

Quietly, the Doctor told them about Cairo, about meeting Hartung and the afternoon at the race-track. Then he told them about what had happened that evening . . .

Mel was wearing a striking creation in sequins and pink organza that she'd found in the TARDIS wardrobe room. She was sitting at a small table at the edge of the ballroom of the Grand Imperial Hotel with the Doctor and Emil. The racing driver was the centre of attention, and so Mel had received more than her fair share of curious looks from the other guests. Although the surroundings were sumptuous, with half a dozen crystal chandeliers hanging from a richly painted ceiling and a full orchestra playing, all three sat staring out of the window, watching owls gently swoop past.

Whooo, ululated the owl, the pitch of its call dropping gradually.

'Fascinating creatures, owls. They've been around for twelve million years,' the Doctor remarked.

'One of the ancient Egyptian hieroglyphs is an owl,' Emil replied.

Illogical though it might be, Mel was afraid of the creatures. 'They give me the creeps,' she admitted.

Emil and the Doctor shared a knowing look.

An owl dived past the window, its feet splayed.

'It's going in for the kill. Do you know they can see well in the dark?' Emil asked.

'Do they have sonar, like bats?' Mel wondered. 'You know, they send out a high-pitched squeak and can build up a picture from the echoes. Like radar.'

The Doctor shook his head. 'No, owls have a combination of sharp eyesight and acute hearing. Owls are binocular, with quite a narrow field of vision, and they sometimes have difficulty seeing things that aren't moving. However, an owl is quite capable of tracking voles across a field just by the sound they make when they are chewing grass. As far as I know, only two species of bird use biosonar, the swiftlet and the oilbird. Both breed in very dark caves. It's a fascinating subject: those birds produce twelve clicking sounds a second in the one kilohertz and sixteen kilohertz range and –'

'What's a "kilohertz", please?' Emil asked.

'The hertz is the SI unit for cycles per second,' Mel supplied. She didn't tell him that the word was only coined in the 1960s.

'The really clever thing, of course,' the Doctor said, smiling to himself, 'is that the mouse can't see or hear the owl coming. The poor little thing doesn't defend itself, because it doesn't know it is being attacked until it is far, far too late.'

'Come on Emil, let's dance.'

As Emil took Mel by the arm, an owl, the same they had seen before, swooped up into the night with a mouse impaled in its talons.

* * *

239

'Hang on,' said Benny. 'You didn't tell the Germans how to build stealth planes, all you did was talk about owls?'

'Yes, but that conversation sparked off Hartung's imagination, joined up few of the dots for him. It made a few links explicit, encouraged him to research into echolocation, so he found out about the radar experiments. That conversation was the first link in the chain that led to the building of Hugin and Munin. Careless talk costs lives.'

'But . . .' Roz tried to think about all the things she had told Reed. She remembered the stungun concealed in her jacket and the mass detector in her holdall. It probably wouldn't be diplomatic to mention all this to the Doctor.

'When I learnt what Hartung had built, I hoped against hope that he had got the information from somewhere else. But he hadn't; it was all my fault – without me, none of this would have happened.'

'It's still a bit cryptic, isn't it?' said Roz sullenly.

'When an apple fell on his head, Newton discovered gravity. That's how genius works: making associations, drawing inferences, putting the pieces together. I . . . came across his diary in the Soviet Union. The entry for the eve of the race in Cairo made it clear.'

Benny rolled her eyes. 'So why didn't you tell us all this before we came here?'

The Doctor shifted slightly. 'I didn't want to admit what I had done. Above all, I wanted to tread carefully. This war is a particularly delicate period: everything interconnected, everything so carefully balanced. Take Guernsey. It seems so insignificant, it's just a backwater, with no strategic importance. But the Nazis spent a great deal of time and effort fortifying the Channel Islands. They used resources that could have been used to defend the French coast, and perhaps if they hadn't then the Germans would have been able to ward off the Normandy landings.'

'Doctor,' Benny asked, 'will Ma and Anne be all right?'

The Doctor nodded. 'They both survive the war, Anne's fiancé comes back as a major, and they get married and have two daughters. I visited them once in 1960; Ma was in her eighties, and had just become a great-grandmother. I wondered then why Anne had called one of her children "Bernice".'

'So now it's all over, Hartung's dead, the Germans don't have the planes, and can't build any more. It's all tied up neatly,' Benny concluded. She seemed to accept the Doctor's explanation.

'Nothing ever ends, Bernice. Munin is still sitting there in St James's Park.'

'There is another loose end,' Roz reminded them. 'Wolff.'

The Doctor's head snapped up, and he looked Benny in the eye. 'Joachim Wolff did this to you? He is here?' She nodded.

The Doctor was standing. 'Roz, I'll need your pistol.' Roz drew it and pressed it into the little man's hand.

'I'll deal with Munin,' Roz concluded.

The Doctor weighed the gun, and bit his lip.

'It's time to finish this.'

14

Endgame

Perhaps it happened this way:

The Doctor pulled back the bolts of the cell door and stepped inside. Behind him, seemingly unbidden, the bolts slid back into place. Wolff sat in the corner, slumped on an iron bed, his hands clasped to the back of his head. Even though he was subdued, Wolff was still a huge man. In the forced perspective of the tiny room, the Doctor appeared to loom over him.

'Good evening, Standartenführer.'

Wolff looked up. The Doctor cocked his head, curious about the eyepatch.

'Your friend, the black witch did this.'

'If you're playing for sympathy, Herr Wolff, it won't work. I've seen what you've done to Benny. I know all about what you did at Mallesan.' The Doctor's voice was low.

Wolff laughed.

The Doctor drew the pistol, his arm swinging in a wide arc until the gun was aiming at Wolff's forehead. Wolff paused for a moment, but there was still a grin on his face. 'You're no killer. I can see the fear in your eyes, the sweat on your brow. You're a pacifist degenerate, a coward,' the Nazi concluded.

The gun stayed level and the Doctor gave a wry smile. 'Things have changed since the last time we met: Hugin and Munin have been destroyed, Hartung is dead. The scheme you cooked up with Herr Steinmann has backfired. Now you are in a prison cell, awaiting a firing squad. The British don't have a complete set of plans, so they won't be building any stealth planes of their own. They do have enough information to detect any German planes built along the same lines, though.'

Wolff smiled. 'Have you come here to kill me or to keep me up to date with current affairs?'

'Neither. I've come here to prove that you were wrong, that you have lost. That there is an alternative.'

'Oh yes, Doctor. You've seen the alternative: that Forrester, the woman who took out my eye, she's from the future, isn't she?'

'Forrester is committed to justice and fairness.'

' "An eye for an eye"?' Wolff chuckled. 'She is a vicious animal, I saw the hatred in her eyes. Her kind will be eradicated, we'll protect decent people from creatures like her. I'll do it myself . . . unless you kill me.'

'Killing you would change nothing. It won't bring back the dead, it won't save a single life. There's worse to come in this war: crimes against the universe itself. For now, Auschwitz, Pearl Harbour, Stalingrad, Dresden, Coventry, Hiroshima, Kwai are just names on a map. This war will give the words new and terrible meaning, definitions that will resonate through history. Killing you wouldn't stop it. No, I've come here to reason with you.'

Wolff sneered. 'A very nice speech. It almost brought a tear to my . . . eye. But you won't stop me with reason, you won't talk me out of it, you'll have to use that gun. If you really do kill all the Fascists, drown out our shouts, avenge the murder of your civilians by bombing our cities into the dust, well then, Doctor, it will just mean that Nazism has triumphed.'

The Doctor spoke in German. ' "He who fights with monsters might take care lest he thereby become a monster . . . if you gaze for long into the abyss, the abyss gazes also into you." '

Wolff paused, trying to put what he felt into words. 'If the word Nazi fills you with revulsion, if you couldn't stand to be in the same room as anyone who calls themselves a

Nazi, then how is that different from my hating the word Bolshevik or Jew? You tell me that I can believe what I like, as long as it meets with your approval. You grant me free speech, yet you won't let me say what I truly believe? I would rather you killed me. You can make all the moralizing speeches you like, but when it comes down to it, all you are saying is that you are stronger than me. The only thing that gives you authority is that gun you are holding. The only thing that separates us is that I would use it without hesitation.'

The Doctor pulled back the gun.

'As I thought,' Wolff spat, ' "If I killed you, I'd become as bad as the Nazis." You haven't the stomach for the fight. You'll be swept away, Doctor, you and all the weak. Do you really think Hartung was the only scientist at the Reich's disposal? There are a thousand more, all with their own secret weapons, all with their vision of Nazi destiny.'

'Could you really live in a world built on foundations of human skulls? Cushions stuffed with dead women's hair, candles made from human fat, lampshades with tattoos? A uniform world of concrete, perpetual war and hatred?'; the Doctor said softly, looking down at the heavy black pistol.

'Yes,' Wolff said simply. Then, 'I challenge you to put that gun down and fight me like a man, with honour.'

'Hardly a fair contest, Herr Wolff; you demonstrated your fighting prowess on the beach, and again with my friend, Professor Summerfield. Thugs like you always find it easy to hurt those smaller and more vulnerable than themselves. Your ability to gang up and kill unarmed civilians has never been in doubt. I do have a possible solution, though.'

The Doctor laid the gun on the bed beside Wolff.

The room seemed suddenly dark.

When the Doctor spoke again, his voice rumbled low as thunder in the mountains. 'I challenge you to a game, a contest of equals. Winner takes all.' The Doctor held out his hand; in it were three bullets. 'We'll take it in turns. I'll place the gun at my temple and I'll pull the trigger. Assuming that the chamber is empty, I then pass the gun to you. You do the same. One of us dies, one of us wins. There are three bullets in there, so it's fifty-fifty odds – I believe they call it Russian Roulette. We'll see what our destiny is, and who's the coward. The winner walks out . . .' the Doctor glanced at the cell door, which swung open ' . . . of that door.'

Wolff glanced down at the gun.

'Do you want me to go first? Are you afraid?' the Doctor asked quietly, picking up the gun and pressing it to his temple. He squeezed his eyes shut and pulled the trigger.

Click.

The Doctor opened his right eye, then his left. He sighed, obviously relieved. The Doctor spun the barrel and offered the weapon to Wolff. The German shrank from it. 'This is not a test of skill, but of luck. A childish display – an activity for drunken degenerates, not an honourable soldier.'

'I agree. But by your own logic, if you don't take up the challenge then I win: you've proved that you are a coward. If you kill yourself you've won because you are brave. Lunacy.' The Doctor spun the barrel and again placed the gun at his own temple and pulled the trigger. He kept his eyes open this time.

Click.

'This little game *is* a demonstration of destiny, of bravery, but above all it's a demonstration of futility. You can't create anything with a gun, Herr Wolff, let alone Utopia, authority or truth. You can dress up in a scary black uniform and talk about destiny. You can use the full power of the state to rewrite biology, mythology, genealogy, history and geography. Burn all the books that you disagree with, burn all the people that wrote them or read them. Hold a parade in every street, attend a thousand Party rallies. Gang up on the weak, persecute the minorities. Win the war. It still won't make you right.'

245

The Doctor nervously licked his lips as he pulled the trigger for the third time.

Click.

The Doctor spun the barrel and tossed the gun over to Wolff.

Wolff began to edge the gun up to his temple. Then his arm straightened and the pistol was pointing squarely at the Doctor's chest. The Doctor didn't try to move.

'You are a fool,' the German spat. He pulled the trigger.

Click.

'You're right, I am a fool. But you are a coward, Herr Wolff.'

Click.

'You've got the gun now. You've got the authority – that's what you said. Use it. Force me to obey you. Force me to agree with you.'

Click.

'You cheated me! This gun isn't loaded.'

'You're the one that cheated – if you remember I did stipulate that you pointed the gun at yourself, not me,' the Doctor reminded him.

Wolff checked the barrel.

'There are three bullets there,' the Doctor repeated.

Wolff looked up helplessly, his eye watery and pale. He was aiming the pistol at the Doctor once more, but his hand was shaking now.

'You're beaten,' the Doctor said wistfully. 'There are no more tomorrows for you, Joachim Wolff. You have no authority, you have no destiny. History is written by the winning side, and there's no part for you. You can keep the gun. Goodbye.'

As the Doctor closed the door behind him, there was a single shot from inside the cell.

Or perhaps it didn't happen like that at all.

Forrester stepped up to Munin, ran her hand along its rough underside. Reed had also returned to the plane. He stood peering up into the bomb bay, a shopping bag in his hand. The church bells were still ringing, and now the air-raid sirens had started up, too.

'It's filled to the brim, Roz. There must be ten thousand pounds of explosives up there.'

'Yes,' she said simply.

Benny caught up with the Doctor as he strode through the park towards the TARDIS. She grabbed him by the shoulder.

'Doctor, what happened in there? I heard a shot.'

'I never discuss my patients,' the Doctor said darkly.

'That's not good enough this time, Doctor.'

'He's dead. He'll never do what he did to you again. Not to anyone.'

'Will you?'

The Doctor stopped in his tracks and whirled to face her. 'That was uncalled for.'

Benny was crying again. 'Doctor, one of these days you're going to leave it just a little too late and one of us is going to die.' She couldn't think of anything else to say, and instead she stepped over to Chris.

The Doctor stood for a moment, lost in thought. He looked up sharply, then joined his companions.

'What's Roz doing?' Chris asked, pointing over to Munin.

'I wouldn't stand there,' the Doctor said. He had pulled out his abacus, and after a second or two's calculation, he took nine steps back. 'Move behind me.'

Chris scampered across. 'Why mov–'

Munin exploded, a detonation in the bomb bay lifting the plane slightly, cracking its fuselage into an inverted V-shape. The wings buckled and snapped, then the fuel tank erupted. It was the first time that Benny had seen the outline of the plane. The scene reminded her almost of a Viking funeral pyre. Then, every pound of explosive in the bomb bay detonated simultaneously. There was a hammer-blow deep inside the Earth, a sound so loud it lifted them off their feet and shattered every pane of glass for two miles in every direction. A column of fire hurtled five hundred feet in the air, and scooped a crater twenty feet deep in the soft soil of St James's Park. The lake was seething and boiling and tiny chunks of metal and earth began clattering back down to the ground like rain. A fragment of the wing sliced into the ground where Chris had just been standing. There were shouts from across the park. Fire-watchers.

The Doctor smiled rather smugly.

'We have to be going.' He checked his watch. 'Where's Roz got to?'

'She's got her own unfinished business,' Chris whispered.

'I'll go and collect her. You've got a key to the TARDIS, let Benny in.'

On the other side of the park, George Reed held Roz close. Together they watched the fire-fighters as they milled around the burning wreckage. It was as bright as day here, brighter. In the firelight, Roz's skin was the colour of burnt amber.

The Doctor announced his presence by clearing his throat. Reed turned to see who it was. The Doctor kept a little way back.

'We won,' Reed said simply. There were tears in his eyes. 'Doctor, Roz has told me who you are, told me that you aren't von Wer. Thank you for what you did tonight.'

The Doctor bowed his head to accept Reed's appreciation. 'It's time to get going, Roz.' He looked her straight in the eye. 'Or do you want to stay?'

Reed broke his embrace and stepped back, but Roz caught the officer's hand. 'Yes.'

The Doctor smiled. 'That simple?'

'No.' She hesitated and turned to Reed who, outwardly at least, remained impassive. 'It's so beautiful here. If it wasn't for the war, it would be so peaceful.'

The Doctor chuckled. Roz squeezed Reed's hand.

'You know what I mean,' she snapped.

'Of course I do. I remember the very first time I visited Earth: Paris during the French Revolution. There was so much promise there, a sense that anything and everything was possible. I walked the dirty, wine-soaked streets with my granddaughter, and I realized that the old order could be swept away, that people could be happy. It was a feeling I'd never had before: elation at the sound of empires falling.'

'The French Revolution ended in chaos, Doctor; thousands died,' Reed noted. He took the little man and his story in his stride.

'Would you like to come with us, George? There's always room for one more. You could see the sights, fight epic battles.'

'No, Doctor. There's a war to be fought and won here.'

The little man nodded, as if it was the answer he had expected. 'Is it your war, too, Roz?' the Doctor asked. 'It's your decision. I'll be back at the TARDIS.' He disappeared into the night. Roz looked up at the clouds again, saw them as flying cities, ablaze. Around her she could hear shouting and the distinctive pulsing chirp of energy hand-guns. Elation. Chaos.

'I'm sorry, George.'

Reed managed a smile. 'I know you are. I'll try to keep a stiff upper lip, though, yes?'

'We might meet again. It is possible.'

'We'll meet again some sunny day?'

Roz glanced up at the clouds. 'Then it won't be in England.'

George chuckled, then a thought struck him. 'I almost forgot.' He held out the green bag he was carrying. Roz peered inside, and George continued, 'It's a fur coat. Silver fox, to match your hair. It cost me quite a few coupons, not to mention a few favours, but you were always complaining about how cold it was and –'

Roz kissed him.

'You'll still wear the ring, won't you?'

Roz nodded, holding up the emerald for his inspection. 'Of course, if that's what you want.'

George kissed her cheek, tasting a salty tear there. Roz grabbed the scruff of his neck and pulled him even closer.

Finally, she drew back. 'I better get going.' Roz straightened, tugging her uniform jacket back into shape.

'Goodbye.'

The Doctor's hand hovered over the dematerialization control.

Benny tapped him on the shoulder. He turned. She shook her head. The Doctor withdrew his hand.

The door swung open and Forrester stepped inside. The door closed behind her and she handed the Doctor back his TARDIS key. Chris was grinning, so was Benny. Wolsey brushed against Roz's leg.

The Doctor's hand tapped once at the console and the crystalline column at the centre began rising and falling. Once he was sure they were in flight, he turned to Benny.

'I'm sorry.'

Benny stood impassively. The Doctor looked down sadly, and shuffled out of the control room.

When he was gone, she smiled. 'That's all I wanted to hear.'

Roz glanced nervously between Chris and the console. 'Where are we headed?'

'Don't worry, the TARDIS won't crash into anything. It's quite capable of flying itself,' Chris assured her.

'That's not what I asked.' She shooed Wolsey away from her Harrods bag.

Chris scanned the readout. 'Canterbury. Twenty-first-century time zone.'

'They will have central heating there, though, won't they?' Roz asked Benny hopefully.

The archaeologist yawned. 'Central heating, electric blankets and global warming,' she assured Roz. 'I'm off to my room to write up my diary. It looks like we could all catch up on our sleep. Especially you, Captain Forrester.' She giggled as she left.

'What did she mean by that? Was there an air-raid last night that kept you awake?' Chris asked curiously.

Roz just scowled.

* * *

The Doctor sat alone in the centre of the Infinity Chamber, remembering. Above him holographic stars twinkled far away in a fake night sky.

In another time and another place, the Doctor sipped at his lemonade. He was sitting outside, on the balcony of the Grand Imperial Hotel, watching the moon and stars. It was cool, now. Earlier, Mel and Emil had been the centre of attention on the dance floor, dancing a mean tango. They were sitting in a darkened corner of the ballroom now, and the Doctor knew enough about human nature to give them some privacy.

Was Mel leaving him so soon? She wouldn't stay with him for ever, the Doctor knew that. Then, the last link with his past self would be severed and he would have to make the first move in a new game. There was so much to do, so much unfinished business. Wolves and ravens were gathering at the fringe of the battlefield. Long-forgotten forces from the ancient past and the distant future had returned, and he could feel their eyes watching him.

The Doctor angled his straw and sucked up the last dregs of his lemonade.

There was a distinctive scream from inside the hotel, and Mel came running onto the balcony, hoisting up her skirt so that she could run all the faster. The Doctor was already standing. 'Mel, what's the matter?'

'Doctor, Emil's a German.'

The Doctor furrowed his brow, baffled. 'Well, yes.'

'It's 1936. We'll be at war soon!' she reminded him.

'We? I'm not human, let alone English, and you won't even be born for another thirty years.'

'Twenty-eight. That's not the point. My grandfather died in the war.'

'Hartung didn't kill him.'

'But he's a Nazi, he just told me. He's a Party member.'

'Most Germans were in the 'thirties. Your ancestors supported slavery, workhouses, fox-hunting and burning witches at the stake. Most of them were nice people. Emil's a nice person.'

Mel shot him an accusing look. 'I've got to get out of here.'

The Doctor smiled thinly. 'I know.'

The rocket arced over the forest high into the clear blue sky. It was Christmas Eve 1942. Generalmajor Oskar Steinmann watched the vapour trail rend the sky in half.

The future was unfolding around him. He'd memorized the chapter in Summerfield's book, watched each one of its predictions come true in turn. His warnings had gone unheeded, his actions had made no effect. *24/12/42 – The first test of the 'flying bomb' at Peenemünde.*

It had all changed in the last eighteen months. The attack on Russia had started only a couple of months after the destruction of the Hartung Project. Britain was undefeated, and Germany suddenly found itself fighting wars on two fronts, just as it had in the Great War. At first it had seemed to make sense – there were untold resources in Russia: land, slaves, oil, grain, metals. On the first day of the attack, the Luftwaffe had wreaked havoc – destroying nearly two thousand Russian planes, wiping out an entire country's airforce. German forces advanced forty miles into Russia every day, capturing more Soviet soldiers than they were able to process, moving so fast that the Wehrmacht couldn't establish their supply lines fast enough. The Baltic States fell easily. At the great battles of Bialystock, Kiev and Vyazma-Briansk, the Germans captured over two million soldiers – more men than were in the entire British Army. Soon the Wehrmacht had advanced one thousand miles into Russia, along a two-thousand-mile front. Joyfully, the radio announced success after success. Soon the propagandists had been forced to tone down reports of the victories because no one believed them.

And then, within sight of Moscow, the first snow fell, and the German army ground to a halt. The Russians, prepared for the conditions, fighting for their own land, drove the Germans back. Steinmann had been transferred from Guernsey at that time to shore up the Eastern Front.

His Luftwaffe squadrons had managed to halt the advance of the Russian tanks, fortified and supplied strategic towns, blocked Russian supply routes. The Germans, though, had been forced to all but abandon bombing raids against the United Kingdom and all plans to invade England were shelved.

The character of the war changed at that moment, became defensive, vindictive. Suddenly, Berlin became worried. There were witch-hunts. A lot of good officers were punished, civilian dissidents were ruthlessly purged. No one could question a command now, however insane it seemed. Any talk that Germany might be defeated was treason. Where was the nobility in killing unarmed women and children, whatever race they might be?

And then the unthinkable happened. America entered the war, adding its massive resources to the British and Soviet efforts. Suddenly, it was Germany that stood alone. It was around that time that Steinmann had been called back to develop *wunderwaffen* here. He was working with many of the team that had assisted Hartung; they had pieced together what they could of his discoveries. But it was a hopeless task. *23/4/45 – Russians on outskirts of Berlin; 28/4/45 – Mussolini executed; 30/4/45 – Suicide of –*

'Impressive, isn't it, sir?'

Steinmann glanced over to the seventeen-year-old Unteroffizier. 'It is a magnificent achievement, but won't win us the war.'

'It will strike terror into our enemies and –'

'It is a psychological weapon, that is all. It is still a year and half from any practical application, and will never be able to carry the same explosive payload of even a light conventional bomber.'

'That is defeatist talk, sir. This is our only hope of beating the British – you are saying that we will be defeated.'

'Perhaps I am.'

'Traitor!' the soldier shouted.

'We all have our part to play in history, soldier. But remember that we can't all be on the winning side.'

The Unteroffizier turned away, disgusted by what he had heard.

Steinmann stood for a minute in silence, staring at the vapour trail, remembering the future, remembering all the millions who would die. Then he too turned away.

Glossary

Banzai – Japanese battle-cry, literal meaning 'ten thousand years'.

Chain Home – The British south coast radar stations.

Cromwell – The British code phrase signalling that a German invasion is under way.

Five – MI5.

Gefreiter – German army rank equivalent to corporal.

KdF – (*Kraft durch Freude*; 'Strength Through Joy') – A state-run organization which raised morale among workers and soldiers by promoting heavily subsidized holidays and artistic performances.

Leutnant – German army rank equivalent to lieutenant.

Longbow – A (fictional) secret international intelligence organization, run by the League of Nations. It investigated unexplained phenomenon.

Luftwaffe zbV – The Luftwaffe were the German air force, the zbV (*zur besonderen Verwendung*) were the 'special assignment' division.

Nationalsozialistische Deutsche Arbeiterpartei – The National Socialist German Workers' Party, or Nazi Party.

Nuremberg Trial – The public trial of twenty-two (or according to *Just War*, twenty-three – Oskar Steinmann being the twenty-third) senior Nazis after the Second World War.

Oberst – German army rank approximately equivalent to brigadier.

Rienfenstahl, Leni – German actress and director of such critically acclaimed Nazi propaganda films as *Triumph des Willens* and *Fest der Völker*.

RCS – Radar Cross Section.

SID (Scientific Intelligence Division) – A (fictional) British intelligence organization in which scientists and military personnel liaised.

Speer, Albert – Nazi architect and city planner. After the Nuremberg Trial he served twenty years in prison. He was the author of *Inside the Third Reich* (1970).

SS (*Schutzstaffel*; 'Elite Guard') – Although technically a political police force, during the Second World War the Waffen-SS were fanatical combat troops, dedicated to Fascist ideology.

Standardtenführer – SS rank, roughly equivalent to colonel.

Tausendjährige Reich, der – 'The Thousand Year Reich'.

Ubermenschen – The Nazi concept of the 'superman'.

Unteroffizier – German army rank equivalent to sergeant.

Versailles Treaty – Treaty signed at the end of the First World War in which Germany took responsibility for the war. Under the terms of the treaty, Germany ceded her colonies and some European territory. Germany also promised to pay full reparations and strict limits were placed on the size of her armed forces. Article 231, the so-called 'war guilt clause', established that Germany was entirely responsible for the war.

Wehrmacht – The combined German armed forces. The term was used from 21 May 1935 onwards.

Wunderwaffen ('Wonder Weapons') – Secret and frequently exotic weapons developed by the Nazis for possible use in the Second World War. The only significant weapons actually used were the V1 and V2 flying bombs.

SHADOWMIND
Christopher Bulis

On the colony world of Arden, something dangerous is growing stronger. Something that steals minds and memories. Something that can reach out to another planet, Tairngire, where the newest exhibit in the sculpture park is a blue box surmounted by a flashing light.

ISBN 0 426 20394 1

BIRTHRIGHT
Nigel Robinson

Stranded in Edwardian London with a dying TARDIS, Bernice investigates a series of grisly murders. In the far future, Ace leads a group of guerrillas against their insect-like, alien oppressors. Why has the Doctor left them, just when they need him most?

ISBN 0 426 20393 3

ICEBERG
David Banks

In 2006, an ecological disaster threatens the Earth; only the FLIPback team, working in an Antarctic base, can avert the catastrophe. But hidden beneath the ice, sinister forces have gathered to sabotage humanity's last hope. The Cybermen have returned and the Doctor must face them alone.

ISBN 0 426 20392 5

BLOOD HEAT
Jim Mortimore

The TARDIS is attacked by an alien force; Bernice is flung into the Vortex; and the Doctor and Ace crash-land on Earth. There they find dinosaurs roaming the derelict London streets, and Brigadier Lethbridge-Stewart leading the remnants of UNIT in a desperate fight against the Silurians who have taken over and changed his world.

ISBN 0 426 20399 2

THE DIMENSION RIDERS
Daniel Blythe

A holiday in Oxford is cut short when the Doctor is summoned to Space Station Q4, where ghostly soldiers from the future watch from the shadows among the dead. Soon, the Doctor is trapped in the past, Ace is accused of treason and Bernice is uncovering deceit among the college cloisters.

ISBN 0 426 20397 6

THE LEFT-HANDED HUMMINGBIRD
Kate Orman
Someone has been playing with time. The Doctor Ace and Bernice must travel to the Aztec Empire in 1487, to London in the Swinging Sixties and to the sinking of the *Titanic* as they attempt to rectify the temporal faults – and survive the attacks of the living god Huitzilin.

ISBN 0 426 20404 2

CONUNDRUM
Steve Lyons
A killer is stalking the streets of the village of Arandale. The victims are found each day, drained of blood. Someone has interfered with the Doctor's past again, and he's landed in a place he knows he once destroyed, from which it seems there can be no escape.

ISBN 0 426 20408 5

NO FUTURE
Paul Cornell
At last the Doctor comes face-to-face with the enemy who has been threatening him, leading him on a chase that has brought the TARDIS to London in 1976. There he finds that reality has been subtly changed and the country he once knew is rapidly descending into anarchy as an alien invasion force prepares to land . . .

ISBN 0 426 20409 3

TRAGEDY DAY
Gareth Roberts
When the TARDIS crew arrive on Olleril, they soon realize that all is not well. Assassins arrive to carry out a killing that may endanger the entire universe. A being known as the Supreme One tests horrific weapons. And a secret order of monks observes the growing chaos.

ISBN 0 426 20410 7

LEGACY
Gary Russell
The Doctor returns to Peladon, on the trail of a master criminal. Ace pursues intergalactic mercenaries who have stolen the galaxy's most evil artifact while Bernice strikes up a dangerous friendship with a Martian Ice Lord. The players are making the final moves in a devious and lethal plan – but for once it isn't the Doctor's.

ISBN 0 426 20412 3

THEATRE OF WAR
Justin Richards
Menaxus is a barren world on the front line of an interstellar war, home to a ruined theatre which hides sinister secrets. When the TARDIS crew land on the planet, they find themselves trapped in a deadly re-enactment of an ancient theatrical tragedy.

ISBN 0 426 20414 X

ALL-CONSUMING FIRE
Andy Lane
The secret library of St John the Beheaded has been robbed. The thief has taken forbidden books which tell of gateways to other worlds. Only one team can be trusted to solve the crime: Sherlock Holmes, Doctor Watson – and a mysterious stranger who claims he travels in time and space.

ISBN 0 426 20415 8

BLOOD HARVEST
Terrance Dicks
While the Doctor and Ace are selling illegal booze in a town full of murderous gangsters, Bernice has been abandoned on a vampire-infested planet outside normal space. This story sets in motion events which are continued in *Goth Opera*, the first in a new series of Missing Adventures.

ISBN 0 426 20417 4

STRANGE ENGLAND
Simon Messingham
In the idyllic gardens of a Victorian country house, the TARDIS crew discover a young girl whose body has been possessed by a beautiful but lethal insect. And they find that the rural paradise is turning into a world of nightmare ruled by the sinister Quack.

ISBN 0 426 20419 0

FIRST FRONTIER
David A. McIntee
When Bernice asks to see the dawn of the space age, the Doctor takes the TARDIS to Cold War America, which is facing a threat far more deadly than Communist Russia. The militaristic Tzun Confederacy have made Earth their next target for conquest – and the aliens have already landed.

ISBN 0 426 20421 2

ST ANTHONY'S FIRE
Mark Gatiss

The TARDIS crew visit Betrushia, a planet in terrible turmoil. A vicious, genocidal war is raging between the lizard-like natives. With time running out, the Doctor must save the people of Betrushia from their own legacy before St Anthony's fire consumes them all.

ISBN 0 426 20423 9

FALLS THE SHADOW
Daniel O'Mahony

The TARDIS is imprisoned in a house called Shadowfell, where a man is ready to commence the next phase of an experiment that will remake the world. But deep within the house, something evil lingers, observing and influencing events, waiting to take on flesh and emerge.

ISBN 0 426 20427 1

PARASITE
Jim Mortimore

The TARDIS has arrived in the Elysium system, lost colony of distant Earth and site of the Artifact: a world turned inside out, home to a bizarre ecosystem. But now the Artifact appears to be decaying, transforming the humans trapped within into something new and strange.

ISBN 0 426 20425 5

WARLOCK
Andrew Cartmel

On the streets of near-future Earth, a strange new drug is having a devastating impact. It's called warlock, and some call it the creation of the devil. While Benny and Ace try to track down its source, the Doctor begins to uncover the truth about the drug.

ISBN 0 426 20433 6

SET PIECE
Kate Orman

There's a rip in the fabric of space and time. Passenger ships are disappearing from the interstellar traffic lanes. An attempt to investigate goes dangerously wrong, and the TARDIS crew are scattered throughout history – perhaps never to be reunited.

ISBN 0 426 20436 0

INFINITE REQUIEM
Daniel Blythe

Kelzen, Jirenal and Shanstra are Sensopaths, hugely powerful telepaths whose minds are tuned to the collective unconscious. Separated in time, they wreak havoc and destruction. United, they threaten every sentient being in the universe.

ISBN 0 426 20437 9

SANCTUARY
David A. McIntee
The Doctor and Bernice are stranded in medieval France, a brutal time of crusades and wars of succession. While the Doctor investigates a murder in a besieged fortress, Bernice joins forces with an embittered mercenary to save a band of heretics from the might of the Inquisition.

ISBN 0 426 20439 5

HUMAN NATURE
Paul Cornell
April, 1914. In the town of Farringham, a teacher called Dr John Smith has just begun work. Struggling to fit in, he finds himself haunted by memories of a place called Gallifrey – somewhere he knows he's never been. Can it be true that, as his niece Bernice claims, creatures from another planet are invading the town?

ISBN 0 426 20443 3

ORIGINAL SIN
Andy Lane
The last words of a dying alien send the Doctor and Bernice to 30th-century Earth in an attempt to avert an unspecified disaster. There, Adjudicators Roz Forrester and Chris Cwej are investigating a series of apparently motiveless murders. And their chief suspects are the Doctor and Bernice.

ISBN 0 426 20444 1

SKY PIRATES!
Dave Stone
Join the Doctor and Benny for the maiden voyage of the good ship *Schirron Dream*, as it ventures into a system which is being invaded by the villainous, shapeshifting Sloathes. Watch Chris Cwej and Roslyn Forrester have a rough old time of it in durance vile. Who will live? Who will die? Will the Doctor ever play the harmonium again?

ISBN 0 426 20446 8

ZAMPER
Gareth Roberts
The planet Zamper is home to a secretive organization that constructs the galaxy's mightiest warships. The TARDIS crew are intrigued by

Zamper's mysterious rulers. What is their true agenda? And why have they invited the last remnants of the Chelonian Empire to their world?

ISBN 0 426 20450 6

TOY SOLDIERS
Paul Leonard
The Doctor and his companions are following a trail of kidnapped children across a Europe recovering from the ravages of the First World War. But someone is aware of their search, and they find themselves unwilling guests on the planet Q'ell, where a similar war has raged for the last 1,400 years.

ISBN 0 426 20452 2

HEAD GAMES
Steve Lyons
Stand by for an exciting adventure with Dr Who and his companion, Jason. Once again, they set out to seek injustice, raise rebel armies and beat up green monsters. But this time, Dr Who faces a deadly new threat: a genocidal rogue Time Lord known only as the Doctor and his army of gun-slinging warrior women.

ISBN 0 426 20454 9

THE ALSO PEOPLE
Ben Aaronovitch
The Doctor has taken his companions to paradise: a sun enclosed by an artificial sphere where there is no poverty or violence. But then the peace is shattered by murder. As the suspects proliferate, Bernice realises that even an artificial world has its buried secrets and Roz discovers that every paradise has its snake.

ISBN 0 426 20456 5

If you have trouble obtaining Doctor Who books from your local shops, a book list and details of our mail order service are available upon request from:

Doctor Who Books
Virgin Publishing Ltd
332 Ladbroke Grove
London W10 5AH